T0381019

JAKE
MILLER III:
R A M P A G E

BILL MACK

authorHOUSE®

AuthorHouse™
1663 Liberty Drive
Bloomington, IN 47403
www.authorhouse.com
Phone: 833-262-8899

Published by AuthorHouse 09/10/2024

ISBN: 979-8-8230-3208-7 (sc)
ISBN: 979-8-8230-3209-4 (hc)
ISBN: 979-8-8230-3207-0 (e)

Library of Congress Control Number: 2023911556

Print information available on the last page.

Any people depicted in stock imagery provided by Getty Images are models, and such images are being used for illustrative purposes only. Certain stock imagery © Getty Images.

This book is printed on acid-free paper.

CONTENTS

Chapter 1 1

Chapter 2 7

Chapter 3 15

Chapter 4 25

Chapter 5 34

Chapter 6 46

Chapter 7 53

Chapter 8 63

Chapter 9 78

Chapter 10 92

Chapter 11 101

Chapter 12 112

Chapter 13 123

Chapter 14 140

Chapter 15 150

Chapter 16 159

Chapter 17 171

Chapter 18 183

Chapter 19 194

Chapter 20 203

Chapter 21 221

Chapter 22 232

Chapter 23 241

Chapter 24 256

CHAPTER 1

Jake took the microphone and asked for everyone's attention. The banquet room, at the Polonia Club grew quiet. "First. I'd like to thank you all for coming here tonight, to celebrate my little sister's wedding to my best friend."

It was Saturday, March 16th, 2019. The past eight months had been very eventful for the whole Miller clan. Jake's niece Kathleen discovered that the Community College courses she took, before entering Veterinary School, counted towards her degree. This meant she became a Doctor of Veterinary Medicine on February 1st, 2019, a full fourteen months sooner than she had previously figured.

Dr. Randy Brown, who Katie met in Temple Hospital's ER, while he treated her mom for snake bites, discovered the credit hours for her. Dr. Randy and Kate had been seeing each other since they met last summer. They got engaged at Christmas. They were planning a Destination Wedding in Ireland, in the spring of 2020.

Kate was currently in the process of opening her own Veterinary Hospital.

Jake's sister, Maggie, like her daughter, also got engaged at Christmas, to Cape May Courthouse Police Dept. Captain Tom Hansen. Maggie and Tom started dating about the same time as Kate and Dr. Randy.

She was leaving her nursing job at Fox Chase Cancer Center, at the end of March, to take a job at Cape Regional Medical Center. The pay was a little less, but she would now be working, literally, three blocks away from where her new husband worked.

Not to be left out of things, Jake, himself, had tons going on, in his life. His Private Investigator business would just not wait for him to open his Wildwood office, in February 2019. By the end of 2018, he had so many clients that he needed help. First, he turned his spare bedroom into an office. Then he hired not only his old boss, retired police Lieutenant Art Kaufman, to assist him in his investigations, but also Art's wife, Irene, to take care of the office.

He was getting requests for his services from up in Philadelphia. So much so, that Jake was considering opening a second office, up there. "…and I was honored to escort my sister down the aisle, as well as standing up as Best Man for Tom. I did, however, have to draw the line at being Flower Girl. With that being said, I ask you all to now raise your glasses, as we toast Mr. and Mrs. Tom Hansen. May you have many years of health and happiness. Cheers!"

Later, during the reception, Jake found himself in a conversation with his niece and sister. "So, sis, what are your plans, as far as the house, up here in Philly, goes. You gonna keep it, and rent it out?"

"I think I'm going to sell it, Jimmy. Kathleen doesn't want to buy it, and I don't need the hassle that goes with renting it out."

"How about if I rent it from you?"

"You? Why would you rent it, Jimmy?"

"Well, sis, I'm thinking about opening a P.I. office up here. I'm getting a lot of calls for private investigation services up here. Philly must be the cheater's capital of the world! How about if I rent from you, and if I decide to go all in, I'll buy it off you?"

"I don't know, Jimmy. Do you have any references I can contact?"

"What?"

"Of course, you can rent from me, knucklehead! We'll make plans later, ok?"

"Fine sis."

The bride and groom left for their 3-night stay at the Borgata Casino, in Atlantic City, when the reception ended at 11:00 pm. Most of the invited guests wandered downstairs to finish off the night at the Polonia Club's bar. Jake was on his way to the men's room, before heading downstairs, when he got a call on his cell. He had no intention of answering it, until he looked at caller ID, and saw it was from Philadelphia Police Captain Roy Lemon. Jake wondered what he could want, this late, on a Saturday night.

"Capt. Lemon. How are you?"

"I'm sorry to bother you, Jake. Art Kaufman told me you were in the private investigation business now, and I need help."

"What's wrong, Roy?"

"It's my Granddaughter Monica, Jake. She's missing. I'm at my wits end."

"Missing? For how long?"

"She was last seen leaving Little Flower High School yesterday afternoon, at 2:30 pm. She had her school uniform on, which is a maroon jumper, with a white blouse under it. She's 17 years old, 5' 2" tall, weighs 115 lbs., has shoulder length blond hair, and wears glasses."

"Okay, Roy. I'm assuming there was a missing person's report filed. Does she live with you?"

"No, she lives with her parents, my son Tom, and his wife Rosemarie."

"It goes without saying, that I'll help any way I can, Roy. First thing I'll need to do is talk to her parents. Get her friends names. Have you had her cell dumped?"

"Not yet. My head is spinning. Listen, Jake, I don't want you to think I'm asking for a favor here. I want to hire you. Money is no problem, between me and my son."

"What is a good time to meet with you all?"

"Whatever time you say, Jake."

"How's 9:00, tomorrow morning sound?"

"Fine. I'll text you my son's address and phone number, and meet you there at 9:00 am, sharp."

Jake realized his plans had changed, and he wasn't going downstairs, but straight to his sister's house, where he was staying this weekend. Before he left, he called his niece, Kate, to make sure she was okay. "Uncle J! What's with the phone call? I'm sitting right here at the bar."

"Yeah, Katie, I just got a call from a friend, and he needs my help. I'm gonna have to bail on the after party. Are you okay?"

"That's a shame, Uncle J. Yeah, I'm fine. Tiffany and Harley are here with me, and Randy. They are going to crash at my place tonight. Randy is our designated driver, so we're good as far as getting home. I'm just sorry that you can't stay."

"Not half as sorry as I am, Katie. Give everybody my best, and text me when you get home, okay?"

"Sure Uncle J. Good night."

"'Night Kate."

~~~

Jake was up, showered, and dressed by 7:15. He opened the text from Cpt. Lemon, and checked out the address…7235 Leon St. He hoped the heater in his car worked, on this chilly St. Patty's Day. He decided he had time for a second cup of coffee. He arrived at the house, in the Mayfair section of Philadelphia, ten minutes early and parked in front of their driveway. Roy Lemon was sitting on the steps, smoking. "Good morning, Jake. I can't thank you enough for doing this."

"I haven't done anything yet, Roy."

The two men went into the kitchen, where Tom and Rosemarie Lemon sat, drinking coffee. "Tom, Rose, this is Jake Miller. He's agreed to let us hire him to help find Monica."

Jake extended his hand to the missing girl's father. "Mr. Miller, thank you. Please find my little girl."

"Call me Jake, and I'll do all I possibly can."

After writing down the missing girl's description, Jake began asking questions. "Okay Tom, Rosemarie, I'm going to ask you some questions now. Everything I ask can be useful in finding Monica. Some of the things I must ask are of a very personal nature. I want you to understand that I only ask for information to help my investigation. Okay?"

Both parents nodded. "Now, here is a pad and a pen. Rosemarie, I want you to write down the names of any friends of Monica that you can think of. Anyone she might call, or contact. She has a cell, correct? I'm going to need you to write down her cell number for me, as well. Tom, and Roy, while she's doing that, maybe we could go in the other room, and talk."

After making their way to the sectional sofa, Jake talked to the men. "Does Monica have a boyfriend?"

"No. Not at all", replied the girl's father.

"Let me put it another way. Does she have any friends that are boys?"

"Yes, a couple. Jake, you're wasting time here. We already called all her friends, boys and girls, and nobody has seen, or heard from her."

"Look, Tom, what I've learned, and your dad can back me up on this, is that Monica's friends might not be as forthcoming to her parents, as they would be with someone they don't know. Now, has Monica ever…stayed out late, or not come home before?"

"No, never! Well, she's stayed at different friends' homes, but she always calls us to let us know, so we don't worry. She has never stayed out, or not come home, without calling us."

"Okay. Here's what I plan to do right now. First, I'm going to call a friend of mine with the FBI and have them monitor her phone. They have a program that listens for her phone number to get, or receive a call, or text. They'll call her number. If the phone answers the call, they have a way to pinpoint exactly where the phone is located. After that process is started, I'm going to take the list your wife is making and start interviewing everyone on it. If nothing else, her friends might know someone new she's friendly with, that you two are unaware of. We also have to think that this is a kidnap for ransom situation. Your dad here, can get with the Philly PD surveillance unit, and have your phone tapped, in case someone calls with some sort of demands."

"That's already taken care of," Capt. Lemon stated.

"Good. As for you and your wife, just stay here. You need to be near the phone, in case Monica, or anyone else calls. Here is my number. If you get any new information, or think of anything else, just call. I will be checking in with you guys every few hours. Stay strong. I'm gonna get started."

Jake shook Tom Lemon's hand, retrieved the note pad from his wife, and headed out.

CHAPTER 2

"**N**o problem, Jake. As soon as I hang up from you, I'll ping this girl's phone. Text me your email, and I'll send you a link, that will allow you to see what we see. That way, you won't depend on a phone call from me if the phone is being used or starts moving. Listen, if you need any hands-on help, I'll get you our Philadelphia Branch number, and a contact there, who will help you out. "

"Thanks, Brandon. I really appreciate this."

"Not at all, Jake. Just glad I could help. Good luck and take care."

"Later, Brandon."

FBI Field Agent Brandon Wright, and his partner, Harvey Caldwell, had helped crack a case wide open, last summer. In fact, Agent Wright saved Jake's life, by shooting the Cobra Motorcycle Club leader, as he was about to kill Jake. Both were stand-up guys, and Jake knew he was lucky to have them in his corner. After sending his email address to Agent Wright, Jake started in on the list of names Rosemarie Lemon had provided him with. The first call he made was to Cindy. The Lemons didn't know her last name. The phone was answered by someone Jake assumed to be her father. "Hello. Who is this?"

"Good morning. My name is Jake Miller. I'm a private investigator, looking into the disappearance of a friend of Cindy's, Monica Lemon. Monica's parents provided me with a list of Monica's friends. I'd like to come to your home, and talk to Cindy for a few minutes, if possible."

"She's not here."

"I'm sorry, and you are?"

"I'm the guy who's going to hang up on your sorry ass. I told you she's not here."

"Well, do you know when she'll be back?"

"No. She went to church with her mother."

"Sir, a young girl is missing. It's very important that I talk to Cindy."

"You're a real pain in the ass, you know that? Try back this afternoon." He then hung up on Jake.

Jake put a question mark next to Cindy's name, and muttered "Talk about getting off to a rough start…"

All in all, there were fourteen names on the list. Rosemarie Lemon only knew the addresses for two of them. Hell, she only knew six of their last names! Jake made a mental note that these parents didn't keep as tight a leash on their daughter as they let on.

Next on the list was Barbara Bell. She answered, and said she was at home. Jake asked if her parents were there, and could he speak to them. She put her mother on, who was more than willing to let him speak with her daughter, once Jake explained why he had called. The Bells lived up in the Bridesburg section of Philadelphia, about five minutes away, and Mrs. Bell told Jake to come right over.

Roger Bell answered the door, and led Jake into the family room, where Angie Bell, and her daughter, Barbara were waiting. "Good morning. Thank you all for seeing me."

The interview was quick. Barbara went to school with Monica, but she was out sick Friday, so she hadn't seen her since Thursday. She *was* able to provide Jake with last names for the rest of the people on the list. While she didn't know street numbers, Jake now had last names for all fourteen people, and street names, that eleven of them lived on. She also added a name to the list, Matt Clevinger. Apparently, Monica had met

Matt at a party, three weeks ago, and had been texting him. She told Barbara that they were going on a date. That was all she knew about Matt, but the party she alluded to was at the house of the next person on the list. Jake left his card, thanked them for their time, and moved on.

The next name on the list was Carole Hanratty, who answered the front door, in her pajamas. She appeared to be alone. Jake asked where her parents were. "I think they went to PARX Casino, for the day. They'll be back around 6:00 pm. Earlier if they run out of money."

"Well, how old are you, Carole?"

"I just turned nineteen."

"Oh, happy belated Birthday. Is that what the party was for?"

"What party?"

"The one that Barbara Bell, and Monica Lemon came to...where Monica met Matt Clevinger."

"I didn't have a party for my birthday. The last party I threw was for the Super Bowl, on Feb 3rd. That was, like five, or six weeks ago. It was off the hook!"

"Were Barbara & Monica here for that party?"

"Yeah, they were here."

"Do you remember Monica chatting with Matt Clevinger?"

"Matt who?"

"Clevinger."

"Don't know who that is, man."

"Dark hair. Close to six feet tall. Thin. Spent most of the party with Monica?"

"Let me think...oh, yeah, the guy I didn't know. I forgot his name."

"Wait. A guy you didn't know was at your party?"

"Well, yeah. Bobby brought him. He was his buddy."

"Bobby?"

"Bobby Regan. He brought this stranger with him. He introduced me to him, but with all the commotion with the game, and all, I forgot his name. Yeah, I remember him now. But it wasn't just Monica hanging with him. Barbara was hanging on him too. In fact, I thought Barb and Mon were gonna battle over him."

"How so?"

"Really? They both thought he was hot, and neither wanted to back off. Personally, I didn't get it. I mean, he was cute, and all, but being around him for two minutes, you could tell he was just looking to hit it and forget it."

"What?"

"You know, get laid. He was a player. He wasn't looking for a girlfriend, or anything. He just wanted to hook up, is all."

"Well, do you know how I can get hold of this player?"

"I guess Bobby. He was *his* buddy."

"Have you seen Monica recently?"

"No. In fact, the Super Bowl Party might be the last time I saw her."

"Ok. Thanks, Carole. If you think of anything else, please call me."

Back out in the car, Jake logged on to his laptop, to check if there was any progress on Monica's phone. There wasn't. It was almost 1:00 pm. He figured he'd try to go see this Bobby Regan, if just to get a line on his buddy Matt. He called Bobby, who wasn't home, but told Jake to come to Chickie's and Pete's, up on the Blvd., and he'd talk to him. Jake got to the bar and dialed Bobby's number again.

"Bobby. It's Jake Miller. I just walked in the front door. Where are you?"

"See the main bar, there on your left? Follow it all the way down. I'm three stools from the end. I got my hand up, waving it."

"I got it." Jake put his phone away and took out his pad and pen.

Bobby Regan was a very large man. He was a good five inches taller than Jake's 5' 10" frame, and Jake estimated he weighed around 250 lbs. "Hey. Bobby Regan. Want a beer?"

"No thanks, Bob. Thanks for talking to me."

"Sure. No problem. That sucks about Monica. I don't know how I can help but ask away."

"Ok. When was the last time you saw Monica Lemon?"

"I guess it was at Carole's Super Bowl Party. Monica is too young to hang in places like this, and I mainly hang in Sports Bars."

"Did you talk to her at the party?"

"Only to say hi. Her girlfriend, Barbara was with her. I kinda like her."

"All right, then. I won't bother you much more. If you could tell me how to get in touch with your friend Matt Clevinger, I'll be on my way."

"Maverick? Oh, yeah, he was sniffing around both girls. He was starting to piss me off, chatting up Monica *and* Barbara."

"Maverick?"

"Yeah, you know, like in Top Gun. He would fly in, pick up a hottie, hit it, and fly away."

"So, how would I get in touch with.... Maverick?"

"Don't really know, man."

"Excuse me? He's your friend, and you don't know his phone number?"

"Sure, I do. But, you see, Mav, he goes through phones like shit through a goose. And every time he gets a new phone, he gets a new number. I think he does it just so none of his girls can corral him in, if you know what I mean. I just called him last weekend, and it said the phone was no longer in service. I won't get his new number until I run into him somewhere, or he calls me, which he hardly ever does."

"Well, where does he live? Does he work?"

"He lives down in South Philly, somewhere. I'm not sure where. And yeah, he works."

"Where at? I'll go to his job and talk to him there."

Bobby spit the beer back in his mug, laughing... "Oh man. Don't think you want to do that."

"Why?"

"Well, Mav is a male stripper. He works at that place down on Columbus Blvd. Near Home Depot. Club Risque, I think. Upstairs, they have guy strippers, a few nights a week. And don't ask me what nights, 'cause I have no idea. You won't catch *me* going in there. Mav says I should. That there's like, 95% chicks, and they're mostly all horny. But know what, I don't want anybody to think I'm one of the other 5%, if you know what I mean."

"Yeah, I know what you mean. Thanks. Call me if you think of anything else."

"You got it, chief."

It was quarter to three when Jake left the bar. He decided to try one more person. That would be Cindy Reeves, the girl who was at church with her mother earlier. This time it was a girl's voice, that answered. "Hello?"

"Hi, is this Cindy?"

"Who wants to know?" Jake told her who he was, and what he wanted, and asked if he could speak to one of her parents, for permission to talk with her.

"Wait..." then to someone else... "Mom! Some guy wants to come over and ask me about Monica. Okay? You know Monica. She's missing, and this guy is looking for her."

"Mr. Miller?"

"Yes, Cindy."

"Mom says it's okay. Come on over. Do you have the address?"

"Yes. I'll be there in about a half hour."

Jake was shown to a seat at the dining room table, and was soon joined by Cindy, and her mother, who was also Cindy. Jake directed his questions at the younger Cindy. "I spoke with your father this morning. Is he here?"

"*Stepfather*. My dad's dead."

Her mother interrupted "No. Mr. Miller, my husband is out right now. He won't be back until dinner time."

"Dinner time! Since when? He's at the bar and won't be home until he's falling down drunk."

"Cindy! Mr. Miller is here about Monica. What your dad…"

"*Stepdad!*"

"Stepdad does, is of no concern to him."

"Okay, let's get back on track here. Cindy, how well do you know Monica?"

"She doesn't know her very well."

"Mrs. Reeves. If you don't mind, I'd like to hear Cindy's answers. Cindy?"

"We're, you know, friends. That's all."

"Really? That seems kind of odd. See, when I asked her parents for a list of her friends, they put your name right at the top. See? Now, it's been my experience, that when parents list their children's friends, they start with their closest friends, and work down. Are you sure you're not real close to Monica?"

"Well, we *used* to be best friends, until about six months ago."

"Yes Mr. Miller. Monica used to be here all the time."

"Very good. What happened six months ago, Cindy?"

"I, uh, I'm not sure. I'd invite her over, and she would make excuses. If I wanted to see her, I had to go to her house. Finally, she just stopped returning my texts."

"And you have no idea why?"

"She told you she didn't know, Mr. Miller."

"So, if I understand you, Cindy, you haven't had contact with Monica since… before Christmas, right?"

Cindy was now staring down at the table in front of her. "That's right."

"Okay then. I'll be on my way. Here's my card. If you think of, or remember anything else, please give me a call. Thanks for your time."

As he handed Cindy his business card, her mother reached in front of her, and took it. "Show Mr. Miller to the door, Cindy."

When they reached the door, Jake turned and thanked Cindy again, and offered his hand. When she took it, she also took the business card he had palmed in it.

CHAPTER 3

Back out in the car, Jake called Art and Irene Kaufman, to tell them he would be staying up in Philadelphia, for a few days. He told Art to just use his judgement on whether to take any potential clients that happened to call, while he was away. He explained the details of the case to Art, who told him to take as much time as he needed. They would be fine. Jake then called Phil's Doggie Daycare, and arranged for Assault and Battery, his Yellow, and Chocolate Labrador Retrievers, to stay with Phil, until Jake came down to get them. He then ate his dinner and cleaned up when he was done. This consisted of throwing the Boston Market containers in the trash. Finally, he opened his laptop, to keep a check on Monica's phone, spread out his notes on the table, and went about sorting through what he knew, and didn't know.

After a few minutes, it became clear that he had way too many questions, and virtually no answers. No one had called, looking for a ransom. Jake was thinking less and less that it was a kidnapping. No, as he saw it, there were only two possibilities. Monica Lemon was either taken against her will, or she went willingly with someone, basically making her a runaway. There was a third option, but Jake forced it back into the recesses of his brain. He did not want to believe that she could have been killed by someone, whether purposely, or accidentally, and the perpetrator had panicked, and done something to hide the body. No, this was only an option to think about when all other options were proven to be not feasible. Right now, Jake's best lead was Matt Clevinger. 'Maverick' was a love 'em and leave 'em guy. Apparently, Monica was… smitten with him. Maybe they hooked up this weekend, and Monica will come walking in the house tonight, or tomorrow. Jake knew that he also had to look at the parents, Tom, and Rosemarie. It was clear to him that they didn't know their daughter as well as they professed to. Maybe she had a huge fight with one, or the other, and took off somewhere. Jake would have to investigate that angle, as well as Maverick. And what about the Reeves family. There was something off with them. Why would Monica suddenly drop Cindy as a friend?

As if on cue, Jake's phone rang. Caller ID said it was Cindy Reeves. "Hello? Cindy?"

"Yes, Mr. Miller. It's me."

"Cindy. Is there something wrong? I can just about hear you."

"I'm in my bedroom. I don't want my mom to hear me."

"Why not?"

"I just don't. Look, about why Monica stopped coming over here… I think I know why."

"Go on."

"I think my stepdad tried to molest her."

"What? Cindy, you *think*, or you *know*? It's very important."

"I'll just tell you that the last time Monica was here, my mom was at bingo, and my stepdad came in, from the bar, drunk. Mon and I were sitting on the sofa, watching TV. He sat between us and put his arms on the back of the sofa. I was embarrassed, plus, I had to pee, so I went up to the bathroom. Coming back down, I heard Monica say *NO!* And when I got to the bottom of the stairs, he was getting up from the sofa, and he staggered up to bed. Monica was shaking, and her blouse was half unbuttoned. She jumped up, and said she had to go."

"OK. Cindy, did you tell anyone? Your mom?"

"No. I didn't actually see anything, and Monica wouldn't tell me if he did anything."

"But you're pretty sure he did. You should have told your mom."

"Why? She didn't believe me when I told her he molested me, so I know she wouldn't believe me if I told her what he did to Monica."

"Cindy. You need to report what happened to you to the police. If not, he'll just do it again, if not to you, to somebody else."

"Mr. Miller, I did report it to the police. They investigated, and he denied it, and said that I was angry at him for not letting me go to a concert I wanted to go to, and I was making it all up. My mom backed him up and said he couldn't have done what I said because she was home all night, the night I said it happened. The police said they would keep an eye on him, but that only lasted a week or so. Then they stopped checking in with us. He's never touched me again, but I go up in my room, and lock the door, whenever he's at the bar, and my mom's not home."

"Cindy, you should talk to a counselor at school, or something."

"Yeah, maybe. Look I gotta go."

"One thing before you go. Do you think your stepdad has something to do with Monica disappearing?"

"I don't think he would hurt anybody, at least not on purpose. No, I don't."

"Then I have to ask you why you called me, and told me what you did?"

"I'm not sure. Maybe I just needed to say it out loud and have somebody hear it."

"All right, Cindy, good night. And listen, if he ever touches you again, or you just need to talk, don't hesitate to call me, any time of day, or night."

"Thanks, Mr. Miller. Good night."

Jake stared at the phone for what seemed like an eternity. Instead of eliminating suspects, and reasons for Monica's disappearance, the list of possibilities was just growing. This was not good. He really had his work cut out for him. He wished Tom Hansen wasn't on his 'mini'-honeymoon. Tom was a great idea man. Great at planning a course of action.

Jake's brain was fried. He was done for the day. He made a list of things to do on Monday. That list included talking to the Philly detectives handling the case, to see if they knew anything he did not; talking to Matt Clevinger; checking out Paul Reeves; and contacting the remaining seven names on the list of friends. But on the top of that list, was a second conversation with Tom and Rosemarie Lemon.

Monday morning was exceptionally chilly for the middle of March. After breakfast at Mary's Luncheonette, Jake called the Lemons to see if he could come up and talk to them again. He posed it as a progress report. Rosemarie told him to come up any time. He knocked on their door at 8:30 am. Rosemarie let him in and walked toward the kitchen. "Let's sit here, at the table, Mr. Miller. The light is much better in here."

After she had given him a cup of coffee, and got one for herself, she sat down across from him. "So, what have you found?"

"Well, if it's all the same, I'll wait for Tom to join us, so you both hear the same thing."

"Oh, Tom won't be joining us. He had to go to work. He's a computer programmer, and they can't spare him right now."

"Really? So, you two haven't heard from, or seen Monica, since Friday morning, and her dad doesn't even miss a day of work? I'd think he wouldn't be able to concentrate on work."

"Well, Tom is a workaholic. That's how he deals with things."

"Ok then. As far as finding Monica, what I have are a whole bunch of questions. Have you ever heard Monica mention the name Matt Clevinger?"

"No. I don't think so. Do you think she is with him?"

"I don't have any hard facts yet, Rose. While talking to her friends, his name popped up, as a guy that Monica thought was cute, we'll say, and wanted to go out on a date with him."

"That's impossible. I'd know if my daughter was seeing a boy."

"With all due respect, Rose, you only knew two of Monica's friends' last names, and none of their addresses. When she went to a party, or to a friend's house, you had no idea what neighborhood she was in, let alone the actual address. That's not what I call keeping a close eye on her."

"Well! If you're just here to tell me I'm a bad parent, you can leave!"

"Rose, I'm not saying that at all. What I'm trying to get through to you is that even the best parents only know what their child wants them to know. I need you to have an open mind when I ask you a question, and not dismiss the question, by saying 'Not my child.' The way this works is, I come up with a list of all the things that could have happened to Monica. Then, by asking questions to everyone who knows her, I try to eliminate the things on that list, one by one. Most kidnappers contact the parents within 24 hours. It's been almost 72 hours since anyone has seen Monica. With each hour that goes by, it becomes less and less likely that she was kidnapped for ransom, and I will no longer focus on that aspect. Now, I need you to listen. I'm not saying this is what happened. What I'm about to say are possibilities. *If*, and again, I say *if* Monica was not kidnapped for ransom, there are basically 3 options, as to what could have happened to her. She could have been in an accident, is injured, and the hospitals can't identify her. The other two options are that she could have gone off somewhere willingly, or she was taken against her will. Your father-in-law told me when he called me Saturday night that there were no reported accidents involving any teenage, unidentified, girls. He also checked all the hospitals in the area, and there were no 'Jane Doe' patients. He got the same result at the morgue."

"Don't even say that!"

"Rose, that's a good thing, okay? So, as of right now, I'm focusing my investigation on two possibilities. That she went off somewhere willingly, or was taken somewhere, against her will. This Matt Clevinger *does* exist, and Monica *has* been in contact with him. You've never heard her mention him at all?"

"No, I haven't."

"Okay, let's move on. How have you and Tom been getting along with Monica. I know seventeen-year-old girls can be a handful. My niece was stubborn, and knew everything, at that age. Any arguments?"

"No. Nothing that would cause her to run away, if that's what you mean. Just the normal teenager/parent arguments."

"Like what? Give me an example."

"Let's see… well, about a month ago, Monica wanted to go to a party. It was on a Thursday night. Her dad said no, because she had school the next day. They argued back and forth, and it ended with her screaming she hates him, and going up to her room. She doesn't really hate him, though, she was just angry."

"Well, how did *you* feel about her going to the party?"

"Oh, I didn't think it would hurt, if we let her go. Just give her an 11:00 pm curfew, or something."

"And…?"

"And nothing. I don't get involved with that stuff. Tom handles all the permission and punishment stuff."

"So, why didn't you say anything?"

"Well, I didn't want to get involved."

"So, Monica didn't go. How long was she mad at her father?"

"Oh, no. She did go. When she went upstairs, she snuck out onto the kitchen roof, and went to the party anyway."

"And her father never found out? How did you know she left?"

"Oh, I saw her climb down from the roof, into the yard, and go out the gate, while I was doing the dishes. She was back by 11:30 pm. I know what time it was because Action News was on. After the news went off, I went down and locked the front door."

"Let me see if I understand. Your husband told Monica she wasn't allowed out. She snuck out anyway. You saw her sneak out, and you didn't say anything to Tom. Is that right?"

"Yes."

"Rosemarie, can you tell me why you didn't say anything?"

"Why would I? Tom felt good about himself for his parenting. Monica was happy. And I didn't have to listen to either of them fighting. Everybody was happy. I took that as a win-win-win. You don't understand, Mr. Miller. Tom and Monica are both very headstrong. Neither one is going to give in. So, when they get into it, and I think Tom is wrong, I tell Monica to go to her room. Tom thinks I'm taking his side, and that he won. Monica knows when I tell her to go upstairs, that I'll look the other way when she does whatever it is Tom told her no about, and everything is quiet."

Jake shook his head. He realized he would get nowhere continuing the conversation. He thanked Rose, told her he'd update them this evening, and headed over to the 15th Police District, home of the Missing Persons Bureau.

Out in the car, he jotted down a few notes about Monica Lemon. She was, according to her mother, both stubborn, and defiant. Used to getting her own way. He flipped over to a new page and went in to find Capt. Lemon. He figured he'd get less pushback, if Roy Lemon walked him down to Missing Persons, and asked them to cooperate with Jake. He found the captain in his office, and he was glad to take Jake to the detective squad. During the trip there, Jake let him know what he had deduced from talking to Rosemarie Lemon. When they found

Detectives Tanner and Hill, Lemon introduced them to Jake, and told the detectives that he would consider it a personal favor for them to be forthcoming with Jake, and he would do the same. When the captain. left, Detective Ronnie Tanner offered Jake his hand, and then a seat. "Welcome aboard Miller. Take a load off."

"Thanks. And it's Jake."

"Jake it is. Hey, wait! Jake Miller! Aren't you the guy who set up that big drug bust over in Pennypack Park last summer?"

"Well, I was involved. Tony Valentino ran the show."

"No, you're being modest. Tony's a good friend of mine, and he said that you put them on to the whole thing. Yeah, and you were responsible for exposing that scumbag Pete Lansing too, right?"

Ronnie's partner, Tony Hill chimed in "Damn, Jake, you busted more cases than most cops that actually work up here!"

"Just being in the right place, at the right time, guys. So, where are we with Monica Lemon?"

"Well, Jake, we caught the case late Saturday afternoon. We sent Surveillance over to the house to hook up taps on the phone, in case somebody calls asking for a ransom. That looks like a dead end. We spent most of yesterday checking citywide for abductions, accidents, involving a white seventeen-year-old female, in a maroon jumper... no luck."

"Yeah, and while Tony was doing that, I was checking all the hospitals in the city, and in a thirty-mile radius, looking for seventeen-year-old female Jane Does being admitted. No luck there either. We were just gonna head over to talk to the parents, if you want to tag along..."

"Just came from there. The father went to work."

"Wait. The daughter disappeared Friday afternoon, and dad goes to work Monday. What's up with that?"

"My thought exactly. Mom claims that's how he deals with stress."

"So, what kind of vibe did you get from mom?"

Jake shook his head. "Kind of a screwed-up family. According to mom, dad and daughter would battle over things, and mom tells daughter to go to her room, which is a code phrase telling her to just go away. Then mom would go behind dad's back, and let the daughter do, or get, whatever they were arguing about."

"That's messed up."

"Maybe we should wait until both parents are there. You got any other leads, Jake?"

"A couple. Here's a list of Monica's friends that I got from her parents. There are fourteen names here, and when I got the list, there were only two last names, and no complete addresses. I filled in the last names and residences, at the first stop I made, Barbara Bell. I interviewed the first seven people on the list. When I got to Captain Lemon's office, he had his secretary make three copies of my interviews. One for him, and one for each of you."

Jake then proceeded to tell them what he knew about Matt Clevinger, and the conversation he had last night with Cindy Reeves, about her stepdad, Paul.

"Damn, Jake! You're a bad man! Well partner, looks like we got three leads to check out. Here's what we'll do, Jake. We'll give this Paul Reeves to Converse, over there. He's our resident computer geek. By the time we get back this afternoon, he'll have a file on this guy for us. In the meantime, Tony and I will check out the other seven names on this list, while you see if you can track down this Clevinger."

"Hey, Ronnie, give Converse Clevinger's info too. See what he can dig up on him. We might get lucky. Jake, since this is the captain's granddaughter, we got extra bodies at our disposal. You want somebody to ride with you?"

"No thanks. I kind of work better as a solo act."

"How about you take Dawes with you, just as a backup. Believe me, Jake, there aren't many 'gentlemen', at that Gentlemen's Club you're heading to. It's a rough crowd."

"No, I'll be okay. Thanks, though. Listen, we'll meet later this afternoon, to compare notes?"

"Sure, give us your card, and we'll call you later, to let you know what time we figure to be back here."

And with that, the three men were out on the street.

CHAPTER 4

Jake walked into Club Risqué and was approached by the doorman/bouncer. "$10 cover charge. Be respectful of the ladies or you'll be thrown out. The $10 gets you a free drink."

Jake showed him his old Detective's badge. "I'm not here for the girls."

"Oh, so it's like that? You want to go upstairs, sweetie?"

This got a laugh from the guy working behind the counter, at the cash register.

"That's funny. I showed you my badge. I need to talk to the Manager."

"And there's a $10 cover charge to get in, bitch," said the bouncer, as he stepped in front of Jake.

In a flash, Jake spun the big man around, and splattered his nose all over the pole he had been leaning on. While he crumpled to the floor, Jake grabbed the second guy by the collar and pulled him halfway over the counter he was behind. "Am I gonna have any trouble from you?"

Before the stunned bouncer could answer, Jake heard a voice behind him. "Whoa there, cowboy! Take it easy! Don't be beating up all the hired help."

Jake turned to find a middle-aged fat guy, with a horrible comb-over. "Who are you?"

"Tommy Randolf. I'm the manager, here." Jake released his grip, and the manager told the guy, "Go get him cleaned up, and then get back behind the counter. Now, what can I do for you, Mister...?"

"Miller. Detective Jake Miller. I need to talk to an employee of yours."

"Detective, huh? I know lot of cops. Don't know you. What Precinct you work out of?"

"I don't. I work out of Cape May County."

"Cape May? In Jersey? You're a long way from home, cowboy. Who is such a desperado, that you'd come all the way up here, to track them down?"

"I'm looking for Matt Clevinger. I was told he works here."

"Name's not familiar. He's a bouncer here?"

"No, a male stripper."

"Clevin... oh, you mean Maverick. Yeah, he works here. Upstairs."

"Does he happen to be working today?"

"Hold on." The Manager picked up a phone on the wall and dialed an extension. "Kamal. What? It's your boss, dickhead! Is Maverick working today? Okay, I'm sending a guy up. *No*, he doesn't want a private show, asshole! He's a detective, and he wants to ask Maverick some questions. Don't fuck with this guy. He'll be right up." After hanging up, the manager turned to Jake. "OK, Detective. Maverick is in the middle of his set. He'll be done in a few minutes. Go right up the stairs over there. Kamal will meet you at the top and take you to Maverick."

"Thanks."

Jake was met at the top of the stairs by Kamal, a guy almost as big as the guy he laid out, downstairs. "You looking for Maverick? That's him, on the stage. You can wait here until he's done. This is his last song."

As Maverick gyrated to the strains of 'It's Raining Men', Jake could see what made him popular with the ladies. As the Weather Girls faded out, the DJ spoke up. "Let's give it up for Maverick, everybody. Don't forget, Mav is available for private shows. If you'd like a private show with Maverick, just see my man Kamal, over there, by the door, and he'll give you the deets. Right now, I'd like you to put your hands together, and welcome to the stage El Diablo!"

Jake thought it was kind of funny that El Diablo came on stage to the song 'Isn't She Lovely'. Kamal tapped Jake on the shoulder. "Come with me."

He followed Kamal over to a table, where three men, in business suits, where pawing at Maverick. As they got close, Jake heard him say, "Whoa, guys. Take it easy. You tipped me to look. You want a private show, talk to Kamal, okay."

"Mav."

The oily naked young man turned to face Kamal and Jake. "You want a private show, big guy?"

"No Mav, this here is a detective. Wants to ask you some questions."

"That's a shame. Okay, let's go in the back." Then, to the men seated at the table, "And don't you boys go trying to get with El Diablo while I'm gone. I'll be back in five minutes."

Jake followed Matt Clevinger into the dressing room that all the strippers shared. Jake noted that on the dressing tables there were all varieties of machines, props, and... 'contraptions', that he neither recognized, nor had a desire to ask what they were. Clevinger put his robe on, sat on a stool, and said "Pull up a stool, and tell me what you want."

"My name is Jake Miller. I'm looking into the disappearance of a young girl. Your name came up as someone who might have seen her." Jake showed him Monica's picture. "Her name is Monica Lemon. You were seen with her, at a Super Bowl Party, and Monica told her friend that you and she were gonna hook-up."

"Yeah. Monica. Hot little number. I remember her. I was gonna hit it that night, but I found out she was only seventeen. Mav don't play around with underage girls. I had to put that on ice, if you know what I mean."

"So, are you telling me that you never had any contact with her, after that party?"

"Oh, no, man! I had plenty of contact with her."

"You'll have to explain what you mean."

"Sure. Listen. Girl's a freak. Here, look." He opened his phone. Jake saw what he guessed were three dozen texts, sent from February 4th, through March 1st. Almost every text included explicit pictures of Monica, in various stages of undress, and doing all kinds of things to herself. "See, man. Read some of the stuff she wanted me to do to her."

"Okay, so what happened after March 1st? No more texts. How'd you get her to stop?"

"What do you mean? I hooked up with her."

"When?"

"When do you think? March 2nd."

"Why March 2nd?"

"Dude, read the texts. See how she tells me what she wants to do, and in almost every text, she says she can't wait for March 2nd, cause that's her birthday, and then we can get busy. And believe me, I met her for breakfast on Saturday March 2nd, and after breakfast, we went to my place, and we did almost all the things she talks about. She didn't leave until 9:00 that night."

"So, you *have* been seeing her."

"No, man. Maverick is like, one and done, if you know what I mean? I told her that before we did anything, you know, and she was cool with it. I haven't heard from her since. Listen, we almost done here. That table of guys out there is good for a hundred apiece, but El Diablo will poach them, if I don't get out there before he's done."

"Almost. Where were you Friday afternoon, between 2 pm and 3 pm?"

"I was here. I worked from 3:00 pm to 9:00 pm. I punched in around 2:30 pm. Can I go now?"

"Yeah, we're done, for now. Write down your address and phone number. I may need to talk to you again."

"Sure, dude. Whatever you say."

As Jake was leaving, Matt Clevinger called him. "Hey, Detective Dude. I hope you find Monica, and she's okay. She's a cool chick."

~~~

Jake sat in his car and wrote down some notes about 'Maverick'. Jake believed you get as much information from the way a person acted, and his body language, as you could from what they said. Jake thought Maverick was telling the truth. That, plus, on the way out, he asked the Manager for Clevinger's timecard from Friday. He punched in at 2:23 pm.

Jake went to John's Roast Pork Shack for lunch. When he was leaving, he checked his watch… 1:15 pm. Too early to hook back up with Tanner and Hill. Suddenly, Jake got an idea. He changed directions, and headed to the Schuylkill Expressway, then north on Route 1, got off at 9th street, and parked in the Little Flower High School parking lot at 1:40 pm. He knew he was cutting it close, so he rushed into the Administrator's Office. Mrs. McNamara hesitated at first, but once Jake explained why he was there, she sprang into action. Five minutes later, she had Monica's roster, and was personally escorting Jake up to 8th period Religion, Monica's last class of the day. They entered the classroom just as class was beginning. "Excuse me, sister. This is an emergency, of sorts. Class, this gentleman, is Detective Miller. As most of you know, Monica Lemon is missing. The last place she was seen was in this classroom. Mr. Miller has some questions. I want you to help him in any way you can. Mr. Miller?"

"Thank you, Mrs. McNamara. Ladies, how many of you remember seeing Monica here, in this classroom, on Friday?" About twenty of the twenty-five girls in the class put up their hands. "OK. How many of you saw her after class was over… you know, outside… getting on the bus… whatever?" Four hands went up. "We'll start with you. What is your name?"

"Angela Reed."

"Hi Angela. Where did you see Monica?"

"We walked out together. We take the same bus home."

"And do you remember if Monica got on the bus?"

"Yeah, we walked out together. I sat next to her."

"Good. Who sat by the window?"

"She did. She always sits by the window."

"Fine. Do you know what stop she gets off?"

"Yeah. She gets off at the end of the line. Cottman and Torresdale Avenues."

"Now, did she ride the bus all the way to the end of the line on Friday?"

"I don't know. I get off at Erie-Torresdale. I take the El to Bridge St."

"So far, so good. Does anybody else take that bus?" Two hands went up. "You are?"

"Tiffany Heller."

"Tiffany, were you on the bus with Monica Friday?"

"Yes. We both rode to the end of the line. I walked across Cottman Avenue with her, we said goodbye, and she waited for the #84 bus to take her to her house. I live at Sheffield St., and Torresdale Ave., so I walked over Torresdale, to my house."

"Great. When you said goodbye, what did you say?"

"I think I said 'See you Monday, Mon.'"

"What did she say?"

Tiffany smiled. "Oh, she always says, 'Not if I see you first.'"

"Thank you, Tiffany. Now, you had your hand up. What's your name?"

"Marge Grant, sir."

"And you were on the bus Friday?"

"Yes, sir. But I get off at Devereaux and Torresdale. By the playground. I live right there."

"And did you say anything to Monica when you got off."

"No, but after Ang got off, I sat next to Monica, until I got off."

"What did you two talk about?"

"She asked me if I had plans for the weekend. I told her no and asked if she was doing anything."

"What did she say?"

"She said she didn't have any plans."

"Thank you, girls. Now did anybody else have a conversation with Monica on Friday?" No hands went up. "Tiffany. Marge. Angela. If you three would please jot your phone numbers here, next to each of your names, that would be great. And while they're doing that, Sister, would you mind if I wrote my number on the blackboard, for the girls to copy down?"

"Certainly, Mr. Miller." As he wrote his cell number, he asked the girls to write it down, and if they remembered anything at all, to please call him. He thanked them for their time and left.

As he made his way down the hall, he heard someone call his name. "Mr. Miller, sir."

He turned to the voice. "Marge, right?"

"Yes sir. Marge Grant, sir."

"What's the matter, Marge?"

"I told Sister I had to… go pee. I needed to tell you something. I didn't want to say in front of the class."

"And what's that Marge?"

"Well, sir, I didn't exactly tell you the truth when I told you what Monica and I talked about. When I asked her if she was doing anything, she did say no, but she also said she was meeting a guy to buy some kind of special pot… you know, marijuana."

"Did she say where, or when, or the guy's name?"

"No, she didn't say where or when, but she called the guy Bug."

"Bug? You sure about that?"

"Yes sir. She said she was meeting Bug to buy some Maui Gold. You know, Maui, like Hawaii? You won't tell Sister, or anybody I told you that, will you? I mean, I don't smoke pot, or anything. I just know what she said."

"Thank you, Marge. That is a big help. We'll keep this between you and I. You better go back to class now."

"Well, now I *do* have to pee…", and off she headed for the restroom.

Jake had turned his phone off while he was in the school. After getting settled in at the car, he turned it back on. He had a missed call, from Tony Hill. He hit the 'call back' button. "Jake! Thank goodness! I thought for a minute that you went to that strip joint and joined the other team!"

"No. Sorry to disappoint you. What's up?"

"We talked to five of the names on your list. Dead end. The last two are still in high school and aren't home yet. Have to get back to them tonight."

"What are the two names?"

"Let's see… Marge Grant, and Angela…"

"Reed." Jake finished it for him.

"Yeah. What are you psychic?"

"No. Cross them off your list. I just left Little Flower High. I interviewed both of them. Are you guys done?"

"Yeah. That's why I called. We're headed back to the station, to see how Converse made out, checking up on Clevinger, and Paul Reeves. You headed in?"

"Yeah. Meet you there in about twenty minutes. I might have a lead."

CHAPTER 5

Jake walked into the 'bullpen' to find detectives Tanner and Hill looking over two files. "Any luck?"

"Nah, Jake. This Clevinger guy, for being a stripper, is squeaky clean. No record."

"Believe it or not, I kind of got that feeling when I interviewed him. He's a player, and might even have a sex addiction, but he told me he wanted to be with Monica since he met her, at a Super Bowl Party. But when she said she was seventeen, he dropped her. She pursued him, sexting him, close to three dozen times, telling him what she wanted to do to him, and she couldn't wait until March 2nd, when she turned 18. He claims he told her all along that he was gonna be with her once, and be done, and after March 2nd, no more texts. Now, her birthday is in May, so technically, he still is guilty of sex with a minor. I *do* believe his story. Plus, he was on stage, at 3:00 pm Friday. What about Reeves?"

"Not much there, either. A couple drunk and disorderly charges. The daughter did report him as a molester, and… Detective Quaid caught that case. Hey Quaid! Got a minute?"

"Sure Ronnie. What do you need?"

"Paul Quaid, meet Jake Miller. Miller's a PI, working on the captain's granddaughter's case. Paul, fifteen months ago, you caught a case. Paul Reeves. Daughter was sixteen at the time. Accused him of molesting her. It got dropped. What happened?"

"I remember that one. I worked on that one with Sarge. Guy retired six months ago. Girl said... stepdad, right? He comes home one night. Mom is at bingo. He's drunk. Starts feeling the girl up and tried to rape her. He was too drunk, and she managed to get away."

"Sounds like a solid case."

"Yeah, not so much. I mean, we believed the girl. But she didn't report it until five days later, so there was no DNA, or anything. And when we go to roust the guy, he denies it. He says the girl was just pissed 'cause he wouldn't let her go to some concert. We still liked him for it, but the mom alibied him. She said they both were home that night, and they sat on the sofa, watching TV. He wasn't even out drinking. We checked the bar that the girl says he goes to, and nobody remembered seeing him there that night. I still had a feeling about him, so we did spot checks for a couple of weeks, but nothing ever panned out. You looking at *him* for the captain's grandkid?"

"Well, Jake here, talked to the stepdaughter, and she said she thinks he tried to molest Monica Lemon, about three months ago. Thanks Paulie."

"No problem. You need a body to knock on doors or anything, let me know."

"Well, Converse says Reeves works at ACME Markets. Cashier. Should be easy enough to see if he was working Friday afternoon. We'll hit that first thing in the morning. What's your new lead, Jake?"

"Well, this kid, Marge Grant, rode home, from school, on the bus with Monica on Friday. She says Monica told her she didn't have any plans, but that she was gonna score some Maui Gold, from some guy named Bug. Another girl, Tiffany Heller, says her and Monica rode the bus to the end of the line. She left Monica on Cottman Ave, in front of St. Hubert High School, waiting for the #84 bus. She Claims that she walked in the house at 3:45 pm. No more than a five-minute walk from where they parted company, to her house, so we can say that Monica was alive and well, at Cottman and Torresdale Avenues, waiting for the #84 bus."

"Hey Ronnie! They just put cameras in the lights at that intersection, didn't they?"

"Yeah Tony, they did. Let's hope they're working. And the school probably has security cameras outside, in that neighborhood."

"Hang out for a minute Jake, while we make a couple calls. Maybe we can get lucky. If this girl got on that bus, she would get off at Leon St., and walk a half block south to her house. I *know* we have eyes at the intersection of Cottman and Frankford. With any luck we might be able see if Monica got off at her regular stop."

Less than an hour later, the three men were sitting in front of Randy Converse's computer, where he had accessed the traffic cam, from Cottman and Torresdale Aves. Detective Hill spoke up. "How'd you get this so quick, Randy?"

"We have the website address for all the city's traffic cameras. I just had to call City Hall and get the serial number for that location. No sweat. Ok, here we go. Friday afternoon."

"Start rolling at 3:30 pm."

"You got it."

After fast forwarding through ten minutes of footage, Tony Hill said "There! Isn't that Monica, with that other girl?"

Detective Tanner chimed in. "Yeah. Gotta be her. SEPTA confirmed that the bus arrived at the end of the line at 3:38 pm. Time stamp says 3:40 pm. "

"Well, why don't we make sure." With that, Randy Converse zoomed in on the girls' faces, and hit a few keystrokes, and the result was a crystal-clear picture of Tiffany Heller, and Monica Lemon, on the North side of Torresdale Ave, crossing Cottman Ave. The four men watched the girls stand on the corner, in front of St. Hubert High School, and chat for two minutes, give or take, and then Tiffany proceeds to walk north on Torresdale, while Monica starts West on Cottman, towards the #84 Bus stop. At 3:47 pm, the bus pulls up, and the five people waiting get on. Except for Monica Lemon. After the bus pulls away, she walks back toward the intersection, and begins to cross Torresdale Ave. The camera loses sight of her, so Converse switched to the camera pointing north on Torresdale. He was able to pick up Monica crossing Torresdale Avenue, and then lost her. A switch to the camera facing east on Cottman gave them enough of a view to see Monica head into the park, before they lost sight of her. "That's all I can do, guys. I have a call into St. Hubert's. I know they have outside surveillance. They're going to send me the videos, which will include the cameras facing the park. Now, that being said, we have state-of-the-art stuff in our traffic cams. We have to be able to read license plates clear enough to hold up in court. What we'll be able to see depends on how state-of–the-art the school's cameras are. I should have the video first thing in the morning."

"Thanks Randy. There you have it, Jake. We know she made it from Little Flower High School to St. Hubert High. We know she didn't get on her bus. We know that at 3:51 pm, she walked into the park. Hopefully, we'll be able to see who she met in the park, if anyone, and what happened next."

"Good. What about this guy Bug? Anything on him, Ronnie?"

"That would be Tony's department, Jake. Tony?"

"I reached out to a pal of mine in the Narco Squad, to see if they know this guy. My friend should be... wait! That's my phone now. Manny! Thanks for getting back so quick. Any luck? Good. Yeah, go ahead." Tony Hill wrote down the information that this friend told him. "Thanks, Manny. Appreciate it. Later, man." After he disconnected the call, he looked up at his partner, and Jake. "Well, boys, Narcotics knows a small-time dealer that works out of the park. Benedict Heller. Twenty-three years old. 5'7". 160 lbs. Kids refer to him as 'Bug', because his thick glasses make his eyes look huge... bug eyes. Lives with his parents. Got an address on Sheffield St."

Jake did a double take. "Wait! Did you say Heller, and he lives on Sheffield St? Tiffany Heller, from the traffic cam, lives on Sheffield St. What do want to bet that the conversation we saw her and Monica having on the corner, was her telling Monica to meet her brother in the park, in ten minutes?"

"Let's go, partner. Jake, you riding with us, or driving yourself?"

"I'll follow you."

It was just before 5 pm, when the 3 men arrived at the Heller residence. Tiffany answered the door. "Detective Miller. What are you doing here?"

"Tiffany, we have some questions. Can we come in?"

"I guess. Mom! Dad! Police are here!"

Jake was out the door, like a shot, when he heard the back door of the small row home slam shut. "He's running!"

Now, the three detectives were in pursuit of Bug Heller. He ran past Jake, heading towards the park. Though at least five years older than the two Philly detectives, Jake clearly had the best chance of keeping up with Bug. He was at least thirty yards behind him, and slowly, but surely, losing ground. As they reached the park, Jake knew the only chance he had was if Heller ran out of gas, or made some other blunder, to slow him down. Fortunately, Bug did. As he jumped over the last of three park benches, he mistimed his jump, caught his foot on the bench, and ended in a heap, on the ground, writhing in pain. Jake could see the way he landed, that he dislocated his shoulder. Tony Hill arrived on the scene, and took out his phone, to call for an ambulance. "Hold up a minute Tony. I'll think he'll be okay."

With that, Jake grabbed Heller's hand, put his foot on his armpit area, and yanked viciously. Benedict Heller howled in pain. "Relax, kid. It'll stop hurting soon. You dislocated your shoulder. I popped it back in place. Hold your arm over your chest, like you have it in a sling. Here. Sit on this bench. Feels a little better already, doesn't it?"

"A little."

"Do you two mind if I ask Bug a few questions?"

"Go ahead. You caught him."

"Okay. Bug. Before you answer my questions, I want you to look at the traffic light there at the corner. See those round things under the lights? They are cameras. Now, look over at St. Hubert's. See those poles every fifty feet, with those big things on top? They are cameras too. So, you see, Bug, between those traffic cams, and the school surveillance cams, we can see everything that happens in this park. Remember that next time you pick a place to do a drug deal. Now, my questions. See this girl? Her name is Monica. Friday afternoon, Monica came into this park, around 4:00 pm, to buy some Maui Gold from a guy named Bug. That's not my question. I'm just gonna assume that you're the guy she was buying from, yes?"

Bug looked from pole to pole, and the six cameras outside the school. He nodded yes. "What did you sell her? "

"I didn't really sell her anything."

"Bug? You're lying."

"No. No. I didn't *sell* her anything. I *gave* her three joints."

"You *gave* her three joints? Out of the goodness of your heart? Do we believe him, guys?"

"No frigging way! Let's take him in, Jake."

"In a minute, detective Hill. Maybe Bug has something else to say, or are you going to stick with that ridiculous story?"

"It's true! She didn't have any money! I told her she could work it off, and she said OK!"

"Work it off?"

"Yeah. Right over there. Behind those trees. She got on her knees and, you know..."

"And then what, Bug?"

"Then nothing. I gave her three joints, and I left."

"What did she do?"

"I don't know man. She said she was gonna fire one up, as I was leaving. I don't do drugs, or nothing, man. I went home, ate dinner, and went to my room."

"And you were there all night?"

"Yeah."

"Ok detectives, I'm done. You guys have any questions?"

"No, we're good. Now, Bug, we're going to go verify what you just told us, and I hope for your sake that your parents tell the same story as you did. Tony, why don't you and Jake head over to the house. I'll call an ambulance for this knucklehead. One of us has to go to the hospital with him. I'll go. Tony, I'll call you from the hospital, and you can pick me up."

"Roger that partner."

Back at the house, Tiffany Heller, and her parents were sitting at the kitchen table, when Jake and Tony Hill got there. Mr. Heller spoke. "Where's Ben? Is he ok?"

"Ben's fine, Mr. Heller. He mistimed his jump over a park bench and dislocated his shoulder. It's back in place, and Detective Tanner is at the hospital with him. After he's released, he's going to be arrested for resisting arrest, and possession with intent to distribute marijuana."

"Is he in a lot of trouble?"

"Well, sir, that depends on you two."

"What do you mean?"

"First of all, Jake and I came back here to arrest your daughter, Tiffany here, as an accomplice in the distribution of a controlled substance."

"Tiffany? That's preposterous!"

"Maybe so, Mr. Heller, but your son just admitted to us that Tiffany, here, came home from school, Friday afternoon, and told him that a girl named Monica Lemon was waiting to meet him in the park, to score some pot. That makes her an accessory, after the fact, doesn't it Jake?"

"Sure does, Tony."

"Please don't take my little girl!"

"Mrs. Heller, we don't want to arrest a 17-year-old girl, but, unless the three of you can give us the information we need…"

"We'll give it to you! Tiffany, tell them whatever they want to know."

Actually, first question is for all three of you. Now, nobody say anything until I tell you to. Details of what happened last Friday, from 4:00 pm, through the rest of the night. Tiffany, you go upstairs, while your mom and dad answer. Jake, why don't you take Mrs. Heller, here, in the living room, and I'll stay here with Mr. Heller, and take down their answers."

"Sure, thing, Tony."

Once seated on the couch, Jake asked Sheila Heller, "Ok, Sheila, tell me about Friday."

"Well, at around 4:00 pm, I was starting dinner."

"What did you have?"

"Our usual Friday dinner, Mrs. Paul's fish sticks, and I made macaroni and cheese."

"All right. It's 4:00 pm. What happened?"

"Let's see. My husband Mark, was sitting in his recliner, right there, drinking a beer, watching Action News. Tiffany came in from school and asked where Ben was. Her dad said upstairs, and she went up. At 4:30 pm, I called up to her, and Ben that dinner would be in 15 minutes."

"Ben was home all afternoon?"

"I guess he was up there. I didn't see him go out, but he could have."

"Ok. It's 4:45 pm. Time for dinner."

"Mark was the first one at the table. He's always the first. As I was getting the macaroni out of the oven, Tiffany came down. I remember, because the bowl of mac and cheese was heavier than I thought, and I asked her to give me a second potholder, so I could use both hands. We said grace and ate."

"Was Ben there?"

"Yes. He came downstairs right behind Tiffany."

"What happened after dinner?"

"Well, the kids finished in, like five minutes, and they went up to their rooms. They eat too fast. What's so important on those computers that can't wait fifteen minutes, so you can eat properly. I doubt if they even taste the food."

"You're right. Then what?"

"Mark and I talked about our day. About 5:30 pm, I poured him a second cup of coffee, and he went to his recliner. I did the dishes and put everything away. The World News was coming on as I sat on the couch, so it was 6:30 pm."

"What about the rest of the night?"

"Well, we watched Jeopardy, and Wheel of Fortune, and then I think Shark Tank."

"That takes us up to 9:00 pm. The kids were still upstairs?"

"No, Tiffany went to a party, at one of her friends' houses. She left at 7:30 pm. She got in a little after midnight. We were in bed, but I never sleep until the kids are in."

"And what about Ben?"

"He was in the house all night."

"You're sure about that?"

"Yes, my husband asked for some ice cream, right after Shark Tank, and I hollered up to Ben, to see if he wanted any. He answered me no. And I heard him in the bathroom while I was waiting for Tiff to get home."

"Thanks, Mrs. Heller. That will be all."

"Did I do ok?"

"You did fine, dear. Just wait here, until I see if Detective Hill is finished with your husband."

Jake went into the kitchen and gave Tony Hill the notes he took from Mrs. Heller.

"Jake, why don't you send Mrs. Heller out here, call Tiffany down, and she what she was to say."

"Roger that." Jake's discussion with Tiffany lasted about five minutes. Her version echoed her mother's, except that she went to a club, to see a band. She admitted to Jake that she told her parents she was going to a party at a friend's house. When they were done, they joined the group in the kitchen.

"Well, Tony?"

"Jake, Mr. and Mrs. Heller's versions agreed exactly with each other, except Mr. Heller said it was chocolate chip ice cream, and his wife said it was mint chocolate chip."

"Mark Heller, you know the ice cream was green! We never get the plain chocolate chip!"

"It's alright, Mrs. Heller."

"What about my Tiffany? Are you going to arrest her?"

Jake answered. "Well, that depends on how she answers this last question I have for her. Tiffany, tell us again where you went when you went out Friday night."

"Huh?"

"You heard me. Where did you go when you went out?"

Tony Hill took out his handcuffs. "Ok. I went to a club. A bunch of us went, to see this band that was playing there."

"Tiffany!"

"Daddy would never let me go, if I said that's where I was going, so I lied, and said I was going to Nancy's."

"I think we're good. Good night." Jake and Tony walked out to the cars.

"Nice touch, Tony, bringing out the cuffs."

"I figured she lied to them and seeing handcuffs might tip the scales in favor of her fessing up."

"What are you guys going to do with Bug?"

"Oh, he's getting locked up."

"For what? He didn't have anything on him."

"We have a rule, Ronnie and me. If they make us run, they're going to jail. We'll most likely keep him overnight, then kick him loose in the morning."

"So, we know that Monica was in the park until at least 4:30 pm, or so, and that she had three joints in her possession. I guess in the morning, we check out the cameras from the school, and see if we can get a timeline on Monica's movements, after 4:30pm."

"Sounds about right, Jake. You headed home?"

"Yeah, I want to give Captain Lemon a report on what we found so far."

"You know, Jake, you might not want to mention the BJ in the park."

"Yeah, I'll edit that out, for now. See you in the morning. I'll check out Reeves' alibi at the ACME before I head over."

"Sounds like a plan."

Jake grabbed dinner on the way to Maggie's, called Roy Lemon, and filled him in on the day's proceedings, and what the plan was for tomorrow. Lemon thanked him and said he would pass the info along to his son and daughter-in-law.

CHAPTER 6

Jake made his way to ACME's customer service desk and asked to speak to the manager. The young girl accessed the store intercom and requested a manager to customer service. A few minutes later, a tall, bearded man approached the desk. "Amy, you paged me."

"Yes, Mr. Hughes. This gentleman asked to see you."

"How can I help you?"

"Good morning. My name is Jake Miller. I'm a detective, and I need some information from you. Is there somewhere we can talk privately?"

"Sure. Right this way, detective."

He led Jake into a tiny cubicle that he called his office. "Now, detective, as soon as I see your ID, I'll be happy to help you."

Jake flashed his badge. "Cape May County? What are you doing up here?"

"I need some information about an employee, Paul Reeves."

"Paul? One of our best cashiers. Been working here 15 years. Has he done something?"

"I'm not at liberty to discuss the case. I just need to know if he worked last Friday, and, if he did, what hours he was here."

"Sure. Sure. Give me a minute to log into the computer and access the payroll function... there! OK. His payroll number is 08962. Got it. And you want to know his hours on Friday, March 15th, 2019? Got it! Here you go. Paul worked from 9:00 am, to 3:30 pm."

"Can you print that out for me?"

"Sure. Is that it?"

"Well, one more question. Do you know if Paul drives to work?"

"No. he lost his license years ago. He takes SEPTA."

"So, he took the bus home Friday?"

"As a matter of fact, no, he didn't. The girl at Customer Service, Amy, had to stay late Friday. She lives near Paul and offered him a ride home. You could check with her to make sure, though."

"Thanks, I will."

Jake left the cubicle/office and went back to the service counter. "Amy?"

"Yes sir."

"Amy, did you drive Paul Reeves home Friday?"

"Yes. First time, and last time."

"What do you mean?"

"Well, I live about two blocks from the Reeves. I know Cindy. I'm two years older than her. We're, you know, friends. So, like, I usually get done at 2:30 pm, but Mona called out sick, so I stayed an extra hour, so, you know, we'd have coverage here. So, I'm clocking out, and I'm behind Mr. Reeves. Just to be nice, I ask if he wants a ride home, 'cause I know he takes the bus. Well, he has me drop him where else, at Stanzak's, the bar on the corner of his block. He, like, you know, hangs there. So, we're like, three blocks from the bar, and he, like, starts hitting on me! I was glad to get him out of my car."

"And what time did he get out of your car, Amy?"

"4:02 pm, exactly! I remember, because he said 'Perfect timing. You got me here just in time for Happy Hour.' Then he asked me if I wanted to come in and get happy with him. What a creep!"

"I agree. Thanks Amy. You've been a big help."

Jake called Tanner and Hill from the car, to tell them to cross Paul Reeves off the list. Ronnie Tanner told him they got the surveillance footage from St. Hubert's, and that Hill was getting it set up, for viewing. Jake said to tell Hill not to wait for him. He was about 20 minutes away.

As he walked into the detective squad room, Jake heard Tony Hill finish a sentence. "… next camera we'll see her leaving. Hey, Jake."

"Good morning, guys. What's up?"

"Well, so far, Bug Heller seems to be telling the truth. We just watched Monica and him meet. They talk for a while, then they go over behind those two trees. Five minutes later, you can see her standing up, and him giving her something, most likely, three joints. He walked north, as if he was going home. She lit up a joint and sat on a bench. The last thing this camera showed was her kind of staggering away, South towards Cottman Ave. She's out of the frame of the camera now. Tony has to cue up the next camera."

"Great." As the next camera was fast forwarded to the last timestamp from the previous camera, they saw Monica weave her way along the path. She passed by a bench that was occupied by what looked to be a young man, in a navy-blue hooded sweatshirt, wearing gloves. Only she didn't pass by.

"Look, guys. It seems like she is passing by, and he says something, or calls to her. She stops and looks at him."

"Yeah, you're right, Jake. She stops and talks back to him. Now it looks as though he's asking her something. Look, she nodded her head."

In the video, Monica made her way over to him, and as she neared him, he stood and put his arm around her, to steady her, and guide her. In doing so, he turned to face the camera. Tony Hill stopped the camera, zoomed in on the man's face and printed out the screenshot. He was wearing a scarf over his face, and dark sunglasses. "Okay, Tony, start up the tape again. Look, Jake, this guy's no good. See how he's keeping his head down? He knows where the cameras are!"

Jake nodded his agreement, as he watched the man and Monica make their way to what appeared to be a silver, or white Toyota Celica. Jake estimated the car to be about five to six years old. They watched the White, or Hispanic man, help Monica in the backseat. Then he got behind the wheel, pulled out, and headed South, on Torresdale Ave. The timestamp said 5:30 pm.

Tony Hill called Randy Converse, to have him cue up the traffic cams in and around St Hubert's, for Friday night, at 5:30 pm. Ronnie, Tony, and Jake went upstairs to Converse's cubicle. As they walked in, Tony Hill said, "If nothing else, we ought to get a license plate from the traffic cam."

At 5:33, a silver Toyota Celica made a left-hand turn, from Torresdale Ave, onto Eastbound Cottman Ave. Converse stopped the footage long enough to print out a clear shot of the Pennsylvania license plate. Ronnie Tanner went to the next cubicle, to run the plate. Meanwhile, Randy Converse picked up the surveillance of the Toyota. The camera at Cottman and State Road, showed the car making a right, onto State Road, and the camera at the next light, Princeton Ave., showed the vehicle turning left, to get on the ramp to I-95 North. Jake spoke. "Now what?"

"No problem, Jake. Him going onto I95, is a home run for us. In the city limits, they have cameras every mile, and once they get out of the city, there are cameras at every exit. Unless he parked on the side of the highway, and abandoned the car, we'll see him."

Sure enough, they were able to follow the car all the way up to the Rte. 413 exit, in Bucks County. The vehicle exited the highway at 5:58 pm, on Friday evening. The car was in the camera's view long enough for them to see that the driver turned right, heading towards Rte. 13.

While Converse called Bucks County, to see if they had traffic cams, and where, Ronnie Tanner came back with the results of the license plate search. "OK. The plate belongs to a silver Hyundai Elantra, registered to Mary Reynolds, of the Mayfair section. I called her. Her car is in front of her house. She went out, took a picture of her license plate, and sent it to me. *It* belongs on a silver Toyota Celica, belonging to Jose Santiago, also of Mayfair, who reported it stolen on Friday afternoon, at 2:30 pm. Looks like our guy stole the Toyota and switched plates with the Hyundai. I put a BOLO out on the 2012 silver Celica, with the Hyundai plate, and an FOP sticker on the back window."

Jake thought it ironic that the bad guy stole a car with a Fraternal Order of Police sticker on it. "The car was last seen getting off 95, at Rte. 413, Ron."

"Ok, I'll update the BOLO, with a last seen added on. I already included the Bucks County cops, and the State Police."

Randy Converse informed everyone that Buck's County did not have any traffic cams operational in, or around that area. They were blind again. The Toyota could be, literally anywhere. It could have gone North, to anywhere. Or, it could have crossed over the Burlington-Bristol bridge, into New Jersey.

Ronnie Tanner called the Bucks County Police, to update the BOLO for the silver Toyota, with the last seen near intersection of Rte. 413 and Rte. 13 information. The officer who took down the information asked Ronnie to hold a minute, for Radio Car officer Pete Hardwell. "Detective Tanner?"

"Yes. You are?"

"Officer Pete Hardwell."

"What can I do for you, officer?"

"Well, sir, you asked us to Be-On-the-Look-Out out on a silver Toyota? I saw that vehicle, sir. Friday night. Right around 10:00 pm.

I was coming out of the WAWA, and I turned behind it. The driver made a left turn, onto Farmers Landing Road. He cut right in front of oncoming traffic, almost causing an accident. I reached for the siren, to give chase, but I got an officer needs assistance, on a domestic violence call, so that takes priority. I took the time to write the plate number down, to run it later, and just forgot. When I saw the BOLO, the plate number sounded familiar. I checked my notes, and bingo!"

"Good work officer, but you saw the car Friday night. It could be in Ohio, by now."

"Well, that's just it, sir. Farmers Landing Road is about a two-mile-long stretch of road, with about ten farms on either side. It dead ends. If that car went down that road, odds are that he was going to one of them farmhouses."

"Very good, Officer. We'll take it from here." As dialed the State Police Barracks, in Trevose, PA, Ronnie Tanner told Jake and Tony what he had learned. After a quick chat with the State Police Captain, Tanner hung up and said "Grab your coats, boys. Time to go earn our money."

On the ride up to Farmers Landing Road, and Rte. 13, Tanner explained that the State Police would meet them there, with a ten-man detail, and they would proceed up Farmland Road, checking each house, for Monica Lemon.

The trio met up with the Troopers in the WAWA parking lot, which was about ¼ mile from Farmers Landing Road. According to the map that the Lt. in charge had with him, there were seven properties on that road. It was decided that the group would stay together, blocking the road, to prevent any escape, and searching one property at a time. Two hours, and three unsuccessful searches later, they approached house #4. Tony Hill was the first to notice a silver Toyota parked behind what he assumed to be, a barn.

As the team approached the house, Hill and Tanner checked out the car. It was, indeed, the car they were looking for. The team entered the house. It was empty. There was evidence that someone had been there recently. Trash, mostly. Food scraps that were not too far along on the going bad train. But it appeared that whoever was there, was gone now. No clothes, toiletries, personal effects. Jake and Tony Hill entered the barn structure, which was about 30' wide, by 50 ' long. The inside was completely barren. Just a dirt floor, and two support columns. Nothing. Jake ordered everyone outside, while he checked for boot prints, or other clues. The ground had been raked, with a leaf rake. As he walked over an ever so slightly raised area, his shoes sank a bit deeper into dirt. He stopped and got on his hands and knees. With his gloved hand, he pawed at the dirt. The raised area was looser dirt, than the surrounding area was. Jake's heart sank. He knew that something was buried there. He went outside, and leaned against the barn door. "Well?"

"I think I found a grave, Tony."

Jake, and the two Philly detectives went back into the barn with a small shovel and proceeded to dig up the body of a young girl in a high school uniform. It was not Monica Lemon. This girl had a Hallahan High School uniform on and had dark hair. Jake had seen enough bodies, in various stages of decomposition, to know that this girl hadn't been dead that long. His guess was no more than a few days. Without disturbing her body, they stood up, and called the Philadelphia Police Forensic Unit. When he finished the call, Ronnie Tanner said to Jake and Tony "We better wait outside. We don't want to contaminate the gravesite."

Jake agreed. They started out. Jake looked back. "Tony! Come on. We had better wait outside. Tony!"

Tony Hill stood stone still. He turned slowly, and quietly said "Tell them to bring cadaver dogs. I can see a couple more raised areas over there."

CHAPTER 7

When the sniffing and digging was done, the sun was starting to rise. Four bodies were discovered. All teenage girls, dressed in their high school uniforms. All died by suffocation. All were dead less than a week. Monica Lemon was not one of them. Tony Hill spoke. "I don't get it. We saw Monica get in that car. The car was there. Why didn't we find her."

"Haven't figured that out yet, Tony. Anything, Ronnie?"

"Well Jake, best I can figure is these girls were dead before our guy grabbed Monica, and for whatever reason, he's not done with her yet."

The girls had all been identified. Calls were made to Goretti/Neuman, Archbishop Ryan, St. Hubert's, and Hallahan High Schools, based on the uniforms the girls had on, and each school had reported a girl missing. School photos had been used to make identifications. Ronnie Tanner stared at the whiteboard, containing the names of each girl, and what they knew about each. After several minutes, he turned back to his partner, and Jake. "Guys, look at this. First girl abducted on her way home from school, Friday, Feb. 15th. Then one the following Friday, and the next Friday, ending with the last girl abducted on her way home from school, on Friday, March 8th. M.E. says all four were probably killed and buried within hours of each other. They were all dead before he snatched Monica. So, what, our guy grabs one girl per week, keeps them alive until he has four, then kills and buries them, and starts over?"

"Well, if that's so, Monica is still alive, and we have a little more than three weeks to find her. "

"Right Tony, and we can expect another girl to go missing this Friday."

It was Jake who now spoke. "Look, I'm an outsider here, but I gotta say, we're dealing with a real bad dude here. Not for nothing, but I think you guys should contact the FBI about this. They have resources, and access to data banks that you couldn't imagine."

Ronnie and Tony looked at each other. "What do you think, Tone?"

"Boss won't like that, Ronnie."

"Yeah, I know, but Jake's right. We got no plan. This guy is a serial killer of some kind. I think maybe we need some help with this one."

"Hey, look, none of my business, but I can call a guy. Real pro. Agent Brandon Wright. If nothing else, he can run interference for you with the Philly branch of the FBI."

Neither detective said anything. They looked at each other again, and both nodded at Jake.

FBI Agent Brandon Wright answered on the second ring. "Jake. What's up?"

"Brandon, I have you on speaker. I'm here with Philadelphia Detectives Ron Tanner, and Tony Hill."

"Morning men. You working the Monica Lemon case?"

"Yeah Brandon. They are."

"What's the problem?"

"Well, Brandon, we haven't found Monica. What we did find was a mass grave, of high school girls."

"Wait! 4 graves? Each taken a week apart? All killed and buried the same day? Out in the country, or in a big field?"

"Exactly! How did...?"

"Listen fellas, it's just about 10:00 am. My partner and I will be up there by 2:00 pm. You're at the 15th Police District? And the bodies were discovered Tuesday, March 19th? See you soon."

"What the hell was that, Jake?"

"Best I can figure, Tony, is the FBI is tracking a case with the same MO. I mean, he knew how many graves there would be, and that there were 4 girls taken, 1 week after each other, and they were killed at the same time. Either our perp has done this before, or agent Wright *is* our perp."

"Well, either way, we're out."

"What do you mean, Ronnie?"

"Tell, him, Jake."

"Tony, if the FBI is coming up here from Washington, odds are they're going to take over the case."

"Yeah, T, they'll be sending us out to get them coffee, and shit. No skin off my nose, though. They may get the glory, if we get the girl back, but we won't have to be the ones to tell Captain Lemon, if they don't find her. All that responsibility is off our plate now, Tony."

About 1:45 pm, FBI agents Wright and Caldwell found their way into the detective squad. Jake made the introductions. "Detectives Ron Tanner, Tony Hill, these are FBI Field Agents Brandon Wright, and Harvey Caldwell."

"Nice to meet you, detectives. Jake. Could one of you take Harvey here, to talk to the captain? We need to let him know we're here and are taking over jurisdiction."

"Brandon, the girl we're looking for is the captain's granddaughter. Harvey, you might want to keep that in mind, when you talk to him."

"Roger that." Tony Hill and Harvey Caldwell headed downstairs to see Captain Lemon.

"Now, Detective Tanner, we'll be taking the lead on this case, but you and your partner will be working hand in hand with us. We will be working out of our Philadelphia Office. Let me tell you what we know already, about these guys."

"Guys? As in more than one? Because we didn't find any evidence of a second perp."

"I'll get to that, Detective Tanner. Let me continue. We believe this is a gang of at least three, possibly four bad guys. We call them The High School Rapists. They struck in Baltimore, back in October. Then they turned up in Wheeling, West Virginia, in the middle of December, and the last time was in January, outside of Memphis. In trying to get ahead of them, their path was leading them further south. Didn't expect them to come up this way."

"Well, what exactly is their deal?"

"Okay. They only snatch girls dressed in high school uniforms. Always on a Friday afternoon. One a week, for four weeks. The girls are apparently used as sex toys. They seem to keep them alive, until they have four, and then they smother all four, and bury them. These girls have been used over and over. The M.E. has concluded on each of the 1st three cases that the first girl taken, who is kept for a little over three weeks, has been used for sex well over fifty times, by the time she is killed. Even the last girl taken, who is only kept for four days, or so, has had dozens of sexual encounters. That's one reason we believe there are multiple perps. We have no DNA evidence. They never have had unprotected sex. They must wear gloves 100% of the time, while they are in their kill houses. It looks like they pick their victims at random, but never from the same school twice. They pick schools that are far apart from each other. By the time the alarm gets sounded at the surrounding schools, they've got four girls, and are gone. Same MO for the abductions. Steal a late model car, silver, or tan. So far, all

Nissans, or Toyotas. Switch plates with a car the same color. We think one guy makes all the grabs. We got a little help, when we think they were stealing a Toyota, in Wheeling, and the owner caught them, and they took off. Citizen described them as a thin black male, and a white male, average height, about 250 lbs. Three blocks away, a silver Sentra was stolen, twenty minutes later. The guy who does the grab, has been caught on traffic cams. Always wears a hooded sweatshirt, and scarf over his face, and sunglasses. Appears to be white, but thin. That's why we think there are at least 3. They find an empty farmhouse and make that their kill house. When they're done, they clean the place immaculately, and torch the stolen car. Obviously, they have a second vehicle, that they travel from place-to-place in. In the first 3 cases, the girls were buried in shallow graves, inside a barn, or some other structure. I think that's it, as far as physical evidence. Sound like your case?"

"Yeah. Identical. Right down to the scarf and glasses."

"*Almost* identical, Ron. They grabbed a 5th girl from this area. The captain's granddaughter. And they took her with them."

"You're right, Tony. So, it looks like it's the same crew. What's your plan, Agent Wright?"

"From what we've learned, Jake, there will be three more abductions, one each Friday, for the next three weeks. We need to get the word out to every school within a hundred-mile radius, to be extra vigilant, especially on Fridays. Have them set up a website, and have every girl email, or text, when they get home. That way, we'll know immediately if someone gets abducted. We know that, up till now, the kill house has never been more than a twenty-minute ride from where the girls were abducted from. Obviously, the next girl taken is extremely important, because we can then set up a perimeter of how far you can travel in twenty minutes, and we assume we'll have two weeks to locate the house, before they're gone again."

"Brandon, couldn't we contact the schools and have their girls not wear uniforms on Fridays?"

"Jake, I don't want this to sound callous, but we need them to grab another girl, if we are to have any chance of finding Monica alive."

"Wait! You *want* them to take another girl?!"

"Look, Detective Tanner, unless we get a break, we have no idea where they took Monica. They could be in North Jersey, or the Poconos, or Hershey. What we *do* know, are the horrible things they are doing, right now, to that poor girl. If we can narrow our search area, that would be great. Right now, the only way we can do that, is if we get word that they grabbed someone else or tried to. I want these guys, Detective. Our Medical Examiner described the unspeakable things…"

Agent Wright stopped talking when he saw Jake's eyes widen. He turned to find his partner, Detective Hill, and Captain Roy Lemon, standing behind him. "Captain Lemon? Brandon Wright. Sir, let me say that the full might of the FBI is doing everything possible to bring your granddaughter safely back to you."

"I know you are. You have the cooperation of the Philadelphia Police Department, at your service, Agent Wright. Carry on."

With that, Roy Lemon turned on his heels, and slowly left the squad room. "Damn! Put my foot in it big time."

Jake rescued him. "Forget it, Brandon. The captain shoots from the hip and wouldn't have it any other way. Listen, you don't need me hanging around here, getting in everybody's way. I'm gonna head out. Goodluck, everybody."

"I'll walk out with you. Harvey can coordinate with the detectives and map out a strategy."

When Agent Wright and Jake were out in the parking lot, Agent Wright spoke up. "Listen, Jake, one of the perks of working for the FBI is that I have, basically, a blank checkbook, at my disposal. The Bureau would like to hire you, to run point for us in this case."

"Whoa, Brandon! I'm not a cop anymore."

"No, you're a Private Investigator. And the FBI would like to hire you. Jake, I'm serious. Look, you're already working for Lemon, right? Well, you do the same things, only you'll be getting paid by Uncle Sam. How about it?"

"Who do I take orders from?"

"Nobody, really. You'll know what we're doing, and you work independently. You'll have all our intel and data bases at your disposal, and any information you dig up, you throw in our pot. Jake, if I didn't think it was worth it, I wouldn't offer."

"What if I want to hire some extra help?"

"No problem. Just try to keep it around $3,000/week. And it works out perfectly."

"How so?"

"Your brother-in-law is due home from the Borgata this afternoon, right?"

"Wait! How did you know…?"

"Jake, I've seen, firsthand, what you and Tom Hansen can do together. Part of my job is to keep up on any assets, that The Bureau may be able to use."

"Okay. What's your play?"

"Our profiler is on her way up here, as we speak. I'm gonna have her brief us at, say, 8:00 pm, here in the precinct. We're gonna spend most of our manpower this afternoon, and tomorrow, contacting schools. Any ideas?"

"Yeah. I was thinking on concentrating on their travel vehicle. It *had* to be at the kill house, on Farmers Landing Road. Add to that, a black guy might stick out in that area. I figured to canvass the neighbors, maybe get lucky, and get a line on their vehicle."

"Good idea. That'll leave our manpower free to warn the schools and monitor stolen car reports."

"Okay, then. See you tonight."

Jake called Tom Hansen. "Hey, Tom. How was the Borgata?"

"Fantastic. We're crossing the bridge, into Philly, in about five minutes. We should be in Port Richmond, and home, in about a half hour, or so. Are you still up in the city?"

"Yeah. I hope that's alright?"

"Yeah. Sure. I'm off until next Monday. You and your sister, I mean, my wife, can show me around. You okay, Jake?"

"Not really, Tom. I caught a case. That's why I'm still up here."

"Really? What kind of case?"

"You remember Roy Lemon?"

"Yeah. Art Kaufman's buddy. Great guy."

"Well, his granddaughter was abducted Friday afternoon, and he hired me to track her down. I've been working with the Philly detectives. We found a mass grave yesterday, up in Bucks County."

"Geez. So, she's dead?"

"No. Tom, we stumbled onto a gang of serial rapists. The FBI named them the High School Rapists. I called Brandon Wright. This crew has been abducting high school girls, in their uniforms, one a week, for four weeks. They keep them…wait! Maggie can't hear this, right?"

"No, you're good. Go on."

"After they get four girls, they kill them all, bury them, and move on to the next town. Monica Lemon was the first girl taken."

"Jesus, Jake, if you need any help."

"That's why I'm calling, Tom. I'm not working for Lemon anymore. Get this. The FBI hired me to work independently from their investigation. I was wondering if you would be up to help me for a few days. The job pays $150/day."

"How many victims so far, Jake?"

"The four we found yesterday, brings the total to sixteen, that we know of. Tom, I know you just got married. I wouldn't ask, if…"

"Say no more Jake. I'll see you when we get home."

"Thanks Tom."

Jake was waiting in the kitchen, when the happy couple came in. His sister threw her arms around him. "Jimmy! I'm so glad you're still here."

"Look at you! You've been married, what, four days? And you look like an old married couple. Have you gained weight, Mags?"

"What?! I'll knock your block off, Jimmy Miller! Is there any food in the house? I'll get dinner started."

"No, sis, the cupboard is bare. We're going to Georgine's restaurant tonight. In fact, we have a 4:30 pm reservation. Let's get a move on."

"Okay. Let me run up to the bathroom. I'll be right down."

When Maggie was out of sight, Tom asked, "So, what's the plan?"

"Well, Tom, right now, I have to make two calls. One to Katie, to see if she wants to join us, and one to Georgine's, and hope I can get a 4:30 pm reservation."

Kathleen couldn't make it. Jake, Tom, and Maggie had a nice dinner. When Tom excused himself to go to the men's room, Maggie took Jake's hand, and told him "Tom told me that he agreed to work on a case with you. He was worried that I'd be upset with him."

"Mags, this really is an emergency."

"Hush, Jimmy. I know that it must be life or death, for you to ask for help. You tell Tom that I'm okay with it, will you? I told him, but I don't think he believed me."

"I will, Mags."

"And Jimmy, you keep him safe."

"I'll do my best, sis."

"That's good enough for me. Now, pay the bill, and let's get out of here. You must have something scheduled tonight. You checked your watch a dozen times, in the hour and a half we've been here."

As Jake and Maggie left the table, they saw Tom coming towards them. "Turn around husband. Why don't you ride with Jake, and I'll drive myself home. That way, you two can go to wherever it is you need to be, and I can go home, and call my daughter."

Jake smiled and slapped Tom on the shoulder. "You got your hands full with that one Tom."

CHAPTER 8

Jake and Tom entered the roll call room, just as Brandon Wright was introducing the FBI Profiler. "Jake. Tom. Just in time. This is Justine Whitlock, our FBI Profiler."

"Good evening, men. Please, call me Jay. I know that Agent Wright is anxious to get moving, so I'll get right to it. This particular group has done this four times, that we know of. The fact that they are targeting high school girls suggests they possess an anger towards that age group. A likely motive for that choice is revenge, for the rejection they likely received when they were in high school. In identifying these men, we are making a leap of faith. While the first attack, in Baltimore, could have been planned well in advance, the following attacks happened very close to when the previous attacks ended. There would not be sufficient time for them to plan ahead. Locating a kill house and finding the schools in each area would have to be done on the fly, so to speak. And why such varied locations? We're fairly certain that the areas chosen were, at one time, home to one of the perps. For them to set up their operation, in Wheeling, for example, they would have to have known ahead of time about the vacant farmland, that is almost exactly 10 miles from each school a girl was abducted from. We believe that one of the perps spent enough time in Wheeling, to know the lay of the land. The same with here, in Philadelphia. There is probably more open space for them to find a kill house, South of Philadelphia, or West of the city, but anyone who has spent any time on the roads of the city, knows that going South on I-95, or West, on the expressway, is horrible, traffic-wise, in the late afternoon. The one direction that offers a semi-continuous flow of traffic is North. Even at that, going ten to fifteen miles further North would have produced many more options for finding a secluded place. Because they stopped in Bucks County, we feel that one of them grew up in the area or spent a good portion of their life there. But if they all were from different areas, how did they meet? The two answers we arrived at were in the service, or in college. We have one team looking into the military service option, and one looking into the college angle. Yes, detective Converse. Question?"

"Yeah, how in the world can you figure out if these guys went to college together?"

"Not easily. Agent Caldwell is heading that up. We can assume these men are smart. We are starting with the two smaller areas, Memphis, and Wheeling. Harvey is checking the high schools in those areas, going back ten years, for male students in the top half of their class, who went to college. Once he has a list of the colleges attended by these men, he can cross-reference the college's records, to see if there were any students there at the same time, from Baltimore and Philadelphia areas. Once he gets a list of the colleges that had students from all four areas, he can check majors, fraternities, etc., to see if he can find a common thread, where the students' paths crossed. I agree it is a long shot, but you never know. Basically, we're probably looking for men who were not popular with girls in high school, and probably after. The rage with which they attack these girls indicates they need to control them, and want to punish them, for the bad way they were treated by girls in the past. They also seem to want to prove to law enforcement that they are smarter than we are. They made no attempt to hide the stolen vehicles when they left. Almost as if they wanted the cars to be found, to prove how smart they were. They want us to know they did this, and kind of, get off, thinking they outsmarted us. Any other questions…? Thank you, and good luck."

Branden Wright stepped back to the podium. "Thanks, Jay. OK. First thing tomorrow, you'll all be given a list of high schools from here to Hershey, and fifty miles into New Jersey. You will contact each school on your list. By Friday morning there will be a website set up for each school. You have the address. You will tell the school administrator that they should have every girl log onto that website when they get home from school on Friday. Now, with tomorrow being Thursday, we only have one day to spread the word. You'll each have a list of about thirty schools that you must contact. OK. That's it. Be back here at 6:00 am, tomorrow morning."

As the officers and detectives gathered their belongings, Brandon approached Jake and Tom. "All right, fellas. Here are two sketches we have, of the black guy, and the heavy guy. Also, here's a photo of the guy driving Monica Lemon away. I want you to do what you planned, canvassing the neighborhood. Hopefully, someone will be able to give us a line on their getaway vehicle. Good luck. Keep in touch."

"Goodnight Brandon."

On the ride back to Maggie's house, Jake asked Tom for his opinion. "Well, pard, these perps have been living on the road for the last four months or so. They don't seem stupid enough to use plastic to buy food, and such, so they have a stream of income, or are independently wealthy. After we talk to the neighbors up there on Farmland Road, we might want to show these pictures around in any fast-food joints, or restaurants."

"Sounds like a plan."

~~~

Thursday morning saw Jake and Tom head up to Farmland Road. Even though there were seven houses on the stretch of road, there were only three that the township had listed as 'occupied'. The others were in various stages of foreclosure. Two were at the furthest end of the road. They were the pairs' first stop. It was a quick stop. Both parties were retired and rarely left their homes. They had no idea anyone was staying at the old Wilson place. They didn't see, or hear anything, and certainly didn't recognize anyone in the pictures. The other occupied home was about five hundred yards east of the Wilson place. The perps would have to drive past this house every time they went anywhere.

Harriet Abrams answered the door, and invited Jake and Tom in. She was a thin woman, about seventy years old, with bright blue eyes, and a sing-song voice. "Come. Sit at the table. Can I get you some coffee?"

"Thank you. That would be nice."

"I can make you breakfast, if you like. It won't take but a minute or two."

"No thank you, ma'am. We ate already. Coffee will be great."

After filling their mugs, and sitting down with them, Harriet asked, "Now what are you two good looking gentlemen doing here?"

Jake spoke. "Well, Miss Abrams…"

"Please. Call me Harriet."

"OK, Harriet, we want to ask you some questions about the Wilson place, across the street."

"Oh, Marie Wilson was a wonderful soul. She was my best friend. The saddest day of my life was when they moved away. Next to my Harry passing on, of course."

"Of course. Now, Harriet, the last few weeks, did you notice anybody over at the Wilson place?"

"Oh, yes! That's right. Yes! That police officer asked me on Tuesday, and I said I didn't think so, but then yesterday, I remembered that I did. The officer gave me a card to call if I remembered anything, but, silly me, I misplaced it. I was just upset, what with all the commotion over there, on Tuesday, that I got confused. Thank goodness you two showed up today. Will you tell that officer that I *did* see something?"

"Of course, dear. Now, what did you see?"

"Well, the police told me that some people were living there for a month! I told them, that I never saw a light, or smoke come out of the chimney, or anything."

"Well, what did you see?"

"At first, nothing. I was on my porch last Friday night, a little after 6:00 pm. The mail man delivers the mail around 5:00 pm, but I'm eating dinner then, so I go out to get my mail after I'm done eating and cleaned up. My mailbox is right on the wall, by my front door. So, I put my sweater on, and went out to get the mail, and I heard somebody yell. They hollered 'get off me!'. Now, it's real quiet around here, so when you hear a noise, you really hear it, you know? Well, I don't move as fast as I used to, and, luckily, it was still a little bit lighty out, and when I turned toward the Wilson place; that's where the noise came from, I thought I saw the storm door on their place close."

"Very good Harriet. Now, the person yelling, was it a man's voice?"

"No, it sounded like a young girl. I'm sorry I didn't see anybody, just the door closing. But that made me keep a look out. On Saturday, I saw a gray car come from there."

"Are you sure, Harriet?"

"Absolutely. I thought it came from down the road, because it didn't come out of Wilson's driveway. "

"Then how do you know it came from there?"

"Well, I stayed in the living room waiting for it to come back. It gave me something to do, for the afternoon."

"And it did come back?"

"Oh, yes. About 1:30 pm."

"And it pulled into the Wilson's driveway?"

"No. It went past the driveway. But I saw a young black man driving, and we don't see many of them here, so I watched to see where it was going. Well, he drove past the Wilson's barn, and turned in behind it."

"And did you see him go in the house?"

"Yes. Yes, I did."

"Was he carrying anything?"

"You mean like groceries, or such? No. He just had a little pouch-like bag. Very small. Too small for food."

"And do you remember what time the car left, dear?"

"Yes. I watch the Mass every morning, at 10:00 am, and it's over at 11:00 am. It was right after that I saw the car."

"Did you see any other cars, Harriet?"

"No other cars. But there was a black...thing, they drove away in, on Monday, I think."

"What do you mean by black thing?"

"Well, it wasn't a car, and it wasn't a pickup truck. It was different."

Tom quickly brought up a picture of a Range Rover. "Did it look like this, Harriet?"

"Yes. But it was a Ford."

"OK Harriet, did you happen to see the license plate?"

"Oh, yes! I don't remember the numbers, but it was from Tennessee. My Harry and I would play that license plate game with our children, when we were going on a trip. I just got in the habit of checking license plates. That's the very first Tennessee license plate I ever saw come down this road."

"One last question, Harriet, then we'll leave you be. Did you get a look at who was in the black Ford? You said, 'they left'."

"Well, I couldn't identify them if I saw them again, if that's what you mean. I'm seventy, you know. My eyes aren't what they used to be. But I did see the black man driving. And there was a man in the front with him, and 2 people in the back."

"So, you saw four men leaving in the Ford, on Monday?"

"No. There were three men. The 4th person was female. And before you ask, it was around noon."

"Harriet, you've been a big help to us. Thank you so much. You mentioned trips you'd take with your children? Do you see them often?"

"My son, Harry; I have a son and a daughter, and four grandchildren; my son comes to see me twice a year. He's single. My daughter and her family come once a year. They live in New York. And they have me up at their home, for Christmas."

"That's nice, Harriet. Here is my card. In fact, I'll give you two of them, in case you misplace one. If you think of anything, or you need anything, you just call me, okay Harriet?"

"Thank you so much! Good luck finding those men. Bye boys."

Back in the car, Jake asked, "What do you think, Tom?"

"Pard, I think that profiler knows her job well. It appears that at least one of the perps is from Memphis, and there are three. Wouldn't surprise me if these three know each other from Baltimore, and decided to do this there, and then went to different places, that are probably familiar to one of them. I believe there's only three of them, because up till now, they seemed to set up in an area, and then started grabbing victims. This time, they grabbed the first victim before they left."

"And...?"

"Well, think about it. They take the first girl here, in a place that's familiar. Let's say they went into Jersey. Now they have a week to find a place and check out the area. Or better yet, what if the routine changes now. Grab a girl on the way out of a place, then skip a week. That gives them two weeks to scout around."

"Makes a lot of sense, Tom. We should call Brandon and let him know what we found."

"Roger that. Somethings bothering me, though, Jake."

"Like what?"

"What Harriet said about the black guy driving the gray car. You'd think that they'd venture out only when necessary. You know, for food, clothes, necessities. But she said he went out Saturday morning, at 11:00 am, and came back a couple of hours later. And he only had… like a sandwich bag with him. What was so important in that sandwich bag, that he'd be willing to travel out, right before they split from the Wilson place?"

"Your guess is as good as mine, Tom."

Jake called Brandon Wright and filled him in on their meeting with Harriet Abrams. Agent Wright agreed with Tom's assessment, and said he was going to have Agent Caldwell have someone concentrate on colleges in, and around Baltimore. After Jake informed him what he and Tom planned to do next, Brandon wished him good luck, and disconnected the call.

Tom and Jake spent the next two hours going in and out of every restaurant, bar, deli, and convenience store, on, or near Rte. 13, asking if they recognized anyone, or remembered a black Ford SUV, with Tennessee plates. They came up empty. They decided to stop for lunch, at a small, hipster-looking place. They were seated at a table in the front. Jake had no idea what was on the menu, but the waitress was smoking hot. He had Tom take the seat facing Rte. 13, while he sat with a view of the new love of his life. He told Tom, that he was a married man now, and he wasn't allowed to be looking at other women.

Tom said, "I could care less about the waitress. Did you see the prices on this menu? $15 for hamburger!"

"Don't worry about the cost, Tom. The FBI is paying." While they were waiting for their $15 hamburgers, Jake asked Tom, "Have you figured out what was bothering you, about the bag our guy was carrying into the Wilson house, Saturday?"

"Well, yes, and no."

"Oh, good. As long as you're sure."

"Hear me out, Jake. We figure the perps are in the age range of millennials, right? Now, what do we know about millennials?"

"They think they're smarter than everybody."

"Check. What else?"

"They're addicted to their cell phones, and computers."

"Exactly. They are checking their phones all the time. Now, they're living in a house, for almost a month, with no electricity. So, how do they get their internet fix?"

"I *hate it* when you play this game. Can't you just tell me, Tom?"

"No, you learn better if you figure it out."

"OK. They get their internet fix on their cell phones. Simple."

"Right. I know you've gone binging on your phone, watching porn, or playing solitaire. How long can you play, before that '*your battery is at 20%*' message comes on?"

"Maybe four hours. Maybe a little less."

"And what do you do when that happens?"

"What do you mean? I hook the phone up to the charger...which *they* can't do, with no electricity!"

"You're catching on. And it takes about a little more than an hour to charge again, right? We'll get back to that in a minute. The profiler said they must be independently wealthy, or have a stream of steady income, didn't she? For the sake of argument, let's say that they're not wealthy. That means at least one of them has some steady income, from maybe investments."

"Or a job."

"Right. Now, what kind of job could somebody have, that they could move around the country, and still do the job?"

"Something to do with computers."

"Good. Only two more questions. Assuming somebody had to keep track of their investments, or their internet business, what's the one thing they'd need to do that?"

"They'd need access to the internet."

"Now, for the big money, where could they go, to get internet access, and charge their phones, at the same time?"

"One of those Internet Cafes, or a Coffee shop, with internet access, but we've gone about five miles from Farmland Road, and we haven't come across any places that have internet access. Sorry, Tom, but this area just doesn't have the call for a place like that."

"You're right, Pard. Think outside the box for a minute. Where else?"

"I don't know. A friend's house?"

"Possible. Not likely. Turn around and look out the window."

Jake turned in his chair, and looked across the highway, at The Bucks County Free Library. "The library! Of course!"

"There you go. Like I always say, you're not just another pretty face."

Twenty minutes later, they were at the Librarian's desk, having identified themselves. "Mr. Hoffbauer, what is the procedure, if I wanted to go online?"

"We would scan your library card, and assign you to a computer, and you'd have an hour. But if we're not too busy, and we hardly ever are, you can stretch that hour, if you need to."

"What if I'm visiting the area, and I don't have a library card?"

"That depends. If it's a onetime usage, we might just let you sign in, but if you're going to be in the area, and plan on coming back in, we'll issue you a temporary card."

"And you do that here?"

"Oh, no, Mr. Miller. We have a desk back in the computer room, where all that takes place."

"Thanks. One last question. Who would've been working back there last Saturday?"

"That would be Miss Levine. She's there Tuesday through Saturday, from 9 am until 5 pm. She's there now. Go on back, officers."

"Thanks."

Jake and Tom found their way back to the computer room, which contained ten computers, three of which were currently in use. Abby Levine looked up from her desk, pushed her glasses back where they belong, and asked "Do you gentlemen need to use a computer? Just scan your card, and we'll set you up."

"No, Miss Levine, my name is Tom Hansen. I'm a Detective with the Cape May Courthouse Police Department, and I'm up here following a lead on a case we're working on. Have any of these men been in here to use the computer?"

He showed her the two sketches and the picture. "Well, that could be the black gentleman, that was here on Saturday. Nice young man. Very polite. Let's see...", as she flipped back through the sign in sheets. "Here. Saturday, from 11:45 am, until 1:05 pm. Reginald Logan."

"Did Mr. Logan show you identification?"

"He didn't have to. He's been here quite a few times in the last few weeks. He has a temporary card."

"When he got his temporary card, did he have to show proof of identification?"

"Oh, yes sir. We can relax the rules some, but you can't get a card, if you don't have a valid, government issued, ID."

"And how do you verify that ID?"

"We photocopy the ID, for our records."

"Please tell me you have Mr. Logan's ID on record."

"Sure. I'll print out a copy for you. Here you are. Reginald Logan. He provided a valid Tennessee driver's license."

"Do you know which computer he used?"

"Yes. Number four. He always requested that computer. It's the closest one to the phone charging station. He charged his phone."

"Just one phone?"

"I don't know, but it's one of those plates that you charge the phone by just placing it on the plate. I think it can accommodate six phones at once. I don't know how many he charged."

"Is computer number four in use right now?"

"No."

"Miss Levine, we're going to need to take that computer with us. I'll sign a voucher for it, and we'll return it in a day or so, once we get the information from it."

As Jake and Tom headed back into the city, with the computer, he called Agent Wright, to give him an update. He read Reginald Logan's driver's license info over the phone to him. Wright asked him to take the computer right down to the FBI field office, at the Green Building, located at 6th and Arch Sts., in Center City Philadelphia. While they were sitting in traffic, on I-95, Hansen asked Jake, "Think the Tennessee license is for real?"

"Absolutely."

"Really? Absolutely?"

"Sure. Let's say you're going to get a phony ID. You're going to pick an alias, right?"

"Yeah?"

"You could pick any name. Are you going to pick Reginald?"

"Probably not. Never thought about it much. Yeah, probably not gonna be Reginald, though. But apparently you have thought about it. What would your alias be?"

"Easy. William Raymond?"

"Really? That's a dorky kind of name."

"Yeah Tom, but then I could be known as Billy Ray. How cool is that!?"

Tom chuckled. "Oh, I see. Yes. Very cool. You are a piece of work."

Jake and Tom walked back into the 15th District and came upon a swarm of activity. Brandon Wright saw them from across the room and motioned them into the office that was his temporary base of operations. "Jake, Tom. Close the door behind you, or we won't be able to hear each other. You boys earned your money today."

"ID wasn't fake?"

"No. I didn't think it would be. Would *you* pick Reginald as an alias?"

Tom shook his head. "Great! Another one."

"Seriously, this is a great lead! I had Harvey track Mr. Logan. Twenty-five years old. He went to University of Maryland, at Baltimore, on a full scholarship, as a Computer Science major. Graduated 3 years ago. We're now cross-referencing students from Wheeling and Philadelphia areas that may have crossed paths with Reginald."

"At least we've made some progress. We're still no closer to finding Monica, but if we can put names and faces to these clowns, maybe we'll get a few calls."

"What about the SUV?"

"Nothing registered at all to Logan, but his address is his mother's house, Renee Davis. Ms. Davis has two vehicles registered in her name:

a 2016 Audi, and a 2014 black Ford Explorer. We have agents at her place, as we speak, and a BOLO out on the Explorer, in PA, NJ, and DE. Jake, Tom, I believe the vehicle is going to be their mistake. It's how we're going to catch them. Somebody's bound to see a black Ford Explorer, with Tennessee plates. They never counted on us ID-ing Mr. Logan. "

"Let's not get too full of ourselves, Brandon. They're only using the Ford to move from kill house to kill house. If they stay according to plan, that vehicle has been hidden out of sight, probably since Monday night. And we won't see it again, until they're ready to move on, in a few weeks. I think our best chance is if we get lucky when they steal the next car, and we catch the stolen car report right away. They drive that car on mostly a daily basis. That's what they don't know that *we* know. Something I've been meaning to ask you, Brandon. The other three locations, how did we discover their kill houses?"

"They lit the stolen car on fire, when they were moving on. Like I said. They are showing us what they did. They wanted us to find the graves. We have kept it all out of the papers."

"So, up until now, they've signaled the police when they were leaving an area. Why didn't they do that now?"

"Good question, Pard. My guess would be that they haven't left the area, yet."

"My thoughts exactly, Tom."

"Wait. Both of you think these guys are still in the area?"

"Makes sense, Brandon. They have been nothing, if not regimented. They moved on Monday. You said they've been throwing the killings in our faces, by showing them to us. The only reason I can think of for them not to do that this time, is if they're not done here yet. My gut is telling me that they haven't gone very far. Hell, there's a chance that they don't know that we found the place on Farmland Road."

"Might not be a bad idea to keep an eye on the Wilson place, Brandon. Seems to reason that if they're still around, they'll come back to set the car on fire, when they leave the area. They may even come back just to check it out."

"I don't know, Tom. I'm already stretched thin on manpower. I don't think I can spare the people on a slim chance."

"How about this, Brandon? You're paying me, right? Tom and I will watch the Wilson house. I'm sure Mrs. Abrams won't mind overnight company for a while. And she can make a few dollars, which I'm sure she can use."

"Sounds good, Jake. Let's do it."

"Hold on, there, pard. Tomorrow's Friday, and I got a job I'm due back at, on Monday. I got a wife to support now, you know. But I'll tell you what, I know somebody that would probably be willing to hang out with you up here for a spell."

"Who, Tom?"

"Jamal King."

"Wilt?"

"Yeah, Wilt. I was gonna talk to you this weekend about him. He's been hanging around the squad room, about the last month, or so. He's made great progress in his rehab. In fact, he's getting antsy, looking for something to do. This job would be perfect. Why don't you give him a call?"

"Wilt, huh? That sounds like a plan. I'll talk to Harriet Abrams tomorrow, Brandon, and set it up."

"Good. Look, it's after 5:00 pm. Not that I'm telling you what to do, but why don't you head out. You're only fifteen minutes away, if I need to reach out to you."

"Sounds good to me. Talk to you tomorrow, Brandon. Tom?"

Tom Hansen grabbed agent Wright's hand. "Agent Wright. Until next time."

CHAPTER 9

The phone at the King home started ringing at 7:30 am, on Friday morning. Seven-year-old Patty King answered it. "Hello. King residence."

"Hello, King residence. Am I speaking with Peppermint Patty?"

"Uncle Jake! Mom! Mom! It's Uncle Jake! Uncle Jake. When can we go on your boat again?"

"As soon as it gets warm out Patty."

"Give me the phone."

"Ok. Bye Uncle Jake!"

Patty handed the phone to her mother. "Jake?"

"Hi Denise. I gotta tell you Denise, even my dogs don't get that excited when they see me. How are you all."

"We're good Jake. Jamal has made wonderful progress. God bless Rebecca Lachowicz. She was the only one to get through to him and make him follow through on his therapy. How are you, Jake?"

"I'm good, Denise. I'm up in Philly right now. I'm helping the FBI with a case. In fact, that's why I'm calling. Is Jamal there?"

"Yes, he's just finishing getting dressed. He should be down any minute. Patty! Go get your father. Tell him to pick up the phone. He'll be right along, Jake."

"Denise, how are things financially?"

"Fine Jake. Between what Jamal gets on disability, and I bring home from my receptionist job, we're doing well. Here's Jamal, Jake. It was great hearing your voice."

"Hey Jake. What's up?"

"What's up, Wilt, is I wanted to ask you if you feel up to coming to work for me, for a while."

"That's right, you're a P.I. now."

"Yeah. Listen, they want me to stake out an abandoned house, from the house across the road. Could be anywhere from a couple days, up to a month. I'll guarantee you a week. Your end is $200/day. Meals and your room are covered. What do you say? You'd be really helping me out."

"Can I call you back, in an hour. I need to talk to Denise. She's the boss."

"No problem, Wilt. And tell her you won't be chasing after anybody, or anything. You're just watching a house for twelve hours, then I'll be watching the house."

"Ok, Jake. Talk to you soon."

Jake was pulling into Harriet Abrams driveway, twenty minutes later, when his phone rang. "That was quick."

"Yeah. I'm in, Jake."

"Good, Wilt. When can you leave?"

"Soon as Denise gets back. She went in work and is gonna tell her boss she has to take me up to Philly for tests, and she'll bring me up there."

"No, no, Wilt. Call Denise and tell her to stay at work. You know Tom Hansen, right?"

"Yeah. Captain of the Narcotics Squad."

"Right. You are gonna be filling in for him, on this job. He told me he'd come down and get you and bring you back to my sister's house.

He and her just got married last week. He'll bring you up here, then he and my sister are going down to his place. She'll leave her car for you to use. This is your cell, right? I'll text you the address we'll be working out of. Plug it in to google maps, and I'll see you up here in about four hours. Tom will call you when he's close. He should be there in about an hour and a half. OK?"

"Roger that, boss!"

After calling Tom, and getting him on his way, Jake went up to the front door, and knocked. Harriet Abrams answered, wearing the same house dress she had on the last time Jake saw her. "Hello, young man. It's nice to see you again."

"It's nice to see you again, too, Harriet. Remember what I told you on the phone, about me and my friend staying here awhile and keeping an eye on the Wilson place? And how the FBI will pay you $100 a day, for every day that we're here?"

"I do. And do you remember me telling you that I'd let you stay here, just for the company, and that you didn't have to pay me?"

"You did, Harriet. Now, I told you I'd take you food shopping this morning. You ready to go?"

"Just let me get my jacket and purse, young man."

When she came back out, Jake helped her to the car, then got in himself. He told her, "Buckle up, Harriet, and please call me Jake."

"Jake? Jake isn't a name. That's a nickname. What is your God-given name?"

"James."

"After the Apostle. What a solid, strong name. I'll call you James. Maybe, after I get to know you better, I'll call you Jim…no, Jimmy. I'll call you Jimmy."

"My sister and my mother are the only ones who ever called me Jimmy."

"Would that bother you if I did, too?"

"Not at all, Harriet."

"Jimmy, it is, then."

Two hours later, Jake had unloaded the car, helped Harriet in the house, and helped her put the groceries away. Once all the heavy work was done, she shooed him away. "I thought you were here to watch the Wilson's house. Get in there and do your job."

Jake took up a position, in the front window, and adjusted the blinds, so that he had a clear view of the entire property five hundred feet down the road. A few minutes later, Harriet brought him a cup of coffee, and some buttered toast. "Thank you, Harriet." She just smiled and kissed him on the top of his head. Jake heard her humming a tune, as she went back into the kitchen.

Right around 2:30 pm, Jake saw his sister's car pull in the driveway. Just as instructed, Jamal King pulled around behind the garage, and parked next to Jake's red Hyundai Santa Fe. The first rule on a stake-out is, keep yourself, and your vehicle, out of sight. As he reached to ring the doorbell, Harriet Abrams opened the door. "Hello, young man. My goodness! You are a big one. You're Jimmy's friend?"

"Yes, Ma'am. My name is Jamal. Jamal King. Nice to meet you. 'Sup Jake?"

"Jamal! I believe you're the first Jamal I've ever met. My name is Harriet. Ma'am makes me feel so old."

"Harriet it is, then."

"Well, come in! Come in! You'll be sleeping in the room straight back, as you get upstairs. I guess you'll want to…oh dear! I don't know how to say it. A woman would say 'go freshen up', but that doesn't seem like the right thing to say, to a big, strong man like yourself."

"Freshen up works for me, Harriet. If you'll excuse me, I'll go put my stuff away, and do just that. Be right back Jake."

When Jamal came down, Harriet met him at the bottom of the steps. "Jamal, Jimmy tells me that everyone calls you Wilt. Is that right?"

"When I was a detective, they did, but I haven't heard it that much since I left the police force, almost two years ago. "

"I'm glad. Frankly, I don't like 'Wilt'. That's what your plants do, if you don't water them. In my house, you're Jamal. Can I get you anything?"

"No thank you."

"I'll leave you two then. I'm sure you need to discuss your spy work."

"What do we have here, Jake?"

Jake proceeded to tell him about being hired by Roy Lemon, to find his granddaughter Monica, and how he stumbled onto this ring of psychos, and how the FBI got involved, and how they believe that they didn't burn this car, like they did the previous three, because they are still in this vicinity. "Yeah, Wilt, we all agree that they just moved to another kill house, somewhere not too far away, and they don't want the cops to find this one, until they are done around here, and leave the area. FBI figures they'll come back here and torch the car on their way out. It's logical to assume that they could come back here, to make sure they haven't been found out, yet. That's where you and I come in. The police have filled the graves in, and put the car back where it was, in case they stop by. Perfect scenario would be if we see them over there, and follow them back to where they're staying, call in the cavalry, rescue the girls, and put them away."

"What's the plan if they come back to torch the car?"

"The FBI's plan is we make contact, we call them, and they take over."

"But you're not gonna do that, are you?"

"Hell no, Wilt. Oh, I'll call them, but I'm not waiting. If they come back here to burn the car, it's logical to assume they're leaving this area.

We can't take the chance of them getting away. Besides, if we don't see them until they torch the car, that means that four more girls are dead, and buried, including Monica Lemon. There's not gonna be a trial. They are not gonna get free room and board, cable TV, free internet, and a free gym membership. Not if I have anything to say about it. Now, Wilt, I hired you to watch that house. I don't expect you to get involved in any other... activity."

"Hey, Jake. In for a penny, in for a pound. And Jake, you don't have to worry about me. I'm about 95% back to my old self. When they kick me off disability, I'm probably going back to being a detective. I've been sneaking to the gun range. Just as good a shot as I was before the accident. I've kind of been fudging a little when I go for my disability reviews. I go back in three weeks. Pretty sure they're going to cut me loose. I was hoping maybe you still had some contacts on the force, and maybe pull a string, or two..."

"You kidding? My brother-in-law is a Captain there. Wilt, you say the word, you're back in. How's Denise feel about that?"

"Well, that's gonna take some convincing. But Jake, I ain't cut out to be no lawyer. And even if I went full time, it's like, six years of school. The way I've been doing it, it'll take ten years. I just have to make her understand that I got hurt in a car accident. That could've happened on my way back from dropping the girls off at school."

"Well, whatever you decide, I'm behind you. Say the word, when you're ready, and I'll get you back in."

Jake told Wilt they'd take twelve-hour shifts. Wilt's shift would be 7:00 am to 7:00 pm, and Jake would take the night shift. That would leave him free during the day, to chase down any other leads he might stumble onto. But not today. It was after 3:00 pm, and Jake was going to lay down few a couple hours. He asked Harriet what time dinner was, and she said 6:00 pm. He set his alarm for 5:30 pm. After dinner, Jake helped Harriet with the dishes, and relieved Wilt a little before 7:00 pm.

The front window was in what could best be described as a sitting room. It was sort of separate from the living room, which was good, because Jake didn't want to be distracted by conversation, or the TV.

Friday night was quiet. Saturday morning, Harriet fed Wilt, then he relieved Jake. "How'd it go last night?"

"Didn't even see a raccoon. If these guys stick to their pattern, they grabbed a girl yesterday afternoon. Agent Wright, of the FBI, is supposed to let me know the minute they hear of a girl being abducted. Haven't heard anything yet."

Jake went into the kitchen, poured himself a coffee, and sat at the table, chatting with Harriet, as she busied herself with her chores. "Anything I can help you with, Harriet?"

"Oh no, Jimmy! I just have my little routine, that I do, just to keep me busy."

After about an hour of small talk, Jake excused himself, and headed up to lay down. Last thing he did, before doing just that, was call Brandon Wright, for an update. "Brandon. Good morning. Any news?"

"Hey, Jake. Yes and no. No reports of any girls being abducted yet. Did have a report of a silver 2014 Hyundai Sonata being stolen, in Croyden, PA. We have a BOLO out on 2014 silver Sonata, any license plate. It's a long shot…"

"I know. There must be 5-10 thousand of those in this area. What's your game plan?"

"Until we have hard evidence to the contrary, we're going under the assumption that The High School Rapists are somewhere close to Philadelphia. We're in the process of calling the high schools in a thirty-mile radius, north and west of Philly. Each one we contacted so far has girls that did not check in on the website they were supposed to.

All the schools brought staff in today, in anticipation of this happening, to contact the girls, to verify they made it home. We have one school, Neshaminy High, who just reported that all the girls that didn't check in, had been accounted for. There are seventy-two schools in our radius, so that leaves only seventy-one to go. We really need to get lucky here."

"No such thing as luck, Brandon. You make your own breaks, by doing the little things, just like you are. Be grateful for the help the high schools are giving you. Imagine how bogged down you'd be, if your people had to contact everybody, instead of the schools doing it."

"Yeah, I know you're right. It's just frustrating to sit here, not being able to do anything."

"How is Agent Caldwell making out, tracking down the other perps?"

"That's a slow process, as well. As of last night, he had thirty-five students from a ten-mile radius around Wheeling, that attended U. of Maryland, Baltimore, during the same time Reggie Logan was there. He's got men trying to get a line on them. Again, as of last night there were eighty-three, I think he said, people from the Philly/Bucks County area, that could have crossed paths with Mr. Logan. We also have people down in Baltimore, using the University's database information. Problem there is that the school won't cooperate. They're afraid to let us look at student files, for confidentiality reasons. My guys are sitting around with their thumbs up their asses, waiting for a judge to issue a court order."

"Well, all is quiet here. I'm getting ready to lay down for a while. Any news, hit me up right away."

"Don't worry about that Jake. I have a feeling that those clowns are still right in that area. You're closer than anybody else I have, so you'll be the first call I make. Get some rest."

"Later, Brandon."

Jake put his head on the pillow and was asleep almost immediately. He was awakened by his phone ringing. It was Wilt. "Wilt? Where are you?"

"Where the hell do you think I am? I'm downstairs! Get your ass down here! A car just drove past the place and turned in behind that barn. I don't know...damn! It's coming back. Jake, I'm going out the back and follow them."

"Wait! I'll be dressed in a minute!"

"No time Jake. They just passed the house. I just got to my car. Keep the line open, I'll give you directions to follow. Hurry!"

Jake almost knocked Harriet Abrams over, running through the kitchen. "Jimmy! What's going on?"

"Sorry Harriet! Gotta go! We're following the car we were looking for."

She yelled out the back door at him "I'll keep your dinner warm!"

"All right, Wilt. I'm headed up towards Rte. 13. Which way?"

"Make a left. We've travelled just about a mile. At a light. Perp's making a left, onto Harvard Lane. "

"I see the light, and I see you. I'll be behind you in a minute."

Jake floored it, and just made the turn before the light turned red. He was about one hundred yards behind Wilt, who was about the same distance behind the silver mid-size sedan. They followed the car for almost four miles, when he turned right onto Pine Road. "Wilt, go past the road, I'll take over the tail."

"Roger that, Jake. I'll go up the road apiece, then turn around, and follow you."

Jake could now make out that it was, indeed, a Hyundai Sonata, that he was following. The driver was slowing down and put his right signal on. He was turning into a farmhouse. Jake went around him, as he turned in. He was pretty sure the driver was black. "Wilt, he turned

86

into a driveway. I'm pulling over. There's a whole row of trees, bordering the property, running from the street towards the back of the property. They won't see my car. Pull over in front of me."

"I see you. Be there in ten seconds."

Wilt shut the engine off, and carefully closed the door, so not to make any noise. He joined Jake on the passenger's side, of his Santa Fe. "What's the plan, Jake?"

"I called Brandon. Cavalry is on the way. We are to observe."

"So, we can't observe anything from here. I can't see a damn thing, with all those trees in our way. I guess he wants us to get close enough to watch them, right?"

"Yeah, that sounds right to me. Where that stand of trees runs, we can get to just about fifty feet from the house. Luckily, I carry my binoculars in my trunk. You got a weapon, just in case?"

"Yeah, you want me to work myself around to the other side?"

"No, for now, we'll stay together. Let's go."

The men made their way up to, and through the trees, and took up a position that was just about where Jake had figured. It was a little after 5:00 pm, and, while the sun was setting, there was still enough light to see inside the house. Wilt nodded to Jake, to point out the silver Sonata, then whispered "Jake, I don't see any black SUV. Their M.O. has been to only drive that vehicle when they were leaving, right?"

"Maybe they have it stashed somewhere."

"See anything?"

"I see two guys talking. The black guy, and a heavy-set white guy. Black guy seems upset about something. He's asking the fat guy questions. Fat guy is mostly shrugging his shoulders, as if he doesn't know the answers to the questions. Looks like they got a place that still has electricity, anyhow."

"Yeah, there's a light in the back room there, Jake. Why don't we go check it out?"

"Ok."

They headed back into the trees and made their way to the back of the property. "Jake, those shrubs there, against the house will make good cover. We can look right in that window. It's the only window on this side. What do you think?"

"I think agent Wright will be here soon, so we better go now."

Jake and Wilt crossed the twenty yards of open ground to the side of the house, and edged their way to the back room, which had a window. Wilt peered up over the sill, and after looking around, dropped back down. "Jake, there's at least two girls in there. Naked. Gagged and bound. One looks pretty beat up. What do you want to do?"

"The girls are alive. When the FBI gets here, they have a better chance of getting them out of there than we do. I think…"

Jake stopped talking when the yelling started. "What do you mean, you don't know where he went?! We're never supposed to use my SUV, only when we are leaving! Suddenly, he makes a call, and then he says he has to go out, but won't tell you where? Tell me again exactly what he said."

"Okay, Reg. About five minutes before you got back, I walk in here, and he's on the phone. I hear him say, 'OK, I'll be right there.' He sees me, hangs up, asks where your keys are. I ask him why he wants them, and he says he has to go somewhere. I asked him where, and he says he doesn't have time to discuss it with me, that he'll be right back."

"Did he take anything with him?"

"Just his overnight bag."

"Well, that's everything he had with him! Something's wrong! I think he took off!"

"Okay, Reg, let's us get the hell outta here then."

"We are, right after we off those bitches in the back."

"Screw them, Reg, let's just go!"

"We can't Andy, they can identify us. Let's just go kill them, and then we split."

Jake whispered to Wilt, "Like I was saying, we better get in there, before those girls get hurt. You take the back door; I got the front. Start a ten second countdown. When you hit zero, go through the door, and I'll be going through the front. Announce yourself as police. And Wilt, if they look at you crooked, kill 'em."

"Roger that. Go!"

Jake flew along the side of the house and reached the front door as the clock in his head reached zero.

As Jake burst through the door, he heard Wilt coming in the back. "Freeze! Police!"

"Get him Reg!"

Jake heard the gunshots, as he made his way to the back room. The fat white guy ran into him, as he came rumbling out of the door, into the hallway, flattening Jake against the wall. Jake turned and followed him. As he rounded the corner into the room, Jake ducked in time to miss being hit with a bat. Jake hit him with a right cross, and dove to the floor, to retrieve his gun.

The force of Jake's blow sent the fat guy sprawling onto the couch, where he pulled a gun out of his own, out of a backpack, there on the couch. As he turned towards Jake, he was hit with three shots, center mass. Two were from Jake's Glock, and the 3rd was from Wilt's .45. The fat guy's gun went flying across the room and hit the wall. As Jake gathered himself, Wilt checked the fat guy for a pulse. He was dead. He then picked up the fat guy's weapon. "Asshole still had the safety on, Jake."

"What about the black guy?"

"Took one round. Head shot. Pretty messy in there."

"The girls?"

"OK. Black guy had a pillow over one's head. Was gonna use it as a silencer. When I came in, the white guy took off, and the black guy turned the gun on me. Let's go get the girls out of there."

"Be right there."

Jake dialed Brandon Wright. "Brandon, come straight to the house. Wilt and I had to breach. Sounded like one of the perps took off before we got here, and the two remaining, were going to kill the two girls they have here and take off. Both suspects are dead."

"Save that for the report. You guys okay?"

"Yeah. We're fine. The girls are pretty beaten up but are alive. Bring an ambulance."

"We're two minutes out. We have a Medical Response Team with us. Hang tight."

Jake entered the back room to find Wilt trying to untie the more badly beaten girl, of the two. Jake recognized her as Monica Lemon. She was lashing out at Wilt. Jake realized she was hysterical. "Monica! I'm Jake, and this is Jamal. We're with the police. Your Grandfather, Roy Lemon, sent us to bring you back to him."

Monica froze and stared at Jake. "The bad guys won't hurt you anymore. Listen! Hear the sirens? That's an ambulance coming to take you two girls to the hospital, and then get you back to your families."

Both girls began crying uncontrollably. Jake and Wilt finished untying them and covered them in blankets they found in the front room. Jake heard the sirens stop outside. "Paramedics! We're coming in!"

"Here! In the back room. Two females in need of medical attention!"

Soon, the farmhouse was swarming with Forensic Teams, medical teams, the FBI, and the Coroner's Office. Jake, Wilt, and Brandon Wright were joined in the living room, by Harvey Caldwell, Agent Wright's partner. "Everybody ok?"

"Yeah, thanks to Jamal, here. Two girls on their way to Jefferson Hospital."

"Where's that?"

"Center city Philadelphia, Harvey. Before you ask why there, orders from Captain Lemon."

"And the perps?"

"Two dead, one in the wind. Took off before we got here. Sounded like he got off the phone, got all panicky, and bolted. Left the other two here to take the fall."

"Any IDs on the dead guys?"

"No. The black guy's name was Reggie, and he called the white guy Andy. Forensics printed them before the coroner took them, so if they're in the system, we'll know."

Agent Caldwell looked up from a sheet of paper he was reading. "Andrew Cashman. One of the names we were checking in Wheeling, that went to school with Reggie."

"How about the one that got away? Any luck IDing him?"

"Not really. There were twenty-five males from this area going to school in Baltimore the same time as Reggie Logan. Nothing to connect them, though. No Computer Science Majors...nothing. We'll keep looking."

"Well, Brandon, do you need Wilt and I for anything else?"

"No. We're done here. Take off. I'll talk to you tomorrow."

As Wilt and Jake walked to their cars, Jake dialed a number on his cell. "Hello Harriet. It's Jimmy Miller. Yes. We're okay. We're just leaving, and I wanted to know if you needed anything. What? Okay, see you soon."

"She okay?"

"Yeah. She has our dinner in the oven."

CHAPTER 10

"Jimmy, would you like more pie?"

"No thank you."

"What about you, Jamal?"

"I couldn't eat another bite, Miss Harriet."

"Well, you boys take your coffee in the other room, and I'll be in shortly."

Harriet cleaned up the dessert dishes and joined Jake and Wilt in the living room. "I guess you boys will be leaving tomorrow, then?"

"Yes, Harriet. Our work is done here. We got two bad guys and rescued the girl."

"But I told you that I saw *three* men leaving Monday."

"Yes, you did. One of the men got away before we got there."

"Well, maybe he'll come back to the Wilson place."

"I don't think so, Harriet. But, you know, if you see anything suspicious, you have my number."

"I'll just miss you boys being here."

"Well, I'll be back tomorrow, or Monday. I have to bring your money up to you."

"Jimmy, you don't need an excuse to come see me. You too, Jamal."

"I know, Harriet. And if you get lonely, or need to talk to someone, just call."

"On that note, I'll get myself to bed, and leave you two men to talk. Good night."

"Good night, Harriet."

"See you in the morning."

After Harriet had left them, Wilt looked at Jake. "Jake, don't you think it's odd that the 3rd guy was on the phone about the time we started tailing Reggie, and something about that phone call made him nervous enough to take off, literally minutes before we got there?"

"Yeah, I've been trying not to think about it. It *does* appear that he somehow found out that we were on our way."

"You think one of the Philly cops, or FBI is tied in with these guys?"

"Couldn't happen, Wilt. I didn't call it in, until I parked in front of the house. The Explorer was gone already."

"Well, how then?"

"Besides you and me, there was only one person that knew we were tailing Reggie."

"Harriet?"

"Harriet."

"Come on, Jake. Must be another reason. That sweet old lady ain't hooked up with those psychos."

"Well, if it didn't come from her, where did it come from?"

"I don't know. Maybe the guy who split knew we were watching the house. He might've called Reggie, to find out what he was doing, and Reggie said he went to check out the Wilson place, and the 3rd guy just assumed we'd see him, and follow."

"Right. Except that we heard Reggie ask Andy what the phone call was about, so it wasn't him on the phone."

"It can't be, Jake."

"I know I don't want to think it's her."

"Well, Jake, you know that FBI guy…Wright? He's gonna read our statements and come to the same conclusion. And he don't know she's a sweet old lady."

"I know, Wilt. I'm gonna have to question Harriet in the morning. Just don't want her to realize I'm questioning her. Hopefully I can find something to tell Brandon, when we see him tomorrow, and he asks us."

"Well, good luck with that, bro. I think I'm gonna, as my mama used to say, climb the golden stairs. See you in the morning."

"Good night, Wilt. Good work today."

Jake didn't sleep much Saturday night. He tossed and turned until it started to get light out, and then just gave up, and got himself dressed. Harriet came down to find Jake looking at the pictures on her mantle, with a cup of coffee in his hand.

"Good morning, Jimmy. You're up early. Couldn't sleep?"

"Good morning, Harriet. Yeah, I had a rough night. Didn't sleep much."

"You poor dear. A nice, big breakfast is what you need. I'll go get started."

Jake wandered into the kitchen a few minutes later, under the premise of refilling his coffee cup. "So, Harriet, tell me about yourself, and your family."

"Well, I got married to my high school sweetheart when I was nineteen. His name was Martin. Martin Reeves. We had our daughter, Andrea, nine months later. My son, Harry. He was what they used to call a 'change-of-life' baby. I was thirty-nine. Marty was forty-one. Heck, Andrea was already sixteen."

"I'm a little confused. You said that the Wilsons moving away was the saddest day of your life, next to your Harry passing."

"Patience, young man. When my son, Harry, was four, my husband Marty decided that he didn't want to be a husband, or dad, anymore, and he took off. Oh, I was devastated! It was all I could do, to get up in the morning. *That's* when I met my Harry. Harry Abrams was an usher at our church. He stopped by one Sunday, to check on me, because I hadn't been to church, and I guess he took pity on me, because he started coming around, doing things, you know, men things, around the house. Six months later, he proposed to me. We were married one week after my divorce was finalized. For the next nineteen years, we were inseparable. Then, one day, August 19th, 2005, he was in the yard with my son, Harry, and there was an accident. My husband was on a ladder doing something to the barn, and he fell off the ladder. They said he broke his neck when he fell."

"I'm sorry. So, Harry Abrams is not your children's father?"

"Well, like I said, Andrea was almost a full-grown woman when Harry came into our lives. And my Harry was only 4. I used to call them Big Harry, and Little Harry. Marie Wilson used to say that God knew Harry Abrams would come into my life, that's why He had us pick the name Harry, for my son."

"So, tell me more about your daughter."

"Not much to tell. Andrea was a beautiful child. Well, you've seen her picture on the mantle. She hated living here, in the woods, as she used to call it. She met a guy, right out of high school, got married, had three children, and about eighteen years ago, moved to Syracuse, New York. My oldest Granddaughter, her Lisa, is engaged to be married. I see them once, or twice a year."

"And your son?"

"Harry? What can I say about Harry? Smart as a whip!"

"How old is he?"

"Harry will be 28, on May 7th."

"Do you see him much?"

"Not too much. He calls me once or twice every week. In fact, he called me yesterday afternoon. Right after you and Jamal ran out of here."

"Really? That's a shame. I would've liked to say hi to him. What did you two talk about?"

"Not much really. Usually, we talk for 20 minutes or so, but yesterday, he got another call, and he had to get off the line. I barely had time to tell him about the excitement going on, with you watching the Wilson place, and, just like that, he had to take the other call."

"Harriet, where does Harry live?"

"Oh, he has a wonderful job! He is a teacher, at a college, in Baltimore. They give him a place to live, as part of his salary."

"And what does he teach?"

"Oh, something to do with computers. That's what he took up, when he went to Temple. Computer something or other."

"That's wonderful, Harriet. Oh, I meant to ask you last night. Those guys we caught. They were in a house not too far away from here. Maybe you know them. Do you know anybody that lives on Pine Road?"

"Certainly. My nephew and his family live on Pine Road. They're down in Disney World right now. I say my nephew, but Eddie is actually my Harry's nephew. Eddie Abrams. He lives at the house my husband Harry grew up in, on Pine Road."

Wilt came down and put his overnight bag by the front door. "Good morning, everyone. Any coffee?"

"Sit yourself down, Jamal. Jimmy and I have just been having a nice chat. Breakfast is ready. I'll bring everything to the table."

They ate breakfast mostly in silence. Well, except for Wilt raving about how delicious everything was. As they were finishing up, Jake's phone rang. "It's the FBI. I have to take this."

He excused himself and went into the living room. After helping Harriet clear the table, Wilt joined Jake. "Yeah, no problem, Brandon. See you there, in about an hour." Then, to Wilt, "What we talked about last night? He wants to talk to us about that this morning. We're meeting him at the 15th District, in about an hour. Harriet, we have to go dear. Thank you for everything. I'll call you this afternoon. Take care."

After hugs were dished out, Jake and Wilt were in their vehicles, and heading down I-95.

"Everything all right in our statements, Brandon?"

"Oh, sure. Open and shut. Damn fine police work. No, what I wanted to talk about is the one that got away."

"We figured as much."

"Well, what's sticking in my craw, is, how did this guy know to take off? My first thought was a leak, either in Philly PD, or my group; but none of us knew about you spotting the car, until you called it in, *after* you parked in front of the house, and the Explorer was already gone."

"Look, Brandon, Wilt and I went over this last night. The phone call couldn't have been from Reggie Logan, because we heard him asking the other guy what the phone call was about. And if you eliminate an FBI, or Philly PD leak, and you eliminate me and Wilt, because we were on the phone with each other the whole time, and you eliminate the two dead guys, the list of suspects is pretty thin."

"Thin? More like anorexic. Jake, it's a list of one."

"Right. Harriet Abrams. We came to the same conclusion last night. That's why, this morning, I questioned Harriet. Turns out Harriet has two children. A daughter, Andrea, who is in her forties, and lives near Syracuse, NY, with her husband, and three children. She also has a son, Harry, who will be twenty-eight, in May. She doesn't see Harry much, but he calls her, on average, twice a week. By coincidence, Harry called her yesterday afternoon. To quote Harriet, she had just told Harry about all the excitement, with the police watching the Wilson place, and Wilt and I chasing the car, and he got another call that he had to take and got off the phone."

"Well, I guess we know who the 3rd member of the High School Rapists is. Why didn't you call this in, so we could put a BOLO out?"

"Brandon, I was in the middle of questioning Harriet when you called. I knew I'd be seeing you in less than an hour. But I'm not finished. Harry is some kind of computer guru, or something. He works as a teacher, according to Harriet, at a college, in Baltimore."

"Son of a bitch! No wonder we couldn't find any students from Philly. The guy is a teacher! I gotta let our guys down in Baltimore know. Harry Abrams, right?"

"Right Harvey. But hold on. If that turns up nothing, try Harry Reeves. That's his birth name."

"Abrams *or* Reeves. Got it."

Harvey went into the next cubicle, to make his call.

"So, what do we think? Harriet Abrams is an accomplice?"

"Really? No way this old woman knows anything about what her crazy son is up to. "

"Yeah, Brandon. I have to agree with Wilt. She said he calls her a couple of times a week, to check up on her. It was just our bad luck that he called when he did. If he had called ten minutes later, it wouldn't have mattered. We would've gotten all three of them."

Wilt picked up where Jake left off. "But on the other hand, if he had called fifteen minutes earlier, he might've killed those girls, and taken off with the other guy, Andy."

"Brandon, all the evidence adds up. Harry lives and works in Baltimore. He knows this area. Christ, he grew up across the road from the Wilson house. Lastly, the house where we caught them belongs to his uncle, Edward Abrams, who is currently on vacation in Florida, with his family. Information I'm sure Harry would have found out from his mother."

Harvey Caldwell came back into the meeting. "Bingo. Nothing on Harry Abrams. Plenty on Harry Reeves. Some kind of a whiz kid. Got his PhD at the ripe old age of twenty-five. Teaches Computer Science. Taught Reggie Logan three years ago, and Andy Cashman, two years ago. Proctored the Computer Science Geeks, a computer programming club. Both Logan and Cashman were members. Our people are on their way to Reeve's on-campus apartment, as we speak."

"What's the plan, Brandon?"

"Jake, how much do you think the mother can help us?"

"I kind of got the impression that he keeps her at arm's length, when it comes to his comings and goings. "

"So, you don't think it's worth another conversation with her, to see if she knows anything?"

"I didn't say that. This guy appears to be somebody who likes to be in a comfort zone. He's on the run now. I kind of think he'll go somewhere that he's familiar with, some place he's been many times. I think Harriet could be helpful to us in identifying places that he might go. The only problem is, she thinks the sun rises and sets on Harry. I don't know how she'd react, if she knew why we were asking about him. She might shut down on us."

"Well, you seem to have formed a bond with her. Why don't you and Jamal find an excuse to spend a day or two more with her and see what shakes loose. But Jake, you know the drill. The more time that goes by, the better chances that Harry will go underground, and we'll never find him."

"We'll do our best, Brandon. Let's go, Wilt."

Jake had Wilt follow him down to his sister's house. They went inside. Jake put a pot of coffee on, while Wilt went up to shower. Twenty minutes later they were sitting at the table, discussing how best to approach Harriet Abrams. "Jake, you know damn well if you start asking her about where Harry likes to go, or places they visited often, she's going to ask why you'd want to know that. What answer are you going to give her?"

"That's the problem. She's not stupid. I got what I got this morning, because I just asked her general questions about her family. I'm open to any ideas you might have."

"Jake, if push comes to shove, we're just gonna have to be straight with her. First things first, though. How are we going to convince her we need to stay there a couple days?"

"I think I already figured that out. I'll just tell her that she was right. The FBI thinks the other guy might come back to the Wilson place, and they want us to watch it for a few more days."

"Yeah, that'll work. Maybe we can just get her talking about vacations, or places she liked to go, and just let her talk."

"That might work. But nothing will work, if we don't get back up there. You ready?"

"Yeah, sure. We're just taking your car, right?"

"Yeah, we don't need two cars. I'll call Harriet from the road."

CHAPTER 11

"Thanks for having us back, Harriet. You were right. FBI thinks the other guy might come back to the Wilson place. You should be in charge of the FBI, Harriet."

"Oh, no. Well, come in. Come in. I was in the kitchen making beef stew for my supper tonight. Nothing like a good stew, on a chilly day."

"You're right about that. I don't know about Jake, here, but I, for one, do not like cold weather. You won't catch me taking no winter ski vacations. Uh-uh. When it's cold out, I'd like to be on some tropical island, sipping a pina colada. What about you Jake?"

"Oh, I don't know. When I was a kid, I loved the cold. Now, not so much. How about you, Harriet?"

"Oh, well, I guess I like the seasons. When the Wilsons moved to Florida, I almost moved down there with them."

"Really?"

"Yes. Well, that was over three years ago. My Harry had just moved down to Baltimore, and I really had no good reason to stay in this big old, drafty house. But I don't know, I just couldn't do it. When Big Harry was alive, we used to like to go down to Ocean City, for vacation. The kids and I, well, not so much Andrea, because she had her own family, but Little Harry and I would spend the whole summer down there, and Big Harry would come down when he wasn't working."

"Ocean City, Maryland?"

"No, dear. Goodness, twenty-something years ago, I didn't even know there *was* an Ocean City Maryland. No, we always went to New Jersey."

"Really. My family went there a lot, on our two-week vacation. Where did you stay, up in the North end, or down by 34th street?"

"Big Harry never stayed at the same place twice. Every year, we got a place in a different section of town. Honestly, I liked up in the northern area, at the start of the boardwalk, the best."

"How about your son? What part did he like best?"

"The older he got, the more he liked being away from the crowd. He was always kind of shy and liked to go exploring on his bike. Goodness, he knew that city like the back of his hand. Would you boys like some more stew?"

Jake and Wilt both said no thank you. "No? Well, I better get these dishes cleaned up, and shouldn't one of you be watching the Wilson place?"

"Right you are, Harriet. Come on, Wilt. We'll go get set up."

The two men used the 'alone time' to sit at the front window and discuss their strategy. "What do you think, Jake? Is her kid good for this?"

"Can't say for sure, Wilt, but I'm liking him more and more. We need to talk to him. The college said Harry Reeves is taking a sabbatical this semester. No one's seen him since around Christmas. He's a shy computer geek, who probably wasn't a ladies' man, so he fits the profile. We need to get more information about him."

"You need to tell the FBI to look for him in Ocean City."

"Yeah. When we're done with this conversation, I'll call Brandon, and give him an update."

"What about the sister, Jake? Think she knows anything?"

"Not sure, but it couldn't hurt to chat with her. I'll put that on agent Wright's plate, as well. Okay, it's 6:30 pm. I'm gonna go upstairs, call the FBI, and lay down for a couple hours. I'll relieve you at midnight, and then, in the morning, you can take over around 8:00 am, and we'll work twelve-hour shifts. Okay?"

"Yeah. Sure Jake. See you at midnight."

As Jake headed for the stairs, he said good night to Harriet, telling her that he was going to lay down for a few hours, so he could relieve Wilt at midnight. As he walked by the fireplace, he stole a glance at Harriet's daughter Andrea's wedding photo. It must've been taken in the lobby of the reception hall. In the bottom left-hand corner, the photographer captured a sign directing guests for the Reeves-Cataldi wedding to the Swan Room.

"Hey Jake. What do you have for me?"

"Okay, Brandon. Here goes. Harry Reeves was, according to his mother, a shy teenager, who kept to himself. They spent every summer in Ocean City, NJ. Never stayed in one particular section. Mother said the boy preferred the less populated south-west section, I guess you'd call it. She said, and I quote 'he knew that city like the back of his hand.' If he's our guy, there's a good chance that's where he'll go, at least until he can come up with a plan of some kind."

"Excellent! It gives us a direction, at least. I contacted our Trenton office, and read them in, just in case he headed their way. I'll give them this info and let them run with it. Anything else?"

"Yeah. Wilt suggested that we contact the sister, Andrea, to see if she knows anything. Married name is Andrea Cataldi. Lives in Syracuse, NY. Three kids. That's all I can give you on her, for now."

"That's plenty. I'll send Harvey up there in the morning, to interview her. Good work Jake. Let me update you now. The two girls you guys rescued yesterday, are doing fine. Both will be released from the hospital tomorrow. The second girl is Rachel Morgan. She's a sophomore at Truman High, in Levittown. She said she was walking home when a car pulled over and asked her for directions to Rte. 1. She said she went over to the car and told the guy what he wanted to know. He thanked her, and asked if she would like a ride home, on such a chilly day. She said he seemed kind of nerdy, so she said OK. Once in the car, he offered her a beer. She said no thanks, and he asked her to hand him one. There was a 6-pack on the passenger side floor. When she leaned forward to get it, he jabbed her with a needle, and that's the last thing she remembers. She was only there a little over twenty-four hours, before you found her. They kept her blindfolded and drugged the whole time. Monica Lemon could not ID Reeves, from his most recent college employee ID badge. She picked out Logan and Cashman from a photo array, but the third guy always wore a Spiderman mask, when he came in the room. Anyway, that's the latest."

"Thanks, Brandon. I'm gonna get off the phone, because I have to relieve Wilt in just about five hours."

"Talk to you tomorrow, Jake."

Jake woke Wilt up a little after midnight. "Yo Sleeping Beauty. You're relieved. Go on up to bed."

"Hey, Jake. I figured there was no chance of Harriet coming down here, so I nodded. Hear anything from the FBI?"

"The second girl we found was from Levittown. She was drugged and blindfolded and doesn't remember anything. Monica Lemon IDed Reggie and Andy but said the third guy always wore a Spiderman mask, when he was in the room."

"Spiderman? Son of a bitch! The room I'm staying in? Must've been Harry's. There's an old Spiderman poster on the wall!"

"First chance you get, toss the room. You'll be looking for anything that could point to a possible landing spot for this guy. Brochures, bus schedules, whatever."

"You got it, Jake. See you in the morning."

Jake set his cell phone alarm for 5:00 am, put the earbuds in, and curled up in the window-side armchair.

Harriet came downstairs right before 7:00 am. Jake greeted her with a good morning, and a cup of coffee. "Oh my! The coffee is made! I could get used to this."

"Harriet, you have a programmable coffee maker. You can get it ready at night and set the timer to turn on whatever time you want."

"I'm not very good at those kinds of contraptions, Jimmy. I feel safer just brewing it in my old pot, on the stove. You ready for breakfast?"

"Not right away, Harriet. Wait for Jamal to get up. Why don't you sit, and chat with me?"

"OK, Jimmy. What do you want to chat about?"

"I don't know. Tell me about your children. What were they like, growing up? Did they have any hobbies? Where either of them in the Scouts?"

"Well, let's see. My Andrea, she was…not wild, but she always wanted more. She didn't like 'life on the farm', as she called it. She did everything. Sports, dancing, debate club. She did things she didn't even like, just to get out of the house, and be with other people."

"Was she a good student?"

"Fair. A C+, or B student."

"And Harry?"

"Well, Harry was just about the complete opposite of Andrea. He didn't do sports or join any clubs. He just wanted to be on his computer. Sometimes I would have to force him to come outside and spend some time in the sunshine."

"And he was smart?"

"I'll say. He made the principal's list every year. He never brought home anything less than an A."

"That's wonderful. And how did Andrea and Harry get along?"

"Ok, I guess. As I told you yesterday, Andrea was sixteen when Harry was born. And she got married when she was twenty, so they never really did brother and sister things."

"When Andrea got married, before she moved to New York, did she live around here?"

"I should say so. She lived right up those stairs for six years. Joe, her husband, was in the Army. Big Harry and I didn't see any sense in them living somewhere else, what with Joe being overseas for eighteen months at a time, so we all decided that they would live here, until Joe got out of the service. When he got out, he got a job up in Syracuse, and they went from here to there. My Andrea left here with a six-year-old, a four-year-old, and an eighteen-month-old baby."

"So…Harry was only a few years older than your oldest grandchild?"

"That's right. Harry was born in 1990, and my little Sofia was born in 1994. When they left, Harry was 10, and Sofia had just turned 6."

"That's interesting. And Harry didn't have any friends to play with, growing up?"

"Jimmy, I said he was shy. I didn't say he didn't have any friends. He had his friends from the Computer Society. That was a club, in high school. There were three, no, four other members. Harry loved that club. It was the only thing he ever joined. And he stayed friends with two of them, even after he graduated from high school, and up until he moved to Baltimore, after he graduated from Temple University."

"That's nice, Harriet."

They were interrupted by Jamal, coming down to get coffee, before he relieved Jake. "Good morning, Jamal. Did you sleep well?"

"Good morning, Miss Harriet. I slept OK."

"Just ok? You need breakfast. Let me get started. I'm sure you two need to discuss your stakeout, or whatever it is you call it. Breakfast will be in a half hour. Shoo…."

"Dude, you look like crap! Didn't you sleep?"

"Not a friggin' wink, Jake. You ain't gonna believe what I found up in that room! When I went up last night, I looked around. Didn't really find anything that could help us. Then I went in the closet. I had a glass of water with me, and I put it down, in the closet, while I got this box off the shelf. I accidentally kicked the glass over. I threw the box on the bed and grabbed some tissues, to wipe up the water. When I picked up the glass, there was hardly any water on the floor! I mean, Jake, I spilled what had to be six ounces of water on the floor, and ten seconds later, there was next to nothing there! Now it's hard to see in that closet. I think it must be a 25-watt bulb in there. So, I get my flashlight out, and when I shine it on the floor, I can see where the floor has been cut. This freak made a hidey-hole in the bottom of his closet. I pried the lid off, and, my God, Jake, the sick shit that was in there! A dozen porn mags. Not just porn, but all Bondage Porn. Sick shit! And in the very bottom, he had a photo album. Jake, he had what look like Polaroid pictures, you know, the kind you take the picture, wait a minute, and peel off the picture? All bondage. With a little kid! Jake it looked to me like he was recreating the pictures from the magazines, only using this little girl. She couldn't have been more than four, or five years old. And he had pictures of animals. Dead animals. Like, a squirrel, hanging by it's tail, with it's head cut off! Dead cats, that had been tortured to death! And he had pictures of all different girls and women, naked. Like they didn't know he was there. Jake, he had pictures of his mother in there. I'm telling you; it is some sick shit!"

"I'll take it to Brandon. Maybe his people can use it."

"Jake, this guy is really out there."

"Hold it, Wilt. Come here."

Jake led him over to the fireplace. He picked up the Cataldi family picture that Andrea sent to her mother, in 2001. He pointed to the tallest child. "Is this the little girl from the bondage pictures?"

"Sweet Jesus have mercy! That's her, Jake!"

"That woman in the picture is Harry's sister Andrea. *That* is her oldest daughter, Sofia. She lived here until she was six."

"So, he did that to his niece?"

"Know what's worse than that, Wilt? That little prick was only ten, when he took those pictures!"

"Holy Mother of God! What kind of sick person are we after, Jake?"

"That's a question for people way smarter than us, Wilt."

After breakfast, Wilt took up his post at the window, and Jake went up to go to bed. Only he didn't. He went into Wilt's bedroom, opened the floor, and took out all the evidence contained in there. He bagged the bondage magazines, in evidence bags, and flipped through the 'photo album'. It was as bad as Wilt had said. Worse, even. After looking at the black and white photos for fifteen minutes, Jake had enough. He closed the book and sealed it in a clear plastic evidence bag. He then headed to his room. He didn't make it. Jake almost knocked Harriet Abrams over, as he left young Harry Reeves' bedroom. "Jimmy! I thought you'd be asleep by now. What are you doing in Harry's room?"

"What? Oh. Nothing. Jamal asked me to bring his blood pressure meds down to him. I had trouble finding them."

"Well, what do you have there, in those bags?"

"Nothing. Just some…"

"Why, that's my Harry's photo album!"

"No, its…"

"Don't tell me it's not. I bought that for him for his 9th birthday. We got him one of those Polaroid cameras for Christmas, and Harry loved it. By the time April rolled around, he had dozens of pictures laying around. I bought that album for him so he could keep things organized. Where did you find it, and where are you going with it?"

Jake could think of no lie good enough to fool Harriet. "Harriet, this *is* your son's album. We found it in a secret compartment, in the bottom of his closet. It was in there, with these magazines."

Jake showed her the bag with the magazines in it, and suggested they go downstairs, where they could sit and talk.

Wilt saw them coming down the steps, and he saw that Jake was carrying the evidence. He looked at Jake, who motioned, with his head, for Wilt to join them in the kitchen. When they were all seated, Jake looked at Harriet Abrams, and said, "Harriet, I didn't want you to ever see these things. I was taking them to the FBI, so that they might be able to get some information from them, to help us find your son."

"For what? Those magazines. All teenage boys look at naked pictures."

"It's not so much the magazines, Harriet. It's the pictures in this album, that are why the FBI needs to have this evidence."

"What are you talking about Jimmy? I've seen those pictures! My Harry took pictures of birds, and cars, and trees!"

"Maybe he did, Harriet, but these pictures in this album are not pictures of trees and birds and cars."

"Let me see them."

"I don't think that's a good idea, Harriet."

"I don't care what you think! That album was in my house! I didn't give you permission to search my house! I want to see it, now!"

Jake looked at Wilt, who shrugged his shoulders. "Ok, Harriet. Here."

Jake took the album from the plastic bag, and put it on the table, in front of Harriet. She slowly opened to the first page. There were pictures of mangled and tortured small animals on the first few pages. One picture, in particular, caught her attention. "That cat. That's Flower. That was the Wilson's cat. She disappeared one day. We just assumed she got hit by a car, or a hawk, or fox, got her. Harry, what did you do?"

109

After three pages like the first, she came upon pictures of women, maybe twenty of them. All ages. By now, tears were rolling down Harriet's cheeks. She stopped at the last page of nudes, which was two pictures. One of her, drying off, after a bath, and one of her then twenty-six-year-old daughter Andrea, almost in the same pose. "Harry. Why?"

"You don't need to see any more, Harriet."

He reached for the album. She slapped Jake's hand away. "I want to see!", and she turned to the first page of the bondage photos, with her six-year-old granddaughter as the object of the bondage. "No!"

Harriet collapsed onto the table, shaking from the crying. Jake took the album from her. Just as suddenly, she stopped, and sat up. "Wait! You came back here yesterday. You said you were here to keep watching the Wilson house. But you weren't, were you? You came back because… because you think my son is the bad person who got away, don't you? You came here to 'chat' with me, and snoop around my house, to see if I could help you find my son. Isn't that right?"

"Harriet, we *do* think your son Harry is the third guy we were looking for. The one that got away. We heard the other two guys talking, and one guy told the other that Harry was on the phone, and suddenly, he got off the phone, grabbed his backpack, and left. We believe that someone on the phone told him that Jamal and I were chasing the black guy, in the silver car, and he knew we would find him there, so he took off."

"Well, Harry was on the phone with me, so it couldn't be him."

"Harriet. Think back. You told me that Harry called you right after we left, Saturday, and that you had just got through telling him about all the excitement, and he got another call, and had to go."

"You think I called him and warned him?!"

"No, dear. I think that your son called you, and you were just telling him what was going on in your life."

110

"Well, I want you both to go now."

"Harriet. Don't be like that."

"I said I want you out of here. You got what you came for. Get out!"

Wilt grabbed Jake by the shoulder, and the men went upstairs, gathered their things, and headed towards the door.

CHAPTER 12

Jake called Brandon Wright from the car. "Brandon, I'm in the car with Jamal. We're headed down to see you. Are you still at the 15th?"

"Yeah, at least for today. That may change tomorrow. But yes, I'm here right now."

"See you soon."

After lunch, Agent Wright told Jake and Wilt that Agent Caldwell had made it safely up to Syracuse, and was hoping to interview Andrea Cataldi, within the hour. He also let them know that they would be joined, very shortly, by FBI Profiler Justine Whitlock. "Brandon, any idea what we're going to do, as far as Harriet Abrams?"

"There are FBI agents serving a search warrant to Ms. Abrams, as we speak. Maybe they find another hiding place, or some other clue, as to where this sick son of a bitch could be holed up."

"I meant, is she in any trouble?"

"As of right now? No. I honestly don't believe she knew anything. Going forward, if she tries to impede our investigation, she could be held for that. As soon as we agreed that he was in contact with her on Saturday, I pinged her phone. If she called him, after you left, or he calls her, we'll know it."

"Are we still working for you, Brandon?"

"Absolutely. As I told you when I hired you, I want you out there, working independent of us. We basically have to follow protocol. You are freelancing and can act on a hunch. We have a rule book to follow. If A and B happens, we proceed by doing C. As you have probably figured out already, agent Whitlock is excellent at her job."

"Yeah, she pretty much hit that nail right on the head, as far as where these guys were, and how they operated. So, I guess what I'm asking, since we still work for you, how would you like us to proceed, boss?"

"You guys just hang loose, until Justine has a chance to look over this stuff you brought in. She might want to talk to you, as far as what Harriet told you about Harry. She should be here very soon, and if she doesn't need to talk to either of you, you can take off, because I know she won't have anything for us today."

"Roger that. I'm going to take Wilt here, down to the first floor, and introduce him to Captain Lemon. That's where we'll be, if you need us." Jake and Wilt made their way down to Captain Lemon's office. Jake knocked on the door, and Roy Lemon, who was on the phone, waved them in. He got off the phone, and came around his desk, and hugged each man.

"Roy Lemon, I'd like you to meet my partner, Jamal King." It looked as if Lemon's smile was painted on his face.

"Cap."

"Jamal. What you...what both of you did, for my family! I can never repay that debt."

"Please Captain. Call me Wilt. And me and Jake? We just did what we're trained to do."

"Don't be so modest. Agent Wright told me that it was you two that came up with the idea of watching the house where we found those poor dead girls. You two spotted the suspect vehicle and followed it to where they had my little angel. And she told me that the black guy put a pillow against her head, and was going to shoot her, when you two burst in and killed those bastards."

"Speaking of Monica, how is she, sir?"

"Physically, she is not in too bad of shape. The things they did to her, though…I don't know if she'll ever recover, mentally."

"Roy, when I was a SEAL, part of our training was learning how to help hostages that we rescued. We were taught that if a victim was talking about what happened to them, that was half the battle, as far as them getting past it. It's the victims that shut down, and keep everything inside, that are haunted by it. I think Monica will be fine. It may take some time, and a lot of therapy, but I think she'll be okay."

"From your lips to God's ears, Jake."

After updating Captain Lemon on the progress they had made trying to find Harry Reeves, Jake and Wilt went back upstairs. Justine Whitlock looked up from the picture album, long enough to acknowledge the two men. "Gentlemen, Agent Wright tells me that you showed this album to the suspects mother?"

"Yes."

"Can you recall her reaction to these small animals that have been tortured?"

"She didn't really react, physically. I think some of the pictures repulsed her, but if you mean did she act surprised, I'd say no."

"Mr. Miller, do you agree?"

"Yeah, in fact the only comment she made was when she saw a picture of her neighbor's cat, beheaded. She didn't look away. She simply said that the cat's name was Flower, and the neighbor assumed the cat got hit by a car, or ran into a fox, or hawk."

"How about the naked pictures of all these women?"

"These women were people that are all known to her, and she mentioned their names, as if she were looking at a high school yearbook, or something, until she got to the last two pictures of her, and her daughter. She didn't say anything, but she started quietly crying."

"And the last set of bondage pictures?"

"Man, she freaked out when she saw them. Right Jake?"

"Absolutely. Her reaction to the first two sets of pictures could best be described as disturbed, but not surprised. But she became very upset and agitated when she saw the pictures of her granddaughter bound like that. What does her reaction tell you?"

"A reaction like hers, and, I have to say, this is a premature analysis, is that while she found these pictures disturbing, they were just a validation of something that she knew was going on. I think she knew that he was hunting and killing small animals, and she possibly caught him taking candid pictures. The reason she 'freaked out', as you say, when she saw the bondage pictures, indicate that she had no knowledge that he was into that. Like she realized that she allowed this other behavior, and because she did, her granddaughter paid the price. Again, I could be wrong, based on just these pictures. I'll need to interview Ms. Abrams, and only then can I do more than speculate on the suspect. I can say that Mr. Reeves used this album to chronologically tell us what he was up to. Much in the same way that he wanted us to find the high school girls that he killed, he wants everybody to see his handiwork. Do we know how old he was when these last pictures were taken?"

"We believe, since his niece was around six, that he was ten years old."

"My God! I wonder how many more there are?"

"Excuse me? How many more what?"

"Bodies! Harry Reeves has all the earmarks of a serial killer. He showed us how he started out torturing and killing small animals. When that stopped exciting him, he went to looking at naked women."

"But he was only ten years old! When I was that age, I was only worried about getting out with my friends and playing ball!"

"Precisely. That was your activity. And as you got older, you continued to play sports. You may have 'upped the ante', so to speak, by joining a team, or playing in high school. His chosen activity was bondage and murder. He has continued refining his 'hobby' over the years. Let me ask you Jamal, what sport did you play?"

"Mostly baseball."

"Okay, and you got older, did you get better, or worse?"

"Well, better. The more you do something, the better you get."

"Exactly! The same goes for Harry Reeves. By ten years old, he already had tortured, and killed. And he went from looking at naked women, to performing bondage on them. God! It wasn't even a question *if*, but *when* he was going to escalate to torturing and killing women! And it's eighteen years since he did this to his niece, and we found the first group of high school girls. Who knows how many women are dead at his hands during that time. I need to talk to his mother!"

"Not going to happen, Justine" All three people turned to see Agent Wright hanging up his cell. "That call was from my agents, serving the search warrant to Ms. Abrams. She's dead."

"Dead!?"

"No one answered the door. An agent went to the back, and found the door unlocked. After entering, and announcing their presence, they searched the house, and found Ms. Abrams hanging from the ceiling fan in her son's bedroom. Looks like she took her own life."

"Really?"

"Well, Jake, the coroner is on his way, but my guys say there was no sign of a struggle. She tied a rope around the fan, stood up on a chair, tied the rope around her neck, and stepped off the chair. Hands weren't tied, but a woman of her age, even if she changed her mind, she doesn't have the strength to pull herself up. Of course, the M.E. will make the final call, but that's what it looks like."

"Come on, Wilt. We're going up there."

"Whoa! Not by yourselves, you're not. Neither of you have badges. No agent will let you on that property. I'll go with you."

"Fine. Let's go."

"Hold it boys. The girl needs to go, too. The more I see, the better my observations will be. Two cars?"

"Okay. Justine, you ride with me. Jake, Jamal. If you two get there first, wait for me. I don't need any more problems."

"Roger that, boss."

Once in the car, Jake noticed Wilt was staring at him. "What?"

"You think that little old lady climbed up and hanged herself, Jake?"

"She was extremely upset, but, no, I don't see her doing something like that."

"I agree, Jake. But, if we're right, that means…"

"That means that her no good son was close enough to see us there, watched us leave, then went in and killed his mother."

"Damn, Jake! You think that sonofabitch was in that house we were pretending to watch?"

"I don't know, Wilt. Look, the profiler said that he only felt comfortable in familiar surroundings. He knew we found out about the Wilson place. His mother told him we were watching it. He knew we saw Reggie Logan and were following him. He didn't know that we found out he was involved. In hindsight, it almost makes sense that he would think we had no reason to ever go back to that place, and he could hide out there. He could've seen us come back Sunday. He heard Harriet throwing us out, and figured it was safe to go over there. Once inside, his mother wanted answers, and he knew we were on to him. He killed her, to prevent her from telling us anything. Or I could be completely wrong."

After parking the car, and finding Agents Wright and Whitlock, the four detectives entered the Abram's house. The downstairs was just as it had been five hours before, when Wilt and Jake were last there. "Everything look okay down here, Jake?"

"Yeah. Just like we left it. Wilt?"

"Yeah. One thing, though. Agent Whitlock, this might be of interest to you. I been thinking about when Ms. Harriet was looking at that album. When she saw what that freak did to her grandchild, she lost it. But then, bam! She snapped right out of it and started accusing me and Jake of trying to use her to get Harry. Right Jake?"

"Yeah, that is right. Does that help you?"

"Positively. It tells me that Harry had her undying devotion. No matter what he did, or how much he hurt her, she was going to protect him. She may have killed herself because she felt guilty about giving you any information."

Upstairs, Agent Wright identified himself to the coroner, and asked for an update. "She has been deceased for about two hours. Looks like a suicide."

Wilt saw Jake looking around. "Something wrong, Jake?"

"Not sure. Is that the chair she stood on, over there?"

"Yes."

"Is that where you found it?"

"Yes. When the agents found her, they left the room, and no one entered, until I got here."

"Problem Jake?"

"Don't know, Wilt, but if she stepped off the chair, seems to me she would've knocked the chair over, and it would've been right there, near her body. That chair is a good five feet away, as if it were pulled out from under her."

"Well, detective, it's very possible that she could have swung back, and hit it with her legs. That could almost certainly propel the chair that far."

"Ok, if that happened, she would have been alive when she knocked it over there, so there would probably be some sort of bruise, or mark, where her legs hit the chair?"

"You are probably right. As I said, this is my preliminary report. The body is on its way back to my lab for an autopsy. I will certainly look for evidence of bruising. Agent Wright, you'll have my report before the sun goes down. Good day, all."

Back outside, Jake told Agent Wright that he and Wilt were going over to the Wilson house, to see if there were any signs of Harry Reeves. "Ok Jake. Agent Whitlock and I are heading back to the 15th precinct. I'll call you later, and we can update each other."

Jake and Wilt walked over to the small ranch style house that used to belong to the Wilsons. They spent the next hour going through the five-room property, looking for any signs that Harry Reeves had been there. The search provided no clues. "What now, Jake?"

"We'll check out the barn, but if he didn't leave anything at the house, I doubt if we'll find anything in the barn." Jake was right. Not a footprint. Nothing.

"Maybe he wasn't here, Jake. I mean, we been all over every inch of this place. We didn't even find one footprint, or anything. Nobody's *that* good. Maybe the old girl did kill herself."

"Well Wilt, if agent Whitlock is right, and she has been so far, this guy's been honing his craft for almost twenty years. He's like, the Lebron James of serial killers. No, I think he killed her. Let's get out of here."

"Wait. What about the car? Think we should check it out?"

"Nah. He'd have no reason to go into the car, unless he was going to take it, which he didn't. Why waste any more time."

Jake and Wilt had gotten about fifteen feet when Wilt put his hand on Jake's shoulder, and said, "Look, Jake. You're the boss here, but, what the hell. We're here. It'll take, what, thirty seconds, to look in the car?"

"OK. You're right. Let's go look in the car."

They made their way past the barn door. Wilt was trying to be positive. "You never know Jake. He might have put something in there, you know? Jake? You know?" He turned back to find that Jake had stopped walking. "Jake? You OK?" Without saying a word, he pointed to the back of the Silver Sonata. Wilt turned and looked. It took three seconds for him to see what Jake was pointing at. "Damn Jake! How did we miss that?"

"We never expected that he would go near the car." There on the back bumper was a Tennessee License plate.

Jake called Brandon Wright and told him what they found. He asked if Jake was still at the scene, and if his agents were still at Harriet Abram's house. Yes, on both. He told Jake to give his phone to one of the agents. After talking to Agent Wright, the agent gave Jake his phone back, and said "Agent Wright said that you would take us to another scene that we should process."

"Sure. Right this way."

He explained what they had found, as he led Agent Carlson, and two other agents, to the Sonata. As they began the job of processing the car, Jake and his partner headed back to the city. He had Brandon Wright on speakerphone. "Good work, Jake. He switched the plate so that the truck wouldn't stand out. I'll change the BOLO to include the plate number that was on the Hyundai."

"Not sure if that will do any good, Brandon."

"Why?"

"First of all, my partner is the one who led us to find the plate. Secondly, this guy wants us to know what he's done. He could've gotten a plate from anywhere. He knew we would find that Tennessee plate and assume that he switched it out. He had to figure you'd be looking for the Ford Explorer, with the Sonata plates on it. I'm willing to bet that he put that Sonata plate on some other SUV and put that plate on his Explorer. It's logical that he killed his mom, then took off. That's only been a few hours. He'd expect you to put a BOLO out for a black Explorer, with the Sonata plate."

"Well, what do you think? Is he still in the area?"

"I doubt it. He's an arrogant prick. He's tied up the last loose end. He's outsmarted us again, and he's not gonna hang around, for us to stumble onto him."

"What are your plans, Jake?"

"I'm going to my sister's now. I'll meet with you tonight, after you get the M.E.'s report on Harriet. In the morning, we are heading towards the only lead we have, Ocean City."

"OK. I'll call you as soon as I know anything ."

Wilt and Jake stopped at a diner and had dinner. By 6:30 pm, they were at Maggie's house, trying to come up with a plan for finding Harry Reeves. Just after 7:00 pm, Jake's phone rang. "Brandon. What's up?"

"Just got the ME's report. Harriet Abrams died from a broken neck. Problem is that if her neck was broken from hanging, it would be broken from front to back. Her neck was broken laterally, as if someone violently twisted her neck. Hanging her from the fan was only for effect. Agent Whitlock is here with me. She has a theory. Justine?"

"Yes. Reeves tortured and suffocated all his victims, yet he broke his mother's neck. That indicates that this was a killing of necessity. He couldn't let her live, for fear that she could somehow lead us to him. He hated all his previous victims. Hence the violence. He didn't hate his mother, that's why, in his mind, he did the humane thing and killed her quickly. I believe you're right, in thinking that he is no longer in the area. And if you think he has a familiarity with Ocean City, NJ, that is the best place to start looking."

"Jake?"

"Yeah, Brandon. We're going to take off early tomorrow. We hope to be down there by sunrise. Maybe catch him off guard. If he's going to slip up, and let his guard down, it will be sooner, rather than later."

"Good. I've contacted our Trenton office, and there will be three agents down there searching as well. I'll text you Tom Argent's number, and I gave him yours. He's the lead agent. He'll hook up with you to coordinate. Harvey Caldwell and I will be down there, by the end of the week, after he gets back from NY, and we finish up here."

"Hey, how did he make out in Syracuse?"

"Harvey made a long drive for nothing, basically. The sister never had much of a relationship with Harry. She described him as a loner, a computer geek, and a little strange. She moved away when he was ten, when all this was just getting started, and hasn't had contact with him since. Harvey is staying up there overnight, and he'll be back here tomorrow afternoon."

"OK, Brandon. I'm getting off the line. We have a long day ahead of us tomorrow, and I'm going to grab some shuteye."

"Good night, Jake. Keep me posted on what's going on. If you need me to grease a few wheels with the Trenton Agents, just let me know."

CHAPTER 13

Five o'clock Tuesday morning found Jake and Wilt on their way to the Jersey shore. Jake called his sister and brother-in-law, to tell them they'd be in Ocean City, and did she want her car? She said yes, so Jake made arrangements for Wilt to get a rental in Ocean City, and they'd drive her car down to North Cape May, NJ, on Tuesday evening. The two men met up with FBI Agent Tom Argent, and his two compadres. Wilt had the idea that since it was still March, they had a slight advantage, in that there wouldn't be any tourists down there yet, so it might be easier to spot Reeves. With five vehicles they could cover the whole city rather easily. The plan was simple. They took a map of Ocean City and divided it into five sections. Each man would cruise his section over and over, hopefully spotting Harry in the process. If anyone spotted a black Explorer, they were to run the plates, to see if they belonged on that Explorer. As per Agent Wright's instructions, the FBI agents provided Jake and Wilt with walkie-talkies, so that everybody could be in touch with everybody else.

Fifteen minutes after the men started patrolling, Agent Argent reported that he had spotted a black Ford Explorer, with PA plates. The vehicle came back as belonging to a Joseph Wells, of Blue Bell PA. He was pulling the vehicle over, to check ID, at 7th Ave and Atlantic Ave. The plan was that whoever was nearby would back up anyone stopping a vehicle. Jake was only three blocks away and was there as Agent Argent approached the vehicle. He pulled in front of the Explorer and walked back to where Argent was. There was motion in the front seat, and Agent Argent leveled his weapon on the driver, yelling "Let me see your hands! Put your hands outside the car window, now!"

Jake now had the passenger door open. With his glock aimed at the man's temple, he added, in a calm, steady voice, "I'd do what the agent told you to."

As the obviously shaken man got out of his vehicle, Tom Argent spun him around, and had him cuffed, before he knew what was going on. Jake holstered his weapon and walked around to the driver's side. "What do you have, Tom?"

"When you pulled up, I told him to get out of the car, and he reached for something. You saw the rest. I'm gonna go run his license."

When the agent walked back to his car, Jake turned to the driver. "You ok? You look a little unsteady."

"Really? Unsteady? Of course, I'm unsteady. I think I crapped my pants! You ever have a gun pointed at you?"

"Yes, I have. What did you reach for, when the agent told you to get out of the car?"

"I-I-I was trying to get my phone to start videotaping, in case, you know, there was any police brutality. I'd have proof that I didn't do anything."

"But you *did* do something. An FBI agent told you to keep your hands in sight, and exit the vehicle, and instead of doing that, you reached down for your phone, to make a video. He thought you were reaching for a gun. You came this close to getting shot."

"I don't even own a gun!"

"He doesn't know that."

"I guess I didn't think of that."

Agent Argent was back. "Mr. Brown, how is it that you are in possession of this vehicle? It doesn't belong to you."

"No. It's my brother-in-law's, Joe Wells. Look, I'm a plumber. My wife's brother owns a home down here. He had a leak, and I was coming down to make the repairs. My tools are right there in the back. Joe loaned me the Explorer, in case I needed to get supplies. Look, I'm awful sorry about reaching for my phone like I did. I didn't think of what it would look like to you, standing outside."

"Okay, Mr. Brown. Here's your ID. You have a nice day."

As the Explorer pulled away, Jake looked at the FBI agent. "You okay? You look a little unsteady."

"I almost shot that guy! When he reached over like that, I almost crapped my pants!"

"Seems to be a lot of that going around. Your first time?"

"Yeah. Is it that obvious? I've been with the Bureau for eighteen months. This is the first op I've been on, dealing with an actual person. Most of the stuff I've been doing is internet surfing, and paperwork."

"Well, Tom, it never gets easier, but you'll get your feet under you, in time."

"Thanks for your help, Miller."

"No problem. And call me Jake."

The rest of the day was more of the same. In all, they stopped eleven black Explorers. Part of their plan was to record all the license numbers of the vehicles they stopped, so that everyone would have a record, to try and prevent the same vehicle from being stopped more than once. As the makeshift squad called it a day, a voice came over the walkie-talkie. It was Brandon Wright. "Agent Argent. This is Brandon Wright, and my partner Harvey Caldwell. We just got into town. I need to meet with you and get a sit-rep."

"Roger that, agent Wright. We're working out of the hotel we're staying at. Port-O-Call Hotel. 15th and the Boardwalk. I'm in room 202. I'll be there in twenty minutes."

"Good. Jake. When can I meet up with you?"

"My partner and I have to take my sister's car down to North Cape May. We should be back by 8:00 pm. We're staying at the EconoLodge Motel, on MacArthur Blvd, in Somers Point. Room 110. Do you know where Somers Point is?"

"Yeah. We drove right through there on our way here. 8:30 pm okay, Jake?"

"Roger that. See you then."

Jake followed Wilt down the Parkway, to return his sister Maggie's car. As they were getting close to Stone Harbor Exit, Jake called Wilt. "What up, Jake?"

"Wilt, I told Tom and Maggie to meet us at the Lobster House, so take the Parkway all the way."

"Lobster House! Damn. Don't tell Denise. That's her favorite spot."

"Why don't you call her. See if she can come over."

"Really?"

"Of course, really. FBI's paying for dinner tonight. Those agents are staying at a $150/night Hotel, right on the Boardwalk. We're at a $39/night motel. We'll make up the difference at dinner. Which reminds me, I owe you $1,000, for the past 5 days. Do you want me to write you a check now, or just keep adding it up?"

"Well, let me call Denise, and see if her mom can watch the girls. If she can join us, yeah, I'd like to give her a check to deposit. If she can't join us, well..."

"If she can't join us, we'll stop at your place on the way back up to Ocean City."

Dinner worked out perfectly. Denise King pulled into the parking lot right in front of Jake, and Mr. and Mrs. Hanson showed up a couple of minutes later. The party of five entered the Lobster house in time to make the first seating, at 5:00 pm.

Jake had a great time, mainly just listening to his sister, and Tom, go on about how great marriage is, and Denise and Wilt reconnect, in a way that Jake believed they hadn't, in a long time. When they were leaving Jake walked Denise to her car, while Wilt ran to get saltwater taffy, that he had gotten, for the girls, out of his trunk. Once he was out of sight, Denise King threw her arms around Jake, and kissed him on the cheek. "Whoa! What was that for?"

"That was for making my man whole again, Jake. He needed this job. I can see he's back to 100% now."

"D, he's earning every penny of his salary."

"The money means nothing. I can see that this has made him feel alive again. That's worth more than anything you could pay him."

"Well, it's a good thing you didn't negotiate his salary."

When he got back, Wilt gave his wife the taffy, and a check for $1,000. Jake gave them both some privacy. After all the goodbyes were said, Jake and Wilt headed back up to their motel, and their 8:30 pm briefing with Agent Wright.

Room 110 of the EconoLodge Motel was much like all the other rooms in that establishment. Very clean, with two double beds, a flat screen mounted on the wall, a small round table, with two side chairs. Agent Brandon Wright showed up five minutes early. The meeting consisted of mainly getting Jake's opinion on the FBI agents he was working with. Jake and Wilt filled him in on the day's proceedings. Brandon asked what Jake thought of the strategy they were employing. "Well, Brandon, we stopped eleven black Explorers today. They all checked out ok. We could do this every day. We'll keep checking. If we see a vehicle with a plate we ran already, we'll let it go."

"I hear a but in there."

"Yeah. Me and Jake were talking. What if this guy decides to switch plates with another black Explorer. They're not too hard to find. And say he happens to pick one that we already stopped. He could drive around for weeks, free and clear."

"You're right. So, what would you suggest?"

"Look, Brandon, you guys have to follow protocol. Doing what we're doing is fine, but we're leaving opportunities untried."

"Like what?"

"The personal approach. Harry Reeves is a loner. He's not going to be out on the town every day. He's more likely to be holed up, in some cheap motel, down here. He would've gone out when he first got here, or even on his way here. I believe we would only catch him on the street, when he's hunting. Now Wilt and I can split up, and take his picture, and start hitting all the hotels, and motels, that are out of the way. There's only one supermarket in town. We'll check there. Check out the mini-markets, WAWA convenience stores, places like that. I think he'll only show himself outside, on foot. His past habits show that he keeps the Explorer only for long-distance travel. He's stolen a car, when he's hunting for victims."

"You think he's going to try doing this on his own?"

"I don't think he can help himself. He might not target high school girls, but I think he has to keep on torturing and killing. It's in his DNA." By the end of the meeting, Jake had convinced Agent Wright to change the time of the operation, to checking out the roads from 1:00pm until 9:00pm, and concentrating the early afternoon hours near Ocean City High School. Wilt suggested waiting in front of the school, at 5th and Atlantic, and sort of follow girls that were walking home alone. When they had finished giving Brandon their opinions, he said that he and Harvey would take their places driving around, and they should just do what they felt was best. After setting up another briefing on Thursday, he was gone.

It was almost ten o'clock, when Wilt said "Jake, I gotta get to bed. You had my black ass up way too early this morning. I'm hitting the sack."

"Ok, Wilt. I'm not gonna be far behind you. I just want to look at this Google satellite map for a bit, to figure out what 's the best place to start looking for this clown, in the morning."

"Knock yourself out, Jake. Hasta Manana, amigo."

"Good night."

Jake woke Wednesday morning, to the sight of his partner doing yoga. "Yo, Jack LaLanne, what are you up to?"

"Morning Jake. Did I wake you?"

"No, but I wasn't really prepared to see all this, when I first wake up."

"Part of my Physical Therapy. I do these stretches and such every morning. With all the sitting we been doing the last few days, I'd be like a pretzel, when I tried to get up and walk. And speaking of pretzel, your plan includes us eating breakfast before we go out hunting, right?"

"Yeah, we'll eat first. But don't let me stop your Jane Fonda Work Out there. I'm gonna jump in the shower, then we can get started."

Jake explained his plan over breakfast. "Look, this guy doesn't like to be around people. The least populated area in Ocean city is down at 59th street, before you hit the State Park. There are only a few blocks east to west there, so we ought to be able to make it at least up to 50th street, by the end of the day. We'll park one car at 50th St. and drive down to 59th Street. We park there and make our way up to the first car. Then we can drive back down to get the other car."

"See, that's why you're brilliant, Jake. The first day, I woulda drove both cars as far south as we could, and then we'd have to walk back down there, all tired, and shit, to get our cars. Let's hit it."

The pair made great time, at the start. Being that there are only four North-South streets that far down, they had covered 59th street up to

57th street, from Central to West Aves., by 11:30 am. Then came 56th to 52nd, which, in some spots had twenty north-south streets. It was almost 3:00 pm when they finished that part of the journey. At quarter after five, Wilt said, "Is that our car, or am I seeing a mirage, Jake?"

"No, that's our ride Wilt."

"Thank you, Baby Jesus! I don't know if I could've walked one more block."

"Let's head down and get the other car. Tomorrow will be a little easier. It stays narrow just about all the way up to 37th street. Friday will be a bear, though."

"Maybe we'll find the prick tomorrow, and we won't have to worry about Friday."

"I just hope we're not wasting our time."

"What do you mean, Jake? This is the best way to catch this guy, right?"

"Oh, yeah. I'm not doubting our method. It's just that we don't know for sure, that he even came down here. All this is based on what Harriet told us, and what the FBI profiler deduced. For all we know, Harry Reeves could be on the West Coast by now."

"Jake, we gotta play the hand we're dealt, right? Sure, we could be way off base, looking down here, but this is the best option we have, right?"

"You're right. I know that. I just hate thinking that we're beating a dead horse, by searching in Ocean City. There's the other car. What do you want to do for dinner?"

"Dude, can we just stop at WAWA, and pick up maybe a sandwich, and some mac and cheese? I really am exhausted. I just want to eat something, and crash for the night."

"Sure. Follow me."

When Jake awoke Thursday morning, he found Wilt doing his Yoga stretches, only more slowly than the day before. "You okay, Wilt?"

"All that walking took it out of me yesterday, Jake. It's taking me longer than usual to get myself stretched out."

"Why don't you sit today out, Wilt? I'll start on my own."

"No, I'll be okay. Just need to get myself moving, and I'll be fine."

"Your call, Wilt. But listen, if you need to stop out there, you just stop, and take a break."

"Sure, Jake, sure. Now, let's get going, before I change my mind."

The two men went to WAWA. Breakfast today was going to be coffee, and a WAWA egg sandwich. While the clerk was ringing them up, Jake showed her Reeves' picture, and asked if she had ever seen him. "Don't know for sure. Maybe."

"Annie, it's very important. Take another look."

"Well, he looks like a guy that was in here the other night. Wait." She pressed the button on her communication device and asked for the Manager to come to the register.

A minute later, Annie, the twenty-something cashier, was joined by Assistant Manager Dave, who appeared to be younger than Annie. "Problem, Annie?"

"No, Dave. These guys are looking for this guy."

"Are you guys cops?"

"We're working for the FBI."

"Like I said Dave, these guys are looking for this guy." She showed the young man the picture Jake gave her to look at. "Doesn't that look like the guy who came in here Tuesday night, when we were both working, and brought the sandwich back."

"Yeah, yeah. The cheese guy."

"Cheese guy?"

"Yeah, this guy orders a ham sandwich, with mayo, lettuce and tomato. The girl back in Deli, put cheese on it, by mistake. Ten minutes after he leaves, he's back. He's allergic to cheese, and he can't eat that, because there is cheese on it. Made a pretty big fuss, over nothing. We made him a new sandwich, and refunded his money, for the inconvenience. I'm pretty sure that's him, but not positive."

Wilt asked, "Do you have video equipment in here, and is it working?"

"Sure. Follow me, to the back office."

While Dave was bringing up the video for Wilt, Jake called Brandon Wright. "Jake. Morning."

"Brandon, we may have something. Come to the WAWA convenience store on 34ᵗʰ street. A block West of West Ave."

"I'm on my way. Be there in 10 minutes." When Agent Wright walked into the WAWA, Jake and Wilt were coming out of the office, with two pictures, printed from the store video system. "What's up, Jake?"

"Here's a picture of what appears to be Reeves, paying for his food." The time stamp said 8:31 pm. The second picture showed Reeves, walking back in the store. The time was 8:53 pm. "He brought the sandwich back, because it had cheese on it, and he's allergic."

"And?"

Wilt picked up the narrative. "And, if he was eating the sandwich while he was driving, he would've opened it right away, and been back in, within minutes."

"Right. The fact that it took him 22 minutes to get back, suggests that he took the food to wherever he's staying, opened it there, then drove back here."

"That means that he's most likely staying somewhere within an eight minute, or so, drive from here."

"Well, Jake and me figured it would take 1-2 minutes to pay, and walk to his car, and pull out onto the road. Maybe five minutes from the time he parks the Explorer, gets in the house, opens the sandwich, and heads back here. Another two minutes from when he parks, and walks in the door, at 8:53 pm. That adds up to, roughly 9-10 minutes of non-drive time."

"Meaning he's holed up somewhere within a 6-7 minute walk/ride from here."

"Well, actually, Brandon, if he walked, it would be closer to a ten-minute walk."

"Right. Do we have any parking lot video?"

"Assistant Manager Dave is cueing it up for us as we speak."

As if on cue, Asst. Manager Dave appeared carrying four pictures. Brandon Wright introduced himself. "I'm FBI Field Agent Brandon Wright. What do you have for us?"

"This picture shows your guy getting in this light-colored Hyundai Elantra. You can see the license plate real good. Here he is leaving the lot, at 8:36 pm. These two show him driving back in, at 8:51 pm, and getting out of the car at 8:52 pm."

"Thanks, Dave. Now, my agents will be down here, and they are going to need to get those tapes from you. I'll ask you to make sure nothing happens to them, until my people get here to relieve you of them. Okay?"

"Sure. Whatever you say." Dave went back to his office, presumably, to guard the tapes.

Agent Wright turned to Jake and Wilt. "Now, assuming it took about five minutes before he discovered the cheese mistake and started back; that leaves us with a five-minute drive. Jake, you go right out of the parking lot. Jamal, you go left. Keep under the speed limit. Drive straight for five minutes. I'll bring everybody down here, get more help, and start searching where you two end up. We'll go from the ocean to the back bay, working our way back to here. We're gonna get this son of a bitch."

Jake and Wilt drove off. Wilt pulled over four minutes and forty-five seconds later, when he came to 50Th Street. Jake's journey ended at 28th Street. Both men called in their positions. Brandon Wright told them to return to the 34th street WAWA.

When they entered the store, they were directed to the back office, where Agent Wright had set up a map, on a food preparation table. Ten minutes later, they were joined by the three Trenton agents, and Harvey Caldwell. Agent Wright had drawn a line from the back bay to the ocean, at 28th, and 50th streets. "This is our search area. We search door to door, until we find this creep. Agent Argent, you and your fellow agents from the Trenton office, will start at 28th and Wesley Ave. You'll work your way back and forth, ocean to bay, all the while heading south, back to this location." Each agent had a head shot, from the store video, as well as a picture of the Elantra. "Any questions? No? Good. We have about five hours of daylight left, so let's cover as much as we can. Agent Argent, I'll expect sit reps from you hourly."

"Roger that." And with that the body count in the room was down to four. Agents Wright and Caldwell, and Jake and Wilt. "Okay, we're gonna head south, and work our way back up to here."

"Brandon. Before we do anything, do you have Reeves' history?"

Agent Wright took a manilla folder out from his briefcase, handed it to Jake, and asked "What are you looking for?"

"Just a hunch. I saw something when I was out driving." Jake was now reading Harry Reeves vitals. "...member of MENSA ...PA and MD driver's Licenses ...PhD in computer Science ...bingo!"

"What is it?"

"I noticed that the Ocean City Municipal Airport is right around 30th St., on the bay. Harry Reeves has a pilot's license."

"And?"

"Don't you see? There aren't many places that have garages here on the island. I think he may be somewhere on the airport grounds. I'm sure there are empty hangars, and buildings, he could hide the car in. He may even be planning to fly out of here."

"What do you want to do about it, Jake?"

"Well, Brandon, can you get a couple more bodies to help search here? That would free Wilt and I to search in the airport."

"Go. Earn your pay. I'll have half a dozen more men here in the morning. Just stay in touch."

"Roger that."

Jake and Wilt headed to find Airport Security at the Ocean City Airport. Their search led them to a small building attached to what passed as a flight control tower. They first talked to the Air Traffic Controller, who assured them that every flight had to file a flight plan, or they would not get clearance to take off. When Jake asked how they could stop someone from just getting in a plane, and taking off, the controller thought for a moment, and said "I don't know. Luckily, that's never happened, in the six years I've worked here."

"But it *is* possible?"

"I guess, but why wouldn't you want someone to know where you were going? If you didn't file a plan, how would people know where to start looking for you, if something happened?"

"Thank you. Now, if you could direct us to airport security?"

"Oh, sure. Right out that door over there. It'll be the building right in front of you."

"Thanks."

Upon entering the twenty-foot square building identified as airport security, Jake and Wilt showed their IDs, and sat down to speak with Captain Larry Greene. "How can I help you boys?"

"We drove in here from 29ᵗʰ Street. We passed dozens of hangars, and structures, that appear to be empty. Is that accurate?"

"For the most part. See, when they built this place, they copied Cape May and Atlantic City Municipal airports. They overbuilt. This never quite took off, pardon the pun."

"How does it stay open?"

"Well, there's enough *old* money people down here, that have their own planes, to keep this place afloat. We're open from 5:00 am until sundown. We have two controllers, and our security consists of myself, and Lenny Baldwin, who is out making the rounds right now."

"Since you brought it up, what does 'making the rounds' consist of?"

"Four times a day, we drive around the perimeter, looking for signs of buildings broken into, things like that. And look, here comes Lenny now."

Jake noted that it was 2:05 pm. Soon, the trio became a quartet, as Lenny Baldwin came in, and hung the car keys on the hook. "Hey, chief."

"Lenny, these boys are working with the Honest-to-God FBI."

"Really? Lenny Baldwin. How can we help?"

"Lenny, you just came back from making the rounds. Do you have to log in and out?"

"Yessir. Just going to log back in now."

"Can I see that log sheet? So, you started your rounds at 1:40 pm, and you're back at 2:05 pm. Seems like a lot of buildings to check, in 25 minutes."

"Not really. We just do a visual, as we drive by."

"And the airport is locked down at sundown?"

"Well, there's no more planes landing or taking off, if that's what you mean."

"What I mean, is can anyone get on the grounds after sundown?"

"Yeah. The 29th St. gate is always open. In case somebody left something on their plane, and they need to get it, or something."

"Okay, let's change the subject. Can you rent a plane here?"

"Sure. Tony Utah runs a flight training school, in the building behind us. You can learn to fly, go skydiving, or rent a plane from Tony."

"You think he's there now?"

"Unless he's got somebody up in the air, he's there."

"Thanks, men. Oh, by the way, have you seen this guy around in the last few days?"

"No, he hasn't been in here."

"Jake. All we found out is that if you want to just take off, they can't really stop you; the place is empty after sundown; anybody can drive in here, any time; and the security is a joke."

"Yeah, Wilt, that's about right. Let's go talk to Tony Utah, and see if he asks for ID, when somebody rents a plane."

Tony Utah was a guy about Jake's age. Wilt estimated that he had to have at least fifty teeth in his mouth. "Hi. Tony Utah's flight School. You guys interested in learning to fly?"

"No, Mr. Utah..."

"Please, call me Tony."

"Okay, Tony. We're working an investigation with the FBI, and we'd like to ask you a few questions."

"FBI? Do I need a lawyer?" Tony Utah flashed his million-dollar smile.

"Do you think you need a lawyer?"

Tony's smile quickly faded. "Umm...no. What can I do for you?"

"Have you seen this man in the last few days?"

"No. Haven't seen anybody in ten days. Last person came through that door was a guy that wanted to go skydiving. He's supposed to come back tomorrow."

"And you rent planes?"

"Yeah. $100 per hour. If it wasn't for plane rental, I'd be closed."

"That many people rent planes?"

"Not what you think. There's about seventy-five people that have planes they own, stored here. Do either of you own a boat?" Jake answered yes. "Good. Know the saying 'A boat is a hole in the water that you throw money into?' Same is true about a plane, except that if the engine quits on you, you can't call for a tow back to port. You crash. Most of the rentals I get are from people who own planes here at the airport, but they're not running right, or they're waiting for an oil change, or a part, so they rent from me. My planes are ten-year-old Cessnas. They're the most reliable plane ever built."

"Just a few more questions. Walk me through renting a plane. What's involved?"

"First of all, I'd have to check your license. Then we'd file your flight plan, and off you go."

"And how much advance notice do you need?"

"Five minutes. I have three planes, and they are all always fueled, and ready to go."

"And how far can one of these planes fly, without refueling?"

"They have a range of 250-300 miles, depending on the winds."

"Thanks, Tony. I'll leave this picture with you. If you happen to see this guy around, give us a call."

"Will do."

When they got outside, Wilt asked, "What now, Jake?"

"We're gonna start at the 29th street entrance, and check every building, hangar, whatever, for forced entry."

"Damn, Jake! Just us two? That's gonna take a week, at least."

"I know. Let's get started."

As the two men drove back to their starting point, they drove past a large hanger, about 200 yards from Tony Utah's Flight School. Inside that hangar was a white Hyundai Elantra, a bound and gagged Asian girl, and Harry Reeves, wearing nothing, but a spiderman mask. The 30-something Asian woman was now into her 70th hour of captivity. The torture she had been put through was barbaric. She had been silently praying to die, for the last 65 hours.

CHAPTER 14

As Jake and Wilt were getting ready to leave their motel room, on Friday morning, Jake got a call from Agent Wright. Based on his conversation with Jake on Thursday night, Brandon and Harvey Caldwell would be joining Jake and Wilt at the airport. Jake explained to Wilt about their company. "Brandon got extra agents to help with the search. With the two extra bodies, we'll get through the airport in a day or two."

"Sounds good to me."

They met the FBI men at the 29th street entrance. As they were telling the FBI where they left off, Jake looked about a half mile down the access road and noticed what appeared to be two vehicles parked at, or near the flight tower. When they got to the spot they had stopped the night before, Jake let Wilt out, and said he'd be right back. He wanted to take donuts, that he had purchased as a sort of 'peace offering', down to the security shack. He pulled up as Cpt. Larry Greene was fumbling with the lock on the security office, cursing as he did so. "I swear I'm gonna put my foot up his ass!"

"Whoa, Cap! You're not talking about me, are you?"

"Wha...? Oh, Miller. It's you. No, it's that lame-brain Lenny! That asshole is supposed to open this place up at 8:00 am, sharp! Here it is, a quarter to nine, and the office is still closed. On top of that, I'm gonna have to make a pot of coffee, before I can get a cup. And, if my guess is right, you brought us donuts, and now I can't even offer you a cup for fifteen minutes."

"That's fine Cap. I had my breakfast already. I just wanted to drop these off. Lenny drives the brown Toyota parked out front yesterday?"

"Yeah, when it's running."

"Well, he's probably in with Tony Utah. The Toyota is parked next to Tony's Jeep, at the flight school, behind your building."

"Son of a bitch! We left out of here last night, 5:00 pm. Tony's jeep was there, and that asshole Lenny pulled over, to go see him. Last time that happened, them two got all drunk, or high, or whatever, and Lenny strolled in here the next day, at 10:30 am, not worth a damn. I had to send him home that day."

"Well, look Cap., take these donuts, then take a deep breath, open your office, and put your coffee on. I'll stop next door, and chase Lenny over here. I wanted to say hi to Tony Utah anyway."

"Really? You're all right, Miller. Hey, what kind of donuts did you get?"

"A dozen old fashioned Dunkin' Donuts."

"See, now that's smart thinking on your part. People get seven, eight different kinds of donuts, all you're doing is asking for trouble. Somebody gets pissed off because somebody else ate the last jelly donut, or you didn't get somebody else's favorite. Your way, nobody's feelings get hurt. Everybody gets the same donut. You want one, or you don't."

"You've given this a lot of thought, haven't you? Well, look, enjoy, and I'll send Lenny over."

Jake walked into Tony Utah's Flight School and Plane Charter and found the place empty. After calling out, he went through the back door, which led directly into Tony's airplane hangar. The first thing Jake noticed was that there were only two planes in the hangar. He remembered Tony saying he had three Cessnas, gassed up, and ready to go. As he rounded a partition, he came upon two bodies. Tony Utah, and Lenny Baldwin both had their throats slashed, from ear to ear. The blood on the ground that they lay in had mostly dried up. This told Jake that they died sometime before midnight. He started to back out of the room, so as not to disturb anything, when he noticed something positioned on Tony Utah's chest. He walked over to find the picture of Harry Reeves that he had left Utah. Under the picture now were the words 'LEAVE ME ALONE, OR THERE WILL BE MORE!!' As he backtracked into the flight school office, he noticed a pool of blood behind Utah's counter, that he didn't notice when he came in. He called Brandon Wright. "Brandon! Grab Wilt and Harvey, and get down here, to the Flight School!" As he ran into the security office, he yelled for Capt. Greene. "Cap! Lenny and Tony Utah are both dead! Call it in!"

"Jesus, Mary, and St. Joseph! Will do, Miller."

"After you call it in, secure the Flight School. Nobody gets in before the Forensic Team. The FBI will be here in a minute. Tell them I'm in the control tower!"

"Roger that!"

Jake sprinted the one hundred fifty yards to the control tower and took the steps three at a time. He burst into the control room. He startled the same Controller he spoke with the day before. "Mr. Miller! You scared me! What's wrong?"

"Listen to me carefully. Did a plane from the Flight School take off this morning?"

"Why do you ask?"

"Answer my question, and don't make me ask again!"

"Well, yeah. As I was walking in the door, I saw a plane taxiing down the runway. I hurried up here and put eyes on it; looked at it through my binoculars, and saw it was Whiskey Tango 1016. That's one of Tony's planes. Sometimes Tony will take a plane up, just to maybe watch the sun rise. He'll circle the field and bring her back down. We don't really make him file a flight plan for that."

"What time did that plane take off?"

"Like I said, just before sunrise…maybe 5:45 am?"

"Did the plane come back yet?"

"No, it didn't. In fact, it's been four hours, and I was starting to worry."

"Ok, this is very important. When the plane took off, did you watch it?"

"For a minute or two."

"Do you remember which direction it was headed?"

"Well, he circled the field twice, then headed Northwest, which is odd."

"Why is that odd?"

"Well, any other time Tony did that, he heads due East, out over the ocean, to get the best view of the sunrise. What's going on?"

"The plane was stolen. You can expect the police to ask you the same questions I just did."

As Jake walked out of the control tower, Brandon Wright was walking towards it. "Jake! What the hell!"

"It's Reeves! He killed a security guard, and a flight school operator, and stole a plane!"

"You sure it was Reeves?"

"Yeah. Come on, I'll show you." They joined the other two members of their search party, and approached Captain Greene, who was guarding the door of the Flight School. "Captain Greene. This is FBI Field Agent Brandon Wright. He's gonna need to get inside."

"FBI! I guess if I can let anybody in, before the Forensics Team shows up, it's the FBI!"

"Good morning, Captain Greene. The FBI will be taking over this investigation. Our Forensic team and Coroner will be here shortly. Jake, join me."

Inside, Jake first pointed out that it appeared Tony Utah was behind the counter, apparently talking to Reeves. Jake remembered leaving the flyer with Reeves info on it, right on the counter. "Could be Utah noticed the resemblance, or Reeves saw the picture, but he killed Utah right here, then moved the body into the hangar. Capt. Greene said security officer Baldwin stopped here, on his way home last night, at 5:00 pm. Maybe Reeves came in to ask about renting a plane? Anyway, the guard was killed in here", and Jake led Brandon into the plane hangar.

"He appeared to be killed where he was standing. The pilot was dead before the guard arrived. Reeves heard the guard come in, and hid behind this partition, and grabbed him from behind as he entered. There's no signs of a struggle."

"That's the way I figure it too, Brandon. Checked with the Tower, and one of Utah's planes took off this morning, a little before 6:00 am. It had to be Reeves. The plane circled the field twice, then headed in a northwesterly direction. I talked to Utah yesterday, and he said these planes had a 250–300-mile distance range, on a tank of gas. The average speed is around 100 mph, so, even if Reeves went the max distance, he's been on the ground over an hour."

"I'll still put out a BOLO to all the airports within three hundred miles of here. If he landed at one of them, there will be a record. Let's get back outside, and give Harvey the ID numbers for the plane, so he can get started on that."

Back outside, agent Wright told his partner, and Wilt, what he and Jake had just surmised. "This guy has taken it to a new level. Up till now, he's been killing his victims when he was finished with them.

Could be that killing his mother, a spur of the moment, off the cuff murder, opened a new world to him. Now, he's killed two men. Two men physically superior to him. These were killings of self-preservation. And his note promises more bodies, if we don't stop chasing him."

Wilt offered his opinion. "Look, Jake and I were right here yesterday, at, what Jake, 3:30 pm? You're saying Reeves was most likely in that office between then, and 5:00 pm. From here, me and Jake went back to that gate we came in this morning, and started checking buildings, for forced entries, and such. We checked maybe two dozen buildings, with no luck. Point is, we were here until after 5:00 pm, and if somebody drove in here, we woulda seen them. We didn't see nobody, did we Jake?"

"Wilt's right. Cpt. Greene told me they lock the main entrance at 4:00 pm. That means that Reeves was already here, when we were here."

"And Jake, if he was far enough away, that he had to drive to this spot, wouldn't we have noticed a car driving around? I mean, it was like a ghost town. Seems likely to me that Reeves had to be holed up somewhere within walking distance of this place. And there's only two places walking distance from here. That big old hangar over there, and the smaller building behind it."

By now, the Forensics Team had shown up. Brandon stayed to bring them up to speed, while Jake, Wilt, and agent Caldwell crossed the one hundred fifty yards to the 'big old hangar'.

Ten feet from the front door, the three men realized that not only was the padlock missing from the hasp, but the door was ajar. Upon entering the cavernous hangar, Jake hit the light switches on the wall, and the four hundred square foot room was illuminated, revealing a white Elantra, in the front, and a hanging body of what Jake could only assume, was once a woman. Her breasts were cut off. She had been partially skinned alive! Jake noticed steam still coming from her abdomen, which had been cut wide open, in what looked like some sort of bizarre 'C' section. All three men staggered back outside, as Brandon Wright approached. Wilt was the only one who could speak. "Sick son of a bitch! Don't go in there, man! I seen a lot of sick shit, but I never seen anything that sick!"

Jake took over. "Brandon, the white Elantra is in there. Along with the remains of what I think is an Asian woman. I'm guessing, because I can't be 100% sure of either the Asian, or woman. Brandon, he skinned her, and by the look of complete terror on her face, he did it while she was alive. There is still steam coming out of what used to be her stomach, before he disemboweled her, so she hasn't been dead more than a few hours. I'm guessing he killed those two, over there, and made his plan to leave, then came over here, and spent the rest of the night... it looked like some of her bones were popped out of their sockets. This was an act of utter and complete rage."

"Okay, I'll make the call." The FBI Forensic team was informed they had a second crime scene to investigate.

An hour later, the two FBI agents, Jake and Wilt were sitting in the Airport Diner, drinking coffee. No one wanted anything to eat. Finally, Brandon spoke. "Jake, I want you two to stay working on this case."

"Well, Brandon, we were staying on this case, even if you didn't pay us anymore."

"Good. Do you have any kind of plan?"

"I been thinking. This guy is smart. He wants us to find his bodies, to prove how smart he is. He flew that plane in the direction of Philly. Now, he could've changed course, but knowing how he wants to be places he's familiar with, I'm betting he went to Philadelphia. And I don't think we're going to get any reports of a landing at any *real* airport, because he wouldn't risk that. Besides, if he flew to, say Northeast Philadelphia Airport, he'd have to rent a car. Those Cessnas can land anywhere. No, I think Harry Reeves is going to fly that plane to somewhere he's real comfortable, and land it in a field, or on a road. I think he already has a plan for how to leave, once he gets there. With that in mind, Wilt and I are going to turn his rental in, check out of our motel, and head up to the city. Maybe Bucks County. I have an ex-SEAL buddy, who I'm sure will put us up for a day or two, if need be."

"Fine. You go ahead. Harvey and I will stay here until the Forensic Team is done, and we see if there's any clues as to what Reeves is going to do next."

Three hours later, Jake and Wilt were headed up Route 73, and over the Betsy Ross Bridge, into Philadelphia. Jake had called Tommy Williams, who was more than happy to put them up for as long as they needed. "Tell me about your pal, Jake. The one whose place we're staying at."

"Tommy? The best. Maybe the toughest guy I ever met. Lost his leg when we were ambushed, outside of Fallujah. Stood on the back of a Jeep, on one leg, firing the .50 caliber machine gun, while we loaded three other guys onto the jeep, and made our escape. He got a prosthetic leg, and the Medal of Honor for what he did that day."

"Damn!"

"One other thing. Last summer, his baby brother, Ted, was going to join CMC PD. He was staying at my place. Did you hear about my truck blowing up?"

"Yeah, yeah. Denise heard about it and told me."

"Well, Teddy was in my truck, when it blew up. He was killed. Tommy took it hard. Keep that in mind."

"Roger that."

As they pulled into the driveway of the two-story single home, Wilt said, "Damn, Jake, your buddy only lives a few minutes from Harriet Abrams house."

As the men got out of the car, Tommy Williams came out of the house to meet them. "Tommy! Good to see you!"

"No time for that now, Jake. Since you called me earlier I 've been listening to the police scanner. Seems there's a cop missing, since around 7:30 am. Last report from him was he was checking out an extremely low flying plane, to make sure everything was okay. With the shift change, they didn't realize he never reported back, until almost 9:00 am. His GPS locator isn't working. You said you were looking for a plane, didn't you?"

"Yeah, I did. Get in."

Jake roared out of the driveway and headed back to Farmers Landing Road. "Why you headed here, Jake?"

"It's where this creep lived, Tommy. Since he killed his mother last week, there are only two other families living on this whole road."

"Wait! You're looking for the guy that killed the old lady last Sunday?"

"Yeah, Tommy. Name's Harry Reeves."

Jake made a right onto Harriet Abrams' street and sped to where it came to a dead end. There, in a field, not fifty yards from the last house, was Whiskey Tango 1016, a red and white Cessna, with Utah's Flight School painted on the fuselage.

As the men got out of the car, Jake reached down to his ankle to give Tommy Williams his backup piece. "No need, Jake. I still got my service revolver." They made their way around the barn, to get closer to the plane.

In the back they found the missing police cruiser. Wilt pointed to the dashboard, which was completely destroyed. "Now you know why the GPS isn't working."

About 30 feet between the car and the plane, they saw the body of the trooper, on his back, throat cleanly sliced open. His weapon was missing. Jake motioned the men back to their car. Once there, he dialed 911. "Hello. My name is James Miller. I'm an investigator working with the FBI. I need to speak to whoever is in charge of searching for the missing police cruiser. It's an emergency."

"Please hold."

After a few clicks, Jake heard "This is Captain Wallace, PA State Trooper. Who is this?"

"Sir, my name is James Miller. I was, and still am working with the FBI. I was involved in the murder on Farmer's Landing Road last Sunday. I've located your missing car, and officer. We're located on Farmers Landing Road, where it dead ends. Your Officer is dead. The suspect may still be in the area. We are holding steady, until your people arrive."

"Miller, is it? Who was the FBI Agent in charge at the murder scene last Sunday?"

"That would be Field Agent Brandon Wright. That's who I'm working for."

"That checks. We'll be there in ten minutes."

CHAPTER 15

In less than five minutes, the three men could hear the sirens getting closer. Jake was on the phone with Brandon Wright. "…look, Brandon, I'm gonna tell the state troopers this, but I know you can get the info faster. The addresses are 3 Farmers Landing Road, and 5 Farmers Landing Road. The cavalry will be here in less than a minute. These are the only two houses that were occupied on this road. I'm betting that when they breach, they're gonna find more bodies. Reeves landed here, killed a Trooper, and probably the people that live here. The house at the first address I gave you doesn't have a vehicle anywhere around. I need you to ID the owners of these houses, and any vehicles registered at these properties. Reeves landed here before 8:00 am. He probably stole the car, after he killed everybody, and has been on the road since then. That's at least a four-hour head start. We need to put a BOLO out on the car he's driving."

"I'm on it, Jake. Good work finding the plane so quick."

"Not good enough, Brandon. We're always one step behind this guy. I should have known about his pilot's license. We would've started at the airport right away. We had him. We had figured out his move and were there in time to catch him. We missed our chance, and three people down there, and maybe five more, up here, paid for my mistake with their lives. Call me as soon as you know anything." Jake hung up the phone.

Wilt followed Jake around to the back of his car. "Jake, hold up. None of this is on you."

"Really, Wilt? I read this guy's sheet. We passed that airport, what, four times, in the 3 days we were down there. It was right there, and I missed it."

"Not just you, Jake. The whole FB friggin' I missed it! Hell, it was *you* that figured out to come down to Ocean City in the first place!"

"Yeah, so that this bastard could kill three people, and we could chase him right back up here. Look, Wilt. I appreciate you having my back here but missing the fact that he has a pilot's license was a rookie mistake. One that I shouldn't make. One that Tom Hanson would've never made."

"Well, it's a shame you're stuck with me, then."

"No, wait! That's not what I meant." Wilt was on his way over to talk to Tommy Williams.

"Mr. Miller?"

"Jake, please."

"Jake, I'm Captain Wallace, of the PA State Police. We spoke on the phone a few minutes ago."

"Right. Sorry about your loss, Captain."

"Thank you. I just wanted to let you know that we found two dead adults in 3 Farmers Landing Road, and one dead adult, and one injured adult, in 5."

"Wait! Somebody survived?"

"So far. It's kind of touch and go. The victim's name is Alan Witten. Looks like the perp took him from behind, and sliced his throat, but he missed the artery. Witten went down and hit his head on the coffee table. Knocked himself out cold. Probably saved his life. Perp thought he was dead and turned his attention to Mrs. Witten. She was not as fortunate as her husband."

"Can I talk to him?"

"He's still out of it. They have him stabilized, for now. Getting ready to take him to the hospital. No guarantee he'll survive."

"Captain, can you see what vehicles are registered to the people who lived at 3 Farmers Landing Road? Since the Witten's vehicle is in the driveway, and the other driveway is empty, I'd guess that Reeves is in their car."

"We're working on that, as we speak, Jake. Is the FBI doing anything?"

"Right now, they're doing the same as you."

"Well, Miller, I feed you everything we get, and I expect the same from your people. The Trooper that was killed? Name was Moss, Billy Moss. Four years on the job. Married three years. Has a two-year-old little girl, Allison. His wife, Connie, just gave birth six weeks ago, to his son, William Jr. We were all going to the Christening next month. I want this guy real bad, Miller."

"Captain, I am going to catch this asshole, and when I do, well, let's just say there won't be a trial."

"You ex-military, Miller?"

"Yes sir. Navy SEAL."

"Thought so. Good hunting, marine."

~~~

The ride back to Tommy's house was quiet. Carmen Williams served dinner, and afterwards Jake, Wilt, and Tommy, went out to the sunroom. "So, what's your plan, Jake?"

"Not sure, Tommy. We should've had this guy."

"Jesus, Jake, will you let it go? We're never going to catch him, if you keep beating yourself up over not catching him in Ocean City."

"You still doing that shit, Jake? Taking blame for every single thing that happens in the world?"

"Damn right he is! Look, Jake. You were able to figure out this guy's play once, you can do it again."

"But now, all we have to go on is the car he's in, a red Chevy Impala."

"At least it's something. And they're looking for that car in every state East of the Mississippi."

"Nah, this guy isn't going anywhere that he hasn't been before. We don't have to worry about him turning up in Ohio, or Kentucky. No, he's most likely within a hundred miles of here. We need to get more information on him. What he likes and doesn't like."

"Maybe that Witten guy can help us, when he wakes up."

"You mean, *if* he wakes up. Yeah, maybe he can."

"You know, Jake, I was thinking. Now, I'm no Tom Hanson, or anything...."

Jake rolled his eyes. "What were you thinking, Wilt?"

"When we followed that car to where we found those girls, didn't Harriet tell us that house belonged to Reeve's uncle?"

"Yeah. Name was Eddie! Eddie Abrams! Good idea, Wilt! First thing tomorrow, we head over to Pine Rd. Uncle Eddie should be back from Disney. Maybe he knows something that could help us."

"Jake, you said Reeves is most likely not too far away, right? Now, he killed his own mother, because he was afraid we would get information out of her. What if he thinks his uncle might be able to help us?"

"Jesus, he might try to kill him! We gotta call him now!"

After finding Edward Abrams phone number, from the White pages, Jake dialed. "Good evening Mr. Abrams. My name is...no sir, I'm not a telemarketer. My name is Jake Miller. I'm working with the FBI. We're trying to track down your nephew, Harry. I was wondering... well, sir, I'd like to talk to you, if that's ok. Something that you might think is the smallest thing, could turn out to be huge. No, sir, you don't have to talk to me, but I do have to tell you that Harry killed his own mother last Sunday, and we don't think he'd hesitate to come after, say, a cousin, if he thought the cousin knew anything. I know, sir. I believe you don't know anything. His mother didn't know anything either, but Harry *thought* she did. Now…yes. You're right. I was just going to say that you should have police protection. How that works is my associate, and I would come to your home, check it out, for safety, and determine what kind, and how much protection you may need. Now, during that walk-through of your property, any information you can remember about your cousin's habits, what he likes, and doesn't like. Anything like that will help us immensely in devising a protection plan for you. Yes sir. Whenever it's convenient for you. Right now? Perfect. We will be there in about ten minutes. Yes sir. See you soon."

"Damn, you're smooth!"

"What can I say, it's a gift. Now I have to convince Brandon he has to post guards at this guy's house. Let's go, Wilt."

"Hey, Jake, mind if I tag along?"

"You want to come, Tommy? Why?"

"Give me something to do."

"What about your business?"

"That runs itself. My foreman does most everything now. I just sit home, and cash checks. Come on, maybe I'll like it, and start a second career, as a P.I."

"It's okay with me, if it's okay with Carmen."

"If what's okay with Carmen."

Jake turned to see Tommy's wife standing in the doorway. "Nothing, Honey. I just asked Jake if I could, you know, work the case with him. He said it was up to you."

"Jake, will it get him out of this house, and out from under my feet? By all means, let him help you. Please!"

Jake just shook his head. "Let's go."

On the ride, Wilt asked, "So, Tommy, what kind of business do you have?"

"Home construction, and remodeling."

"That's cool."

"Wait. Tommy. Tell Wilt the name of your company."

"Happy Homes Construction."

"Really? I seen your commercials. The cartoon muscle guy, that chops down trees with his bare hands. My girls love that commercial."

"Wait for it..."

"Hey! In your commercial, you're a white guy! What's up with that?"

"Well, my brother, statistics show that three out of four people that own homes, are white. History shows that white people are more likely to call a white contractor, before they call a black contractor. So, when in Rome..."

"But don't you have to go to their house, to give them an estimate? They will notice that you're black, right?"

"Well, you see, once I get my foot in the door, my charming personality takes over, and they can't resist me. And, of course, if I don't think it's going well, I let them see I'm a disabled Vet, and they always ask what happened. Don't ask, it's just what white people do. When they ask, I tell them that I lost my leg fighting to keep them free. They can't say no then."

"Well, all right!"

"Yeah. All right. We're here. Thank God!"

Jake had already called Brandon Wright and mentioned that Eddie Abrams might be in danger. Wright agreed and made arrangements to have around the clock surveillance on Eddie Abrams home, which Jake planned to use as a bargaining chip, in case Eddie's memory needed jogging.

The Abrams home looked much different than the last time Jake and Wilt were there. Even though the carpets were shampooed, there was still a dark spot visible, where Andy Cashman had bled out. But other than that, it was just like any other family residence. Jake introduced himself, then introduced Wilt and Tommy. After pleasantries were exchanged, with Ed, and his wife Mary, the four men went into the den to talk. Jake started the conversation. "Ed, we are trying to figure out where your cousin Harry is likely to go. We need to find him, and bring him in. Make no mistake, Harry Reeves is a dangerous man. Not to scare you, but in the last twenty-four hours alone, he's murdered three people in Ocean City, and four others, right over there on Farmer's Landing Road. He left another resident there, for dead. To that end, anything you can tell us about him, no matter how insignificant you may believe it to be, could be the information we need to catch him, and make you and your family safe."

"Well, I don't know. Harry was always an odd kid. I'm not sure what he liked to do. I know he would come over here, from time to time, and go hunting for squirrels, and rabbits, and such, in that little wooded area behind my house. Can my wife join us? She is way more observant than I am."

"Absolutely. Let's get her in here."

Eddie called his wife Mary, and when she came in the room, he gave her the sanitized version of Harry's violence, telling her only that Harry has gone off the deep end, and killed some people, and she could help find him by telling Jake anything she could remember about Harry. When she asked, 'Like what?', Eddie told her any habits Harry had, or things he had talked about. Mary Abrams thought quietly for a moment, then said. "Well, Eddie, remember that summer we vacationed down the shore, and Harriet, Big Harry, and Little Harry joined us? It was the summer Harry graduated from high school. Harry and I were on the porch, and I asked if he had any plans. He told me how much he loved it at our house, that we rented for two weeks, and how much he would love to live there. Does that help?"

"Well yes it does, but we're already aware of his affinity for Ocean City."

"We could never afford Ocean City. No, this was in Villas. We rented a place on the bay for two weeks, and Ed's uncle Harry came down for the first weekend. Don't you remember, Eddie? Young Harry stayed with us for the whole first week."

"That's right. I forgot. Yeah, he loved it down there. I remember he said how peaceful it was down there, and that there were lots of woods, for him to hunt there, as well."

"Excellent. Anything else? Did he ever talk about places he'd like to visit?"

Eddie looked at his wife, who shook her head no. "Not that we can recall. I'm sorry we're not being much help, but Harry always kept to himself. He didn't really talk to anybody about anything. Except that summer. He loved it in Villas."

"Yeah, and he loved crab cakes."

"Oh, yeah, one night we went out and brought home crab cakes. Harry had never had them before, and he totally flipped out over them. He wanted them every night."

"Ok, anything else you can remember? Did he ever have a girl friend?"

"Harry? No, he wasn't much of a ladies' man, if you know what I mean."

"Well, Eddie, there was that one girl. Pamela, I think her name was. But that only lasted about a month."

"Was Pamela from around here?"

"Oh no. She was from Philly. In fact, Harry met her on the Boardwalk, in Wildwood, that same week he stayed with us."

"Do you remember where in the city she lived?"

"I don't know much about the areas down there, but one Sunday, he was supposed to go to her house for dinner, and Big Harry's car wouldn't start, so they called Eddie, and asked him to drive him down there."

"Do you remember this, Ed?"

"Yeah, I do. We took I-95 South. I don't remember the exit name, but it was right after we passed the Betsy Ross Bridge. We got off the highway, and right at the bottom of the exit ramp was a playground, with tennis courts. I remember because that's where I dropped him off. He was meeting her there. I offered to wait for her, and take them both to her house, but he said it was only a couple blocks, and he didn't mind the walk. Does any of this help?"

"Yes, it does. Now, Mr. and Mrs. Abrams, the FBI is arranging for a protection detail for you and your family. There will be a car parked either in the street in front of your house, or in your driveway. We have no knowledge that you are in any danger. This is just precautionary. Here is my card. If you think of anything else, or hear from Harry, please get in touch with me. Good night."

As they made their way back to Tommy's house, Wilt asked, "What do you think, Jake?"

"Don't know, Wilt. I'll call Brandon when we get back to Tommy's place, and fill him in. He just might be down in our back yard."

"What about this Pamela? Dead end?"

"Again, I'm not sure. He went out with this girl for a month. For a loser like him, he must've thought he was in love. He might feel comfortable getting in contact with her. Or he could be in the house next door to Tommy, here. Brandon's going to have to get that Profiler on the job. I'll give this all to him, and we'll see what tomorrow brings."

CHAPTER 16

Wilt walked into the kitchen, on Saturday morning, to the smell of fresh coffee, and the sound of Jake talking on the phone. After he filled his coffee cup, Wilt joined Jake and Tommy out on the parking pad. "Morning, Jake... Tommy. Was that agent Wright?"

"Yeah. He had that FBI Profiler up all night. Based on the information we gave her, she thinks there's a bout a 40% chance he's down in Villas, a 10% chance that he's down in Philly, looking to hide out with that Pamela, a 30% chance he's still in this area, and 20% that he is in....'parts unknown.'"

"What do you think, Jake?"

"Well, I think this guy is going to be the last place he thinks we'd look for him. When he had to leave Ocean City, he figured the last place we'd look for him would be his mother's house. Wilt, put yourself in his shoes. If you wanted to go the last place we'd look for you, where would that be?"

"Well, if it were me, I'd assume the law wouldn't look for me around here, where I just killed a cop, and three others."

"You're right, except that he already did that, last Sunday. While you and I were leaving his mother's house, he was a hundred yards away, in the Wilson house. I think he'd have to assume we wouldn't fall for that again; that we'd comb every inch of this area, looking for him. And we know he prefers to go someplace he's comfortable with. That being said, an unknown destination is also not likely. That leaves us with Pamela, and Villas. It's probable that he's not aware that we even know about Pamela, and Villas. Since we don't know if this Pamela is even on the east coast, I'd bet on Villas."

"So, we're going home?"

"No. Brandon, and his crew are headed down there. For right now, he wants us to try and locate Pamela."

"Talk about a needle in a haystack…"

"Maybe, maybe not. Where Abrams dropped Harry off that Sunday was Monkiewicz Playground, at Richmond St. and Allegheny Ave. I grew up in that area of Philly. We know Pamela lived a couple of blocks from the playground ten years ago. Pamela is not a very common name. I still know people that live there. Maybe they will recognize the name. The first call I make is to my niece, Kate. She's in the same age range. She might know Pamela, who lived near that playground. It still won't be easy finding her. I'd say it's more like finding a ten-penny nail in a haystack. After we've found or eliminated her, we head home."

"Any idea when that might be? Denise is gonna ask me, is all."

"We won't be up here more than a day, or two, Wilt. Tommy, it was good to see you. Thanks for putting up with us."

"Anytime, Jake. Jamal, it was nice to meet you."

"Right back at you."

"Listen Tommy, you and Carmen, have to come down, and stay a while. With or without the kids."

"Roger that, Jake. When the weather breaks. Good hunting, marine."

Jake called his sister first, to see if they could stay at her place, if they didn't wrap up before nightfall. He got her voicemail. Then he called his niece. "Hey, Kate."

"Uncle Jake. What's wrong?"

"Nothing is wrong. I need to ask you something. I want you to think back to about ten years ago. Do you remember anybody named Pamela? About the same age as you. She would've lived near Monkiewicz Playground."

"Pamela. Hmmm…not off the top of my head, uncle J. No last name?"

"If we knew her last name, Katie, I wouldn't be bothering you."

"Sorry uncle J."

"Maybe a year or two behind you, or ahead of you, in school?"

"I knew a Pam, when I went to Little Flower, but she lived in Harrowgate section of the city, not Port Richmond. No, I'm drawing a blank. I'll call Tiff, and Harley, and ask them. We ran in different circles back then. Maybe they know her. I'll call you back after I talk with them, Uncle Jake."

"Thanks, Kate. How's that doctor of yours? "

"Randy is fine, Uncle J. Are you going to mom's?"

"Yeah, if we have to stay overnight, we are."

"Give her a hug for me. Later."

As they passed Bridge St., Jake's sister Maggie returned his call. "Jimmy! What can I do for you?"

"Hey, sis. I'll be in the neighborhood, with Wilt, trying to locate a girl, in Richmond. Your daughter says she loves you."

"Kathleen? When were you talking to her?"

"Five minutes ago. This girl we're looking for is in her age range, and lived near Monkiewicz playground, about ten years ago."

"And you didn't think to ask me?"

"Not for nothing, sis, but you're at least twenty years older than this girl."

"Jake, you are a knucklehead. Did you forget that Kathleen's father's family lives on Emery Street, between Allegheny and Clementine St.?

The Haskells have lived there since the trolley cars were pulled by horses! Heck, I met Kathleen's dad in Byrnes Tavern. And he was the oldest of nine children. He has two sisters that are Kathleen's age. If this girl lived around there, one of the Haskells probably knew her. What's the girl's name?"

"Pamela. Don't know the last name."

"Well, how many Pamela's could there be? Let me make a call to Kathleen's aunt Ruth. She might know. Are you coming to my house right now?"

"No, I was going to stop in the old neighborhood first, to see if a could get a lead on this Pamela."

"Well, be here by 5:00 pm, sharp. That's when dinner will be ready."

"No sis, I don't want you cooking for us."

"Try and stop me. 5:00 pm, Jimmy."

"Ok, sis. See you then."

"Wow! You didn't really try too hard to talk her out of cooking."

"That's because I didn't want to talk her out of it. She's a fabulous cook!"

Jake and Wilt spent the rest of the day trying to get a line on a girl named Pamela, who would most likely be twenty-five-ish years old, and lived near Allegheny Ave, about ten years ago. They had no luck at all. Finally, at 4:15 pm, Jake decided to call it a day, and they headed to his sister Maggie's house. When they entered, Maggie had just finished setting the table for dinner. After their hellos, Maggie told both men that dinner would be in about twenty minutes. "Tom up here with you?"

"Yes. He's taking a shower. He'll be down in a minute."

"Did you have any luck calling Ruth?"

"No. I called *both* Ruth and Rita."

"That's right. They're twins, right?"

"Right. And they're a year older than my Kathleen. I got voicemail both times. I'm waiting to hear from them. Here comes my husband now."

"Hey Tom."

"Jake. Jamal. How are you boys making out?"

"Well, I take it you're up to speed on our case?"

"Yeah. Quite a mess. Any leads?"

"That's why we're still here. Trying to locate a girl named Pamela, that Reeves dated for a month, ten years ago."

"Kind of thin, don't you think?"

"No stone unturned, Tom. Anyway, I've just about exhausted all my avenues. If Maggie's calls to Kathleen's aunts don't produce anything, we're going to pack it in, in the morning. There's a chance Reeves is down in our neck of the woods."

"Enough shop talk. Dinner's ready."

~~~

Wilt pushed away from the table, and said, "Damn, Maggie! Jake was right. You are one awesome cook! I never had pork chops cooked in baked beans like that. I'll help with the dishes."

"You'll do no such thing! Thank you for your kind words, Jamal. I'm glad you enjoyed it. I'll clean up my own mess. Thank you, though. And you two could do with some of his manners. Now, in the other room! All of you!"

After the dishes were cleaned, and put away, everyone sat around the dining room table, drinking beer, and telling stories. About 8:30 pm, Maggie's phone rang. "Hello? Ruth! How are you? Oh, I'm fine. Kathleen's fine too. Listen Ruth, you remember my brother Jimmy, right? Well, he's working with the FBI, and they're looking for a girl who is about your age and lived down where you all live. What? Well, they need to find her. They think she might be in danger. Her name?

Pamela. I don't kn… really? Pamela Foster. Thank you so much Ruth. Give everyone my love. Good night."

"Pamela Foster?"

"That's right, Jimmy. She used to live at the same address as the Haskell's, but on Salmon St. She doesn't live there anymore, but Ruthie thinks her mom still does. 3129 Salmon St."

"You're the best, Maggie. We'll head there, first thing in the morning."

Sunday morning, Jake took everyone to IHOP for breakfast, after Maggie came home from 9:00 am mass. He and Wilt had their things packed in the car already, and told Brandon of their plans on Saturday morning, after they left Tommy Williams' house. After breakfast, they took Tom and Maggie home, and by 11:30 am, they were parked in front of the tiny porch-front house, at 3129 Salmon St. When they rang the doorbell, they heard a dog barking. A minute later, Charlotte Foster cracked the door open. "Hello. Can I help you?"

"Good morning Ms. Foster. My name is Jimmy Miller. This is my partner, Jamal."

"Whatever you're selling, I don't need any,"

"No! Ms. Foster. Excuse me, but we're not salesmen. We're working with the FBI."

"The FBI?"

"Yes, ma'am."

"My goodness, what in the world could the FBI want with me?"

"May we come in, ma'am? This concerns your daughter, Pamela. We believe she may be in danger, and we need to locate her, in order to protect her."

"Yes, come in. You two aren't afraid of dogs, are you? My Robbie can be scary."

When they entered the living room, a Chihuahua, who Jake assumed was Robbie, barked at them 3 times, and then flew up the stairs. "Please. Sit."

Charlotte Foster was short, about five feet even, and heavy. "Now, what did you say about Pamela?"

"We think she may be in danger, ma'am. We need to find her."

"Please call me Charlotte. Ma'am is for old ladies. I'm not even 60 yet."

"Of course. Charlotte, do you know where Pamela is?"

"Of course, I do. She's my daughter, after all. And don't you lawmen ever talk to each other?"

"I don't know what you mean, Charlotte."

"Well, that Detective, from the police department, was here just yesterday, saying the same thing you're saying now. You wasted your time coming here. All you had to do is call Detective Reeves, and he could have saved you a trip."

Jake looked at Wilt. "Charlotte, did Detective Reeves leave you his phone number?"

"He gave me his card. Here!"

Wilt took the card. Jake continued. "We're sorry for bothering you again, Charlotte. We'll call this detective, and coordinate everything. But in case we can't get hold of him right away, can you give us Pamela's address and phone number?"

"Pamela lives at 3780 Richmond St. That's just above Castor Ave. Her number is 215 680-0661."

"Thank you, Charlotte. Don't get up. We'll let ourselves out."

As they went down the front steps, Wilt turned and gave Jake the business card. "You know Jake, if Reeves was here, why didn't he kill the mother. He's killing everybody else. I don't understand... Jake? You okay?"

Jake was not okay. The color had drained from his face, and he stood, frozen on the top step, staring at the phony business card. "Jesus, Jake! Sit down! You look like you're going to pass out. What's wrong?"

"The phone number Reeves put on this card? It's my sister's number!"

"What!?"

"This son of a bitch! He *knew* we'd find Charlotte Foster! He didn't kill her, because he wanted her to give us this card! He knows who I am. This is a warning to leave him alone."

"Jesus Christ, Jake. How does he know who we are?"

"His mother. He obviously saw us there, at her house. He must've asked her who we were."

"What are you going to do?"

"You mean what are *we* going to do. If he knows who I am, he knows who you are. We're gonna call Brandon, and get somebody over to your place, and get protection for my family. Call Denise. Is there somewhere she can take the girls until we can get protection arranged?"

"No."

"Tell her to take them to the police station. We'll be down there by 3:00 pm. I'm gonna call my sister, and my niece, then Brandon Wright." The next five minutes were spent calling everyone and getting them protection. Jake wasn't worried too much about his sister. Tom Hansen was more than capable of protecting her. Katie was another story. She was headstrong and wouldn't take kindly to someone following her around all day. Jake didn't have time to debate with her, so he told her the whole truth. He gave her every detail of what Reeves had done to his victims. When he was done, Kathleen was more than willing to accept the protection detail. Then he called Brandon. "...and they need to be protected, Brandon."

"You're right, Jake. When I hang up with you, I'm sending Harvey Caldwell to the CMCPD station to stay with Jamal's family, until we get a protection detail in place, for them and your sister. Then I'll coordinate with the Philly PD, to arrange a detail for your niece. I need you two to take Pamela Foster into protective custody and bring her down here. Good luck."

"What did he say?"

"He's putting the protection in place. Harvey Caldwell will stay with your family, until everything's set up. We're supposed to pick up Pamela and bring her down the shore."

As they approached the front door of Pamela Foster's house, Wilt motioned to Jake that the inside door was ajar. The first floor of the little row house looked immaculate. Not a thing out of place. The front bedroom, on the second floor, was another story. That's where Jake and Wilt found Pamela Foster's mutilated corpse. She was tied to her bed and had a gag in place. The room was covered in blood. Jake guessed at least a dozen stab wounds were inflicted, none of which appeared to be fatal. No, when he finished 'playing' with Pamela, he slit her throat. There was a note covering her battered face. It was held in place, by a nail, that was driven into her forehead. The note was addressed to 'Mr. Miller'. It read: "Mr. Miller, if you're reading this, that means that you didn't get my other hints, or you are just too stupid to figure out their meaning, so I'll spell it out for you. This bitch thought she was better than me. I wonder what she thinks now. I know who you are, Miller. It was easier finding out about you, than it was finding a ten-penny nail, to hammer into this bitch's head. If you don't leave me alone, more people will be punished. People that are close to you. The names Kathleen, and Maggie come to mind. It's amazing the information you can find on the internet these days. *Leave me alone*!! PS- Tell your partner, Mr. King, that I looked him up, as well. Now, I've never touched a child, but then again, I never killed a man before, and when I did, I liked it.

So, Mr. King, if you want your two little angels, Patty, and Angela, as well as your beautiful wife Denise, to stay safe, *leave me alone!*"

Jake called Brandon Wright to tell him that Pamela Foster would not be coming down the shore with them, and that there was another crime scene to process. Brandon called it in to the Philadelphia FBI Office, then called Jake back. "Jake, my people will be there in a half hour, or so. Once you turn the scene over to them, head down here."

"Roger that. Where are you?"

"We're set up here at Congress Hall, in Cape May, where we were last summer. Call me when you're twenty minutes out, or so, and I'll meet you at your house. I've coordinated with CMCPD, and Harvey Caldwell. After you call me, I'll call them, and Harvey will bring Jamal's family, and the protection detail to your house."

"See you in about two hours."

"Well?"

"As soon as the FBI Forensic Team gets here, we're out of here. Denise and the kids will be at my house. That's where we're going. FBI should be here soon."

"You know Jake, something 's bothering me."

"Like what?"

"This guy is smart. He must know by now that we know that he's driving a red Impala."

"I agree."

"Well, if I were him, and I was as smart as he is, I'd dump that Impala, and there's a red Impala sitting right there, across the street. What do you think the odds are that one of the people that live in this row owns a red Impala, exactly like the one that Reeves is driving."

"You're right, Wilt. Impalas are not a very common car. We'll put the FBI Team on that car, over there, when they get here."

"Yeah, fine. But Reeves drove something out of here. When we went in the house, I noticed that this Foster girl had a dish on her TV. In that dish were her glasses, phone, and wallet. Denise does that. She puts everything she needs on the TV, so she never has to go looking for it. Know what wasn't on the TV? A set of keys."

"You think Reeves took her car?"

"If she has one, it makes sense."

"Good thinking, Wilt. Let's knock on a couple of doors and find out if Pamela had a car."

That process took all of three minutes. They knocked on the door of the house next door, that shares the same steps as Pamela Foster. A 40-something year old man answered. "What do you want?"

"Sir. We're working with the FBI. Your neighbor, Pamela, how well do you know her?"

"We're not screwing, if that's what you mean."

"No, sir. I mean, does she have a car?"

"Yeah. A Green Ford."

"Do you know what Model?"

"I just told you, Ford."

"No, sir. What kind of Ford? Taurus, Fiesta? How old is it?"

"It is a Ford…Focus! That's it. It isn't a station wagon, but not a regular car, either."

"A hatchback?"

"Yeah. Hatchback. I don't know the year, but she's owned it at least four years, and she didn't buy it new. Hey, is Pamela in trouble?"

"We're not at liberty to discuss that sir." Jake saw the big FBI Forensic truck slowing down, and he waved to the driver. "Now, Mr…?"

"Anthony. Richie Anthony."

"Mr. Anthony. Thank you for your help. The men getting out of that truck are also FBI. They'll want to get a statement from you, at some point while they're here. Again, thank you."

Wilt was giving the Medical Examiner the details of what they found, and that they didn't touch, or move anything. Jake approached, as he was finishing. "Jake Miller. Okay if we take off?"

"Yes, I think so. Do we need to talk to the neighbor that you were talking to?"

"Yeah."

"Okay. You gentlemen are free to go."

CHAPTER 17

Once in the car, Jake called Brandon Wright, to let him know they were on their way. He gave them the info on Pamela Foster's car. "And the guy next door swears he saw it early this morning, parked out front, around 7:00 am. It's almost 2:00 pm now, so if he's heading down where you are, he could be there already. And Brandon, what about Pamela's mother? She doesn't know yet."

"That's the Forensic Team's job. They'll ID the body, if they can. Then they'll inform next of kin. Come home. We need to talk."

Jake called Phil, of Phil's Doggie Daycare, and asked him if he could bring his two Labrador Retrievers, Assault and Battery, home. He told Phil he'd be home by 4:00 pm, and asked if he could wait there, so Jake could pay him. When they approached Jake's house, Jake thought it reminded him of a three-ring circus. The temperature had peaked at 61 degrees, warm for a March day. Wilt's daughters, Patty and Angela were playing with the dogs in the yard. His wife Denise was on the porch. Members of the police protection team wandered about. Brandon Wright, Harvey Caldwell, and Tom Hansen were huddled off to the left.

When they entered the gate, Patty and Angela ran to Wilt. "Daddy! Daddy! We missed you!"

Right behind them were Jake's 'kids', not to be outdone, in the welcome home department. When the hugs and hellos and handshakes were done, Jake paid Phil Brown, and sent him on his way. Finally, Brandon, Harvey, Wilt, Jake, and Tom Hansen, found themselves alone. "Brandon, what do we need to talk about?"

"Well, Jake, Reeves appears to be going off the rails, here. He's butchering people, in the same way that you or I take a shower. To say he's escalating may be the understatement of the year."

"And?"

"And I think you should consider doing what he says."

"Are you crazy? Look, Brandon, you're right. This guy is ramping it up, almost every day. There's no way this S.O.B. is scaring me off. I *want* him to come after me. I'll feed him his nuts."

"Agent Wright, I know I'm just working for Jake here, but there's no way I'm backing down from this lunatic! I'm with Jake. Step to me, bitch."

"But that's the problem. He's too smart to come after you two. Look, he's told you that he's not coming after you. He specifically named who he will target, if you two don't drop this case. And face it, no matter how hard you try, and how much protection we give your families, there *will* be times they are vulnerable. You know that."

"Tom, this affects you, as well. What do you think?"

"Well, Jake, Brandon showed me a picture of the note you texted him. He's right, in that nobody can be with Maggie, Kathleen, or Wilt's family 24/7. Maybe, at least for right now, you should back off some."

"And let this asshole get away with everything?"

"Now, I never said *that* pard. He seems to know all about you, but he doesn't know about me."

"Hell no, Jake! Ain't nobody gonna threaten my family, and me let it go."

"Hold on a minute, Wilt. What did you have in mind, Tom?"

"The way I figure it, this guy thinks women are just about the most stupid creatures God ever put on this earth, right? Now, he only knows I'm Maggie's husband, if he knows that much. If I were to team up with a woman, that's a team he might not see coming."

"A woman! Jake, what's he talking about?"

"You're talking about getting the band back together, aren't you?"

"Could work."

"Okay, but how will Reeves know we're not working the case?"

"That's the part I haven't figured out yet. How does he know you are? And something's been bothering me. Why did he specifically mention a ten-penny nail, in his note?"

"Holy shit, Jake! That's exactly what you said the other day, at Tommy Williams' house. I asked if we were going home, and you said we were looking for Pamela, and I said that would be like finding a needle in a haystack."

"And I said not exactly. That we did have some advantages, and it would be more like finding a ten-penny nail in a haystack. Were we in Tommy's house when I said that?"

"We were at your car."

It took the FBI technician less than ten minutes to find the bug in Jake's Santa Fe. As per agent Wright's instructions, he silently got out of the vehicle, and showed Jake where it was, then left it right there. Once back in Jake's house, which had been swept for listening devices, and cleared by the Tech Team, Jake, Wilt, agents Wright and Caldwell, and Tom Hansen discussed what the plan was. Agent Wright spoke first. "Okay, we may have our first advantage on this guy. He doesn't know we know about the bug in Jake's SUV. We have to feed him what we want him to know. We might be able to trip him up."

"Yeah, if he's down here. We don't know that, yet."

Tom Hansen took the floor. "You're right, pard. We don't know that yet. Baby steps. We have to deal with one thing at a time. And if we all agree that we need a couple of new players, to track this slime ball down, the first thing we need to do is convince him that you're off the case, Jake."

"And how do we do that?"

"Well, once we proceed under the assumption that he's down here, that's the easy part. You'll drive Brandon here back to Congress Hall, and on the way, he'll fire you. That tech guy said the bug in the Santa Fe is kind of like a motion detector. When it hears voices, it transmits, probably to a recorder. That way, Reeves can play everything back whenever he wants."

"Then what?"

"Then, nothing. You're fired. Oh, you'll argue with Brandon, and make him promise to keep you in the loop. That will keep Reeves listening, to see if Brandon tips his hand."

"That's great! But what am I supposed to do? Sit around with my thumb up my ass?"

"Oh, I don't know, Wilt. I think you'll have plenty to do. See, I realized about a month ago, when you started hanging around the station, that you're ready to come back to work. I have an opening for a Detective, in Major Crimes, where you worked before. Whenever *you* realize you're ready to come back, the job is yours. Paperwork's all filled out. Just needs your John Hancock."

"Huh? You mean I can come back? I just have to sign?"

"Does he always talk in half sentences, Jake?"

"Only when he's flabbergasted."

"Who's flabbergasted?"

"Hey, Denise. Oh, your husband."

"About what? Going back to work as a cop? I've known for about six weeks that's what he wants to do. I was just waiting for him to get the gumption to talk to me about it. He hates lawyering. He loves being a detective. That's what he should do."

"See that, Jamal? You're about the only one who doesn't know you want to be a detective again."

"You mean that, baby? It's okay with you if I go back to being a detective?"

"Sure, it is. Just don't go getting yourself all shot to hell, or anything."

"Tom, I'd like to take you up on your offer."

"See you Monday morning."

Just as planned, Jake drove Brandon Wright back to Cape May, and during the ride, Brandon fired Jake. "Look, Jake. The Profiler said the chances of Reeves being down here, in South Jersey, were, like 30%. I know you're not scared of him, but why take a chance of him going after your family? There's really nothing else you can do, anyway. I have a team of five, and we'll spend a day or two, down here, looking for him, and then start moving North. We know the guy is a freak, and he'll strike again. Then we'll know where he is, and hopefully, we can figure out his next move."

"I still don't like it, Brandon. I put a lot of time into this case."

"And you got paid for your time."

"That doesn't matter."

"That's all that matters. You have a full list of cases people want your services on. All right. How about this? I'll update you every day on any progress we make. That way, you can follow along, and if you have any ideas, I'll listen to them."

Jake made a point of calling Wilt, to let him know they had been fired, on the way back from Cape May. Wilt was furious, and that he didn't want to quit, but when Jake mentioned that he was starting back, as a Detective, on Monday morning, Wilt had to grudgingly admit that he couldn't do both, and he needed the detective job. The idea was that it would be easy enough for Reeves to find out that Jamal King had, indeed started working, as a detective for Major Crimes, in the CMCPD, on April 1st. This would help convince him that he and Jake were no longer looking for him. The first three days, or so, of April, would have the FBI 'suits' out in force, knocking on doors, and then 'moving on', as Brandon Wright had said in his conversation with Jake. Jake would go back to catching cheating spouses, and the other normal duties of a Private Investigator. The hope was that if Harry Reeves thought the FBI had moved north, looking for him, and Jake was out of the game, he would feel secure enough to make his home, at least for now, in Villas. He might even let his guard down, and finally make a mistake. And if he did, Tom Hansen, and his partner, Detective Regina Weaver, a.k.a. Kari, a.k.a. Chantelle, would be there to put him down, like the rabid animal he was.

Everyone knew not to call Jake, for fear that he might be in his vehicle. Oh, he got a call, on Wednesday, the 3rd of April, that the FBI would be moving over into the Wildwoods, and then make their way up the coast, after that. On Thursday morning, there was no FBI presence in the area. They checked out of Congress Hall, and into La Costa Motel, in Sea Isle City. It did appear that they were moving on. In reality, what Brandon Wright was doing was monitoring all stolen vehicle reports in the New Jersey areas closest to Philadelphia. His men were focusing on Pennsuaken, Cinnaminson, Camden, Gloucester, and Deptford areas. In particular they were looking for a late model Toyota, Hyundai, Kia, silver, white, or tan, that had been reported stolen on Sunday, March 31st. The thought was that since Reeves knew Jake and Wilt were going to eventually find Pamela Foster, he knew they would also find her car missing. He wouldn't want to be driving a car with PA plates on it, in New Jersey, so he would dump it somewhere, and steal a different car, as soon as possible. All the searching for Reeves in the Villas, Delhaven, Townbank areas was being handled by CMCPD Tom Hansen and Regina Weaver. What they were mostly interested in, were missing person's reports. Any missing person report, involving a female, was directed to Hansen. There were none, until Friday, April 5th.

The call came in at 5:15, Friday afternoon. Tom Hansen was on his way out the door when his phone rang. He went back to answer it. It was a borderline hysterical Hispanic woman. Tom could hardly understand her. He managed to get out of her that she lived in Erma, on Tabernacle Road, just off on Rte. 9. Her daughter, who was a Freshman at Lower Cape May Regional High School, didn't come home from school today. Tom wrote the address down, called Kari, who said she would meet him there.

Kari got to the home first. When Tom arrived, she had already gotten most of the pertinent details from the distraught woman, who was more comfortable speaking in Spanish, which Kari was fluent in. "Apparently, the daughter, Elena Montez, walks home from school most days. Her last class today ended at 2:00 pm. You can see the high school from their front yard. It's less than a ten-minute walk. The bus that would bring her home goes the opposite direction first, and Elena would be the last drop off, at 2:45 pm, or so. The only time she takes the bus is when it's raining or snowing. She's been calling Elena's phone since 2:30 pm, and there has been no answer. She has stopped at her friend's house, which is about a hundred yards away, on her way home before, but she always calls to let her mother know. Her mother, Luz Montez, went down to the house, and Elena was not there." They got a recent photo of the girl, along with her cell number, and told Luz to stay by the phone. Once outside Regina asked Tom how they were going to proceed.

"Well, Regina, this is how Reeves operates. He picks up girls on their way home from school. All the abductions that I'm aware of have occurred on a Friday. First thing is we talk to the friend who lives down the street. Maybe Elena went with some Romeo, and she didn't want to tell her mother."

Karen Miller answered the door, with her mother at her side. After identifying themselves, and being let in, Tom and Kari sat down with the chubby blonde. "Karen, what time did you get out of school today?"

"2:00 pm."

"Good. did you walk home or take the bus."

"She always walks home. The bus takes too long. She can walk home in ten minutes."

"Mrs. Miller, it's important that Karen answers our questions. She might know some little detail that could really help us."

"I'm sorry."

"It's okay. I know you're just being a mom. So, Karen, you walked home today?"

"Yeah."

"Did you stop anywhere?"

"No."

"So, what time did you get in?"

"Around quarter after two. I'm not sure exactly."

"That's fine. Did you see Elena today?"

"Yes. We eat lunch together, and we have the same Algebra class, at 1:15 pm."

"So, you and Elena are in the same class at the end of the day?"

"Yes."

"Was Elena in Algebra class today?"

"Yes, she sits right behind me. I'm Miller, and she's Montez."

"Good. Did you two walk home together?"

"Look, can't you see my daughter's upset. She already told Mrs. Montez that they walked home, Karen came in here, and Elena started towards her house. If something happened to her, it happened between here and there."

"Mrs. Miller, please. Now Karen, I know Elena is your friend, and you don't want to get your friend in any trouble. And if what your mom said happened is true, that's okay. But if something else happened, Elena could be in real danger, and she won't get in any trouble, and neither will you, if you tell us what really happened."

"You promise you won't tell Elena that I told you?"

"Cross my heart and hope to die."

"Okay, Elena went with some guy."

"What!"

"Mrs. Miller, *please*! Tell us what happened, Karen."

"Well, Elena and me were walking home, like normal, and like, this car pulled up and asked if we knew where Wal-Mart was."

"Do you remember what kind of car it was, Karen?"

"No. It was silver, though."

"Was it a big car?"

"It wasn't real big. About the size of our car, mom."

"We have a Camry."

"And it had four doors."

"Do you remember any part of the license plate?"

"No, but it was Jersey, and it was one of them special plates. You know mom. Like Aunt Patty has. With a lighthouse on it."

"Ok, That's a big help Karen. Now, the guy in the car asks for directions to Wal-Mart. What happened next?"

"Elena starts telling him, and he doesn't understand. He said he's not from around here, and would she mind showing him. He has to buy baby formula, and they are the only ones who sells the special kind he needs for his sick baby. Well, Elena, she says no, she can't go, and he says if she goes with him, and shows him where it's at, he'll bring her right back here, and give her $10."

"Then what, Karen?"

"I told her not to go, but she wanted the money, and she went with him."

"Now, focus on the man, Karen. Do you remember what he looked like?"

"Nothing special."

Tom Showed her the picture of Harry Reeves. "Could this be him?"

"Maybe, but he had a hoodie on, sunglasses, and a scarf."

Tom looked and Kari and scrolled through his pictures until he came to the traffic cam picture of Reeves, when he abducted Monica Lemon. "How about this guy, Karen?"

"That could be him. It looks like the same glasses, and scarf. Do you think he took Elana?"

"I don't know, Karen. But you've been very helpful, and we're going to do everything we can to find your friend and bring her home safely. I'm going to leave you my card, and Detective Weaver will do the same, and if you think of anything else, give us a call. Good night."

It was just about 7:00 pm, when Kari and Tom left the Miller home. "What now?"

"Elena has been missing for about five hours now. Based on this guy's M.O., he's holed up somewhere no further than a 10–15-minute ride from here. And he likes deserted areas. That points right to Villas/Townbank/DelHaven. If we assume he stole a silver mid-size car, his next thing to do, is switch the plates with another car, of the same make and model. The person who had their plates switched may not even notice, and even if we have a BOLO out on the car he stole, it's got different plates. If an officer pulls him over, and runs the plates, they come back as belonging on the kind, and color of car he's driving."

"So, what do we do?"

"He might have slipped up. That personalized plate, with the lighthouse? They cost $20 extra per year to have them. You've seen them. You can get SPCA plates. Save the forests plates. A bunch of things. I'll bet there aren't more than ten thousand lighthouse plates, throughout the state."

"How we gonna check ten thousand plates?"

"We're not. We're going to look for lighthouse plates registered to silver mid-size cars, in Lower Township. I'll bet there aren't more than a couple hundred. And if we eliminate the ones that go with Mercedes, and Lexus, probably less than a hundred. We track them down, find out if they have the right plates on their car. If they don't, we have the plates of the stolen car, and we can change the BOLO to show the stolen car, having the stolen plates."

"Come again? No. Never mind. You could explain that a dozen times, and I'm not gonna get it. I trust you. Let's do it."

"Now, tomorrow morning, what I want you to do is start looking at Real Estate Agencies. Over here on the bay. You're looking for places that have been rented out, very recently, for a month, or so. It makes sense that Reeves isn't going to break into a place down here. Too many year-round residents. Somebody would notice if he did that. And besides, he'd be breaking into somebody's summer place, and you know people start coming down in April, to open the places up, and get them ready for May. He can't take a chance of somebody showing up here, to cut the grass, or turn the water on. For now, I'm headed back to the precinct, to get this paperwork started, and get this girl's picture out there. You head home and get a good night's sleep. I need you to work your magic tomorrow."

"Roger that, boss."

"Kari, as far as this operation goes, I'm not your boss. I'm your partner. Last summer, you saved Jake and me from those motorcycle guys. You have some of the best pure instincts, and interviewing skills I've seen. That's what I need tomorrow. You know how Real Estate can be."

"You got it partner. Good night. And thanks, Tom."

"Good night."

CHAPTER 18

The first Agency Kari Weaver went to was Blue Home Real Estate, on Atlantic Ave, in Villas. The agent she spoke with showed her all the rentals they had, to date. There were none that started before Memorial Day. She didn't have any requests for a rental right now, but she would check with the other agents, and get back to Kari. That's how it went most of the day. She left the Apex Real Estate Agency just after 4:00 pm. Fifteen minutes later, she pulled into the Farrell Agency parking lot. She thought to herself that maybe the shamrock on the Agency sign would bring her some luck. "Hi. How can I help you?"

She produced her badge, and said, "Hi. I need to know if you rented out a home in the area, with the rental starting in the past week, or so."

"What do you mean?"

That answer made the hair on the back of her neck stand up. What does this bitch *think* I mean? "Well, I think it's a pretty straight-forward question. Have you rented any places out recently, with the rental starting within the last week, or so?"

"Why would I rent a house out now?"

"Listen. I'm very tired. I didn't ask you for a reason why you'd rent out now, I only asked you if you did. Simple yes, or no question."

"Well, I don't know."

"Well, would you mind checking for me?"

"I have to think of my client's privacy. I don't know if I'm allowed to..."

"Ok. That's enough! You are going to put your rental agreements on this desk, in front of me, in the next two minutes, or I'm taking you in, for obstructing justice, and we'll have a court order to impound all of your files. We'd probably have them for three months or so. Think that will have any impact on your seasonal rentals?"

"Wait here."

She was back in less than a minute, with one folder in her hand. She gave it to Kari. "This is the only rentals you have?"

"The only rental that started this past Monday."

The house on Texas Ave was rented out to Andrew Lyons, of 3 Farmer's Landing Road, Bucks County, PA. "Did you verify Mr. Lyons ID?"

"He didn't have it with him. He said he'd bring it back, when he picked up the key."

"Explain."

"Well, the place is $1,200/month in season."

"What about out of season?"

"We don't really rent, out of season."

"This agreement says you did, for $1,500."

"I know. Mr. Lyons was desperate. He said he would pay the $1,200, as well as a $300 'out of season fee', in cash. He told me to run the card, and he would be back in 10 minutes with his ID, and the $300."

"But he didn't bring his ID back, did he?"

"I forgot about asking for it."

"Okay, I'm gonna need copies of all this paperwork."

Twenty minutes later, Kari was back on the street. She called Tom Hansen, but it went straight to voice mail. She texted Jake and told him to call her. It was important. She waited five minutes. Nothing. She decided not to wait any longer. She parked her red Mazda Miata at 15 Texas Ave, and walked the last block, to the house at 25 Texas Ave.

She noticed a silver Ford Focus in the driveway. She checked her phone. Still nothing from Tom, or Jake. She couldn't wait.

~~~

Harry Reeves opened the front door to find Kari Weaver's Glock in his face. "Police! If you move, you die! Back up and put your hands up!"

"What's the problem officer?"

"I'll tell you what the problem is. You're a no-good rapist, and I'm putting you away. Where is Elena?"

"I'm sure I don't know what you mean."

"The girl you picked up in the silver Focus parked outside."

"I assure you I didn't pick up any girl. I just rented this place Monday, and I've been inside all week, reading."

"Really? I guess that LCMR High School jacket is yours, then?"

"It was here when I moved in. I put it on the chair to take it back to the Real Estate Office tomorrow."

The house was about 700 sq. ft. There was a living room, kitchen, bathroom, and two bedrooms. The only door that was closed was to the second bedroom. "What's in here?"

"Nothing."

"Open it."

Kari pressed the gun into the small of Harry's back, as he led the way into the bedroom. There, hanging from the ceiling, was Elena Montez. She was gagged and her feet and arms were tied. She was positioned on some kind of table-like contraption, that allowed her to be manipulated, exposing whatever part of her they wanted exposed. A closer inspection showed she had been cut many times, and the smell of burnt flesh verified that she had been branded, as well. Kari gagged a little. That's when her lights went out.

Jake called Tom Hansen just after 6:00 pm. "What's up, Jake?"

"That's what I called you to find out. What does Kari want? She texted me to call her, but she isn't answering her phone."

"She got in touch with you, too? What time?"

"About an hour and a half ago."

"Funny, she left me a message about the same time. She had just left Farrell Agency and needed to talk. Her phone keeps going to voicemail."

"Something's wrong, Tom! She tried to get in touch with both of us, and we can't contact her? That's not like Kari."

"What do you want to do?"

"Call Brandon Wright. See if he can locate her phone. The Real Estate Agency is closed now. We need to get in touch with them, somehow. I'll go over there and see if there's a phone number to contact. After you talk to Brandon, meet me there."

Jake jumped out of his car almost before it stopped moving. There were no phone numbers visible, either on the window, or in the office. He stopped, to collect his thoughts, and come up with a way to contact someone in the Farrell Agency.

Meanwhile, Tom Hansen had just gotten off the phone with Brandon Wright. Using all their technology, the FBI could not locate Kari's phone. Brandon told Tom that either the battery was removed, or the phone was turned off. Tom said he would keep Brandon in the loop, as he pulled away from the precinct. As he turned onto Townbank Road, he heard sirens in the distance. They were getting louder, the closer he got to Bayshore Rd., and the Farrell Agency.

Tom had to park in the street, as the small parking lot was filled with Lower Township Police cruisers. He found Jake, talking with one of the officers. "Jake!"

"Tom. Some kid threw a cinder block through the plate glass window, and took off, on a motorcycle. These guys are responding to the silent alarm that went off."

"Officer. Captain Tom Hansen, CMCPD. Has the proprietor been contacted?"

"Yes sir. Someone should be here any minute. The alarm company contacts them, right after they contact us. In fact, that might be the person in charge right there, crossing the street."

A middle-aged blonde hurried through the parking lot and approached the front door of the agency. To no one in particular, she said "What happened here?"

Jake spoke up. "Miss...?"

"Jones. Beverly Jones."

"Miss Jones, my name is Jake Miller. This is Police Captain Ton Hansen. It appears someone vandalized your office here. We're going to need you to open up, and check inside, to see if anything has been stolen."

"Yes. Of course." After fumbling through her purse, Beverly found her keys. Tom Hansen told the officer that was talking to Jake when he arrived, to keep everyone out of the office until Forensics showed up. Then he and Jake followed Beverly into the office, which was covered in shattered glass. "None of the file drawers are open. Nothing is out of place. Looks like they just broke the window. Why would somebody do that?"

Jake spoke quickly. "Miss Jones, we need your help. There was a CMC Detective here this afternoon, around 4:00 pm. Were you here?"

Jake showed her Kari's picture, on his phone. "Yes, I was here until closing, at five o'clock. I'm the Broker in this office. And yes, I remember this woman. Very pretty. She was talking to Marsha. She got a little loud. I remember Marsha being upset. I asked what was wrong, and she just said nothing was wrong, she had to get some paperwork for the officer. What does this have to do with my window being broken?"

"Probably nothing. Listen, we have reason to believe that female officer's life is in danger. Do you remember what paperwork she got for her?"

"No, I didn't see it. If I knew what she was looking for, I might be able to help more."

Tom now jumped in. "Detective Weaver was in here looking to find out if your agency had rented out any places that were occupied this week."

"I don't think so. 99.9% of our rentals start after Memorial Day. If there was, it would be in our active rental drawer, right over there." As Beverly opened the drawer, she said, "My bad. Looks like I stand corrected. There is a file in here. Looks like an Andrew Lyons rented a place for four weeks."

"What is his permanent address?"

"3 Far...."

Jake finished it for her. "Farmers Landing Road, Bucks County, PA."

"That's right."

"What's the address of the place he rented?"

Jake and Tom made the three-mile trip, from The Farrell Agency to Texas Ave., in Villas, in record time. On the ride, Jake had called Wilt, who was now on his way there. They pulled over behind Kari's car, and sprinted the three hundred yards down to 25 Texas Ave. Jake put his hand on the engine of the silver ford Focus. It was cold.

When they breached the house, the home security alarm went off. A search of the tiny property took all of ten seconds. Both men hit the closed bedroom door together. Inside they found the beaten, tortured body of Elena Montez, lying on the floor, covered in blood. A note was stapled to her chest. *YOU SENT A GIRL TO DO A MAN'S JOB. SHAME ON YOU! I TOLD YOU TO LEAVE ME ALONE! I'LL SEND YOUR GIRL BACK TO YOU, A LITTLE AT A TIME!*

Jake looked at Tom, but before he could say anything, they heard a low moan, coming from Elena. "Jesus, Jake, she's alive!"

Jake took the tape off of the girl's mouth, while Tom called for an ambulance. Elena opened her eyes. "Elena! You're safe now. Do you know where the bad man went.

All she said was one word: "Bomb!"

~~~

Wilt had put his left turn signal on, to turn onto Texas Ave, when the concussion from the explosion almost made him lose control. He saw that the house that once stood at 25 Texas Ave., was no longer there. Parts of it now littered the lawns and street of the tiny little area. He got as close as he could, then jumped out of his car, and ran to the now vacant lot. "Jake! Jake!"

Wilt stumbled through the debris and made his way to where the back of the house used to be. From behind the garage, he saw some movement. Weapon drawn, he turned the corner of the one car garage to find Jake, Tom Hansen, and Elena Montez, sprawled on the lawn, but alive.

By the time the ambulance had gotten there, Jake and Wilt had Elena's neck would treated, and the bleeding mostly stopped. Wilt had field dressed the cuts Tom had received during the explosion. Jake, while banged up, and sore, emerged otherwise unscathed. "Jesus, Jake, what happened?"

"We got real lucky. Reeves thought he killed the girl. Hell, Tom and I thought she was dead. When we went in, we thought we tripped the alarm system. We heard the girl moan. Tom called an ambulance, and I took the tape off her mouth, I asked about Reeves, and she said *BOMB*. I realized we triggered a detonator, not the house alarm, and yelled to Tom that there was a bomb and to get out. He had the presence of mind to go through the sliding glass doors, that led onto a small porch. That's how he got cut up. I followed with the girl, and we just got around the corner, where you found us, when the place went up."

"Damn!"

Just then Brandon Wright and his partner, Harvey Caldwell, pulled up. "Jake! You all right?"

"No. Reeves was one step ahead of us again!"

"We'll get Reeves. As long as you all are okay."

"We're not, Brandon. That son of a bitch has Kari Weaver now!"

It was agent Caldwell that replied. "What!? How did you let that happen? You were, all three of you, supposed to take care of her! Now that psycho has her!"

"What do you mean, 'let this happen'? This happened because Kari didn't wait for backup."

"Okay. That's enough." Everyone turned towards Tom Hansen's voice, as he joined the group, after getting patched up by the EMTs. "Doesn't really matter how it happened, or whose fault it is. Reeves has Kari. We know he didn't kill her, or he would've left her here. Kari is okay, until he finds a new place. However long that takes is how much time we have to track him down. We know what he'll do to her, just based on the note that he had stapled to that young girl's chest. Instead of arguing with each other, how about we figure out where the prick is going, and meet him there, and cut his heart out."

"How?"

"We have to take advantage of the clues we have."

"What clues? Any clue he might have left was in that house."

"You'd think that, wouldn't you, Wilt?"

"What's going through your head, Tom?"

"Well, pard, the way I see it is that Reeves left here, before we got here, and took Kari with him, right? Okay, how did he leave here? There's his Focus, right there. Kari's car is down the block."

"Right. So, he had a second vehicle."

"Exactly, Wilt. And that second vehicle most likely sat out here since he got here. I'm willing to bet that one of these looky-loo neighbors can give us a description of that vehicle, and maybe a partial plate number. Maybe somebody should go talk to them."

"Good thinking, Tom. Harvey, Wilt, let's go."

"Hold on there, agent Wright. Harvey, Wilt, you go ahead."

"What else you got, Tom?"

"The girl."

"Elena?"

"Elena. Look, if nothing else, Kari spooked this guy. He panicked and took off. He didn't get to butcher Elena, the way he likes to. It was only a couple of hours, at the most from when Kari showed up here, until we did. That means that he had to forget his plans and take off. That's why he blew up the house. He didn't have time to sanitize it, like he usually does."

"And, in his haste, he screwed up twice. He didn't kill the girl, and he left too much time on the detonator. His ego wanted us to find the girl, read the note, and get blown up. He didn't count on the girl saying anything to us, and he didn't count on Jake figuring out what the girl meant, when she said bomb. We need to get to that hospital and interview that girl. She heard him say there was a bomb. Maybe she heard something else. An address, a phone number, a name, anything."

"You're right, Tom. I'm on my way."

"Well, hang on a minute, there Brandon. Jake was the one who rescued that girl. She was clinging to him like barnacles on a boat. Might be she'd remember a little better, if she was talking to him."

"Jake, let's go. What about you, Tom?"

"I'll give Wilt and Harvey a hand here. I'll check in with you in a bit."

The Emergency Room they found Elena in had a strong alcohol smell to it. Brandon told the attending doctor who he was, and what he and Jake were there for. "I just gave her something to help her sleep. I don't know how much time you have before she conks out. And don't get her too wound up."

"Don't worry, doc. We just have a couple of questions."

Jake made his way to the side of the bed and picked up Elena's hand. "Elena?" She half opened her eyes. "Elena. My name is Jake. Do you remember me?"

She slowly nodded. "You took me out of there. Thank you."

"You're welcome, Elena. Elena, the man who took you there..."

"S-S-Spiderman!"

"Right Elena, the man wore a Spiderman mask. Did he say where he was taking the other woman?"

"Cop. She was a cop. Came to rescue me."

"Right. Do you know where he took her?"

"K-K-Karl's."

"Carl's? What is that, Elena?"

"Bald man's name."

"What bald man?"

"The one who hit the cop."

"Elena? Stay with me, honey."

"Tired. Need to sleep."

"In just a minute, dear. Tell me what happened when the cop got there."

"She had gun pointed at Spi..."

"Spiderman. She had a gun pointed at Spiderman. Then what?"

"Karl was behind door. When she walked in, he hit her with a bat. Same bat that he used to..." She was sobbing now.

"It's okay, Elena. You're safe now. We're gonna catch Karl, and Spiderman. What happened after he hit the cop?"

"Spiderman told Karl they had to leave. To run home and get his truck. He left. He came back, and Spiderman told Karl he rigged a bomb, to kill any cops that show up."

"Last question, Elena. Then you can sleep. How long was Karl gone, when he went to get his truck?"

"I don't know."

"Okay, honey. You sleep now." Outside, in the waiting room, Jake called Tom Hansen. "Tom. Reeves has a partner. Karl. Bald headed. Lives within walking distance of the house on Texas Ave. Apparently, Kari got the drop on Reeves. Karl was behind the bedroom door, and hit her with a bat, when she entered. Reeves told him they had to leave, and to go home and get his truck. Unless he had another mode of transportation, he went on foot."

"That jives with what he got here, from the neighbors. They say that either an F-150, or a Dodge Ram, backed up to the house, and two guys carried a rug out, and put it in the back, then they drove off. We have two versions of this. It was either ten minutes, or an hour, after they left, that they heard the explosion."

"Well, Tom, this Karl lives, or is staying in the area. Mention his name to the neighbors, see if anything shakes loose."

"Roger that, Jake. I'll get back to you soon."

"What's next, Jake?"

"I'm not sure, Brandon. I'm not really sure."

CHAPTER 19

Brandon Wright, Harvey Caldwell, Jamal King, Tom Hansen, and Jake were sitting around Jake's dining room table. Tom was mobilizing any available body, from Cape May County PD, to help in the search for Regina Weaver. Harvey Caldwell was in a phone conference with FBI agents in Baltimore, checking if there was a student named Karl that was a member of the Computer Science Geeks, down at University of Maryland. "I can't stand just sitting here, doing nothing!"

"I hear you, Jake. But we have to wait until we have something to do, before we can do it. Otherwise, we're just chasing our tails." Jake looked at Wilt.

"Something wrong?"

"I feel like we're forgetting something, Jake. An angle we're missing."

"Like what?"

"Not sure. But it has to do with something Harriet Abrams told us."

"Let's see, she said that Harry kept to himself, and was always a computer geek. Didn't have a lot of friends…"

"Wait! He didn't have a lot of friends, but he *did* have a couple of friends that he kept in touch with, until he moved to Baltimore, four years ago. He was in some club, in high school!"

"You're right, Wilt. Here it is, in my notes. Computer Society. He went to Neshaminy High. Graduated 2008. Brandon?"

"On it." Brandon Wright dialed a number on his phone. "Hank. It's Brandon. Write this down. Neshaminy High School. Class of 2008. A club called the Computer Society. See if Harry Abrams was a member. Looking for a member named Karl. Don't know if it's a 'C', or a 'K'. No last name. What? I need it five minutes ago. It's a matter of life and death. Call me back."

"Think he'll find anything?"

"Hank is a good man. Doesn't matter that it's 11:30, on a Saturday night. He'll get somebody up and get access to their archives."

"Maybe he'll throw a cinder block through the front window and wait for somebody to show up." Tom Hansen was off the phone now and joined the conversation. "That's the way Jake does it. Okay. It's all hands-on deck. Statewide BOLO out on a dark colored f-150 or dodge Ram, with extended cab. State Troopers are checking out the Parkway, AC Expressway, and Turnpike. CMC and Lower PDs are sending men out, going door to door, in all the bayside communities. If he's anywhere down here, we'll find him."

"Don't think he is, Tom."

"Why not, Jake?"

"No matter how much I want this guy dead, I have to give it to him, he's smart. He's anticipated our every move and been one step ahead of us. He took one of our people. He *has* to know we're going to mobilize the troops and look everywhere. No, I don't think he went too far, because he'd figure we'd get a line on his truck, so he'd want to be off the roads within an hour or so."

"Ok, along that line of thinking, let's plot a radius across the state sixty miles from here."

"We don't have to do that, Brandon. Hey, Tom, how far up the Parkway is Atlantic City?"

"Well, it's Exit 38, so that would be thirty-eight miles."

"So, if A.C. is forty miles away, how far is Ocean City?"

"I see what you're thinking, Pard. About thirty-five miles, give or take. A little less than an hour's ride from here."

"There's no way Reeves would go back there. That's just a coincidence that Ocean City is an hour from here."

"Brandon thinks it's a coincidence, Wilt."

"No such thing as coincidence, Jake."

"Hear me out, Brandon. You're right. Nobody in their right mind would go back up there. It's the last place we'd expect him to go. That's why I think that's exactly where he'll go. He can't stay around here. I think Baltimore is too far away. He wouldn't chance it. He'd have to know we know what he's driving, and it would be dangerous for him to be driving around much more than an hour after he left. No, I think he went somewhere very familiar to him."

"I agree, pard. Let's go."

"No, Tom, you and Wilt know these towns better than anybody. You should be here, heading up the search. This is a hunch. I'll head up there myself."

Brandon looked at Harvey Caldwell, who nodded his agreement. "You're not going yourself. Harvey will go with you."

"Yeah. You drive. Let's go."

"Yeah, pard. I'll have your sister come stay over here and watch these mutts."

"It's settled then. Harvey, let's go."

It was just about 1:00 am, when Jake and agent Caldwell got onto the Parkway. "Tell me about Detective Weaver, Jake? How well do you know her?"

"Kari? She's the best. Somebody you want in a foxhole with you."

"You two work together long?"

"Yeah, she was here when I started, back in '02."

"Is she seeing anybody?"

"I don't know. Oh, that's right! I forgot. You two went out last summer, when you and Brandon were here."

"Yeah. Most fun I've had in a long time."

"Kari is fun to be around."

"Wasn't just that. With the way me and Brandon move around, it's hard to have any kind of relationship. Regina and I seemed to click, if you know what I mean."

"So, it's like that, is it? Look, Harvey, Kari, I mean Regina, holds a special place in my heart. I'll go to hell and back for her. I owe her my life."

"Your life?"

"Yeah. You remember last summer, with the Cobras, up in Philly? Well, I had Tom and Kari up there helping me. I sent Kari home, because I didn't need her anymore. Tom and I got jammed up. The Cobras had us in that club up there. We were all tied up. They were going to kill us after the club closed at 4:00 am. Only Kari didn't go home. When she saw my truck sitting outside the place for a couple of hours, she figured we were in trouble. Along around 1:00 am, she got herself upstairs, found us, cut us loose, and, well, the rest is history."

As they pulled into the Econolodge parking lot, Harvey said, "I didn't know that. Hey Jake, I want you to promise me something."

"What's that, Harvey?"

"When we find this guy, he doesn't go to trial, if you know what I mean."

"That's why I wanted to come alone, Harvey. There's no way Harry Reeves, or Abrams, or whatever he calls himself, is going to set foot in a court of law. No, I am going to be his judge, jury, and executioner."

~~~

Jake's alarm went off at 6:00 am. Harvey Caldwell was already in the bathroom. "Didn't sleep well, Harvey?"

"Quit trying, about an hour ago."

"Well, give me fifteen minutes, and we can hit the streets." Jake showered and dressed. As he was getting his and Harvey's weapons out of the room safe, his phone rang. "Brandon? What's up?"

"Everybody in Bucks County, apparently. Agent Hank Barry found Karl."

"Brandon, it's 6 am! How?"

"Hank is like a bulldog. First, he woke up the Principal at Neshaminy High. He wasn't thrilled about opening the school for Hank at one o'clock in the morning, but when you throw FBI, and Federal crime, around, people tend to be more helpful. Anyway, Karl Mount. Graduated with Reeves. Was in the Computer Society with him. Hank went to his address on file and knocked on the door. Karl didn't live there anymore, but his parents do, and gave Hank his address. He lives in an apartment, in Bucks County. Mount didn't answer his door. Hank woke up the super of the building and got a pass key. No sign of Karl in the apartment. Karl drives a 2012 Dodge Ram with an extended cab. I texted Harvey the plate number. He's our guy, Jake. And get this, his family has a shore house in Ocean City. I sent you the address. I'd tell you to wait for us to get there, but I know it wouldn't do any good. Be careful, Jake."

"Roger that." Jake parked the car half a block from the house at 3027 Asbury Ave. "Okay, Harvey how do you want to play this?"

"You're the Navy SEAL. I'm okay with whatever you say."

"Good. Here's what we know. There are at least two bad guys. There could be more, so be alert. I don't see a vehicle, but there is a garage, and it could be in there. Now, we can use the three houses between us and our objective as cover. From the last house, we move to the garage. We establish the vehicle is there, then we move on the house. You go in the back; I go in the front. You ever go through a door before."

"Yeah."

"Okay, when we get to the house, I'll recon the perimeter, to see if I can locate where the bad guys are, and where Kari is. We good?"

"Roger that." They made their way to the garage. It was empty. They silently crossed the twenty yards from the garage to the back corner of the house. Jake motioned for Harvey to stay put, and he started his journey around the perimeter of the property. Ten minutes later, he was back with agent Caldwell. Jake whispered. "We're going in blind. Too dark to see anything. You go in the back. Clear that room. There looks like a bedroom to the left when you go in. After you clear the back room, clear the bedroom. Harvey, if you see Kari when you first go in, you have to ignore her. We'll take care of her after we clear the house. Got it?"

"Roger."

"We breach in twenty seconds from... now!"

Jake made his way to the front door, and froze there, silently counting down in his head. When he hit two, he kicked in the front door, and shouted 'POLICE'! Harvey did the same. Jake heard Harvey yell "Clear!", then the sound of him kicking in the bedroom door. Jake entered the other bedroom at almost the same time. He literally caught bald headed Karl, with his pants down, in the middle of raping Regina Weaver, who was tied to a bed. Jake heard Harvey yell "Clear!" again. Jake hit Karl with a right hand, that sent him sprawling. "Harvey! In here!" Then to Karl, "Where's Harry, Karl?"

"Harry who?"

Jake hit him again, this time breaking his nose. "Where's Harry?" Karl was crying now.

"I don't know who you mean." Jake picked Karl up, and hit him with a right cross, that busted his eye open. "I can do this all day, Karl. Where's Harry?"

"Please. Don't hit me no more. He's crazy! He'll kill me, if I talk!"

"You're in a tough spot, Karl. See, I will, for sure, kill you if you *don't* talk. The way I see it, if you tell me where Harry is, we can kill him, and you don't get killed. But it's a sure thing if you don't talk to me, you're getting killed. Last time, where's Harry?"

"Okay, okay. He went to WAWA, to get breakfast."

"He driving your Dodge?"

"Yeah."

"He's coming back soon, then?"

"No. Whenever he goes out, he calls before he comes back, to check if it's safe." As Karl finished talking, his phone rang. "That's him now. If I don't answer, he won't come back."

"By all means, Karl, answer." Jake put the phone on speaker and handed it to Karl.

"Harry?"

"What's wrong, Karl? You sound like something's wrong."

"Nothing's wrong, Harry."

"If nothing is wrong, why was the front door open when I drove past? Am I on speaker, Karl? Who else is listening?"

Jake spoke now. "The FBI, Reeves. You can't get off the island. Give yourself up."

"I know this voice. This is Mr. Miller, isn't it? Well Mr. Miller, I don't have to get off the island. I'm already off the island. When I drove by, I saw the door open, and assumed something was amiss, so I drove out 34th St., until I got off the island, before I called. And by the way, Mr. Miller, didn't I tell you to leave me alone?"

The phone went dead. Jake turned to find agent Caldwell standing in the doorway. "Harvey? Harvey! You didn't untie Kari yet? Harvey! Watch this scumbag!" Jake went to Kari, who was beaten badly, and was bleeding from everywhere. "I got you K."

"Jake? Jake, is that you?"

"It's me Kari. You're safe now."

The gunshot resonated off the walls. Jake dove for cover and spun to face the enemy. But there was none. Only Harvey Caldwell standing with his gun pointed at where Karl Mount's head used to be.

Brandon Wright arrived about twenty minutes after the ambulance left, to take Regina Weaver to the hospital. He went to Agent Caldwell. "Give me a sit rep, Harvey."

"Huh? Well, Brandon, I just…"

"He just saved my life, Brandon. I entered the room, and subdued Karl Mount. I then went to attend to detective Weaver. I didn't see the gun he had stashed under the pile of clothes on the floor. As he reached for it, Agent Caldwell entered the room, discharged his weapon, saving both detective Weaver, and myself."

As Agent Wright looked at the body, of Karl Mount, sure enough, there was a gun, on the floor, next to it. "That the way it happened, Harvey?"

"Yeah, Brandon. Just like Jake said."

"Okay. Good work."

"Not so good. Reeves wasn't here when we breached. He was making a breakfast run. He saw the front door open when he got back, so he kept going."

"And you know this how?"

"Apparently, they had some sort of signal set up. If he went out, he would call before he came back, to see if it was safe."

"So, he called?"

"Yeah. He could tell by Karl's voice that something was off, so he asked who was here. I told him FBI, and to give himself up, because he couldn't get off the island."

"Good."

"Not good. He anticipated that, so he didn't call until he was already off the island."

"You're right. Not good."

"Gets worse, Brandon."

"How so?"

"He recognized my voice. He knows it was me. He made a point to remind me that he told me to leave him alone."

"I'll make the calls, Jake. Surveillance for your niece, and sister."

"Thanks, Brandon. I'll call you in a little while."

"Where you going?"

"To take Harvey, here, to check on his girlfriend."

Jake parked the car in the Hospital parking lot. As he started to get out, Harvey stopped him. "Jake, wait a minute. Back there. With Brandon. Why did you lie?"

"Because you weren't going to. Look, I told you Reeves was not going to make it into custody. That goes for anybody he's hooked up with. You did the right thing. End of story. Okay?"

"Okay. Thanks Jake. Why did you tell Brandon you were taking me to see my girlfriend? Regina isn't my girlfriend."

"Not yet. But give me five minutes to tell her about how you rushed in and saved everybody's life..." Jake started towards the hospital entrance. "You coming, or not?"

"Right behind you, Jake."

CHAPTER 20

Jake and Harvey sat in the waiting room while Kari Weaver had testing done, and wounds cleaned and bandaged, and some more testing done. Finally, after an hour and a half, the attending physician came out to see them. He told them that she had two broken ribs, a concussion, and severe facial swelling, as well as bruises over 60% of her body, due to what appeared to be a hellacious beating. There were a dozen, or so, burn marks on her upper torso, and about the same number of stab wounds, which were too shallow to put her life in danger. They seemed to be done just to cause pain. The doctor suggested it took the form of torture. He continued, "The patient was sexually penetrated numerous times, with objects, as we discovered wood splinters…"

Jake cut him off. "Thanks, doc. Can we go see her?"

"Yes. Of course. I can't guarantee she'll know you are there, because we've given her some pretty strong pain medicine, to help her rest. But absolutely, you can go sit with her."

When Jake and Harvey entered the room, Jake noted how vulnerable Kari looked, as she lay in her hospital bed. Her left eye was completely swollen shut, and her right eye wasn't much better. Her body was covered, head to toe, in bandages, and she was hooked up to what seemed like six different monitors. As Jake walked to her side, Harvey hung back a few paces. "Hey, Kari."

"Jake? Is that you, Jake? Jake I can't see real good. I think I might be blind."

"No, Kari, you're not blind. Doc says you'll be good as new, once the swelling goes down."

"Jake, I fucked up. I shoulda waited for backup. And I got my ass kicked for my troubles. And Jake what they did to me...' Her voice trailed off, and she started quietly sobbing. Jake held her the best he could.

"Shhhh, it's all right. You're safe now, K. Nobody's gonna hurt you anymore."

"Look at me. I'm all swole up, and now I got snot running out of my nose."

"I think you look beautiful."

"Who's that? Jake, who you got with you?"

Jake stepped to the right and moved Harvey in front of Kari. "It's FBI agent Caldwell, Kari. He was with me when we went in the house to rescue you. In fact, he killed that bald headed sonofabitch, before he could shoot you or me."

"Harvey Harvey?"

"Yes, Regina, it's Harvey Harvey. And I think you look beautiful."

"Jake, I think *he* might be the one who's blind."

"That may be, but I have to go call Tom Hansen, and Wilt, and let them know you're okay. Be right back."

"Jake! Please don't tell my mama. I don't want her to see me like this."

"Sure, Kari, whatever you say."

When they were alone, Harvey said "I was so worried about you when I heard you were taken. If anything happened to you, I don't know what I'd do."

"Harvey, this medicine is really starting to hit me. Don't say anything else, okay?"

"Really? I thought..."

"Let me finish. Don't say anything else until the next time you see me. I want to remember everything you say, and I ain't probably gonna remember any of this."

"Okay, Regina. You sleep. I'll sit here with you, until you fall asleep, and I'll come back to see you later today."

"Okay Harv..." And with that, Regina Weaver drifted off to sleep. Harvey leaned in, and gently kissed her on the forehead, and made his way out to find Jake. He found him, in the waiting area, as he was getting off the phone.

"What's up?"

"She fell asleep. What's going on with Reeves?"

"Well, first off, I called my niece. She's a veterinarian. Just opened her practice. She's getting a local Vet to cover for her, and she's coming down to my place, until we get this bastard. As for Harry Reeves, he's in the wind. Brandon's got people checking surveillance tapes on every bridge out of New Jersey, looking for any dark colored Dodge Ram, extended cab. Checking with the Cape May-Lewis ferry as well."

"Good, so unless he steals another vehicle, he can't leave the state without us knowing about it."

"That's not quite 100% true. You get up near Trenton, there's probably more than a dozen free–to-cross, small bridges, that don't have cameras, so if he thinks of that, he has a way out. We're banking that he won't think of that and make a mistake."

"Well, don't count on that. He hasn't made one yet. This guy has thought of everything, so far."

"You're right, Harvey. That he has."

Jake and Harvey made their way back to their motel. They stopped at a diner to eat. While they were waiting for their meal, Harvey asked Jake if something was wrong. "Jake, you okay? You haven't said two words since we left the hospital."

"Just thinking, Harvey."

"About?"

"Reeves. Back there, when I said we were counting on him making a mistake, you said not to count on it, because he hasn't made one yet. And you were right. We've figured out where he would be, every time, and yet he still has outsmarted us. Hell, he had a contingency plan for when he was away from the house."

"You mean phoning before he came home?"

"Exactly! And, on top of that, he had a backup, not to even call, until he was far enough away, to make an escape, if needed. Who *DOES* that!?"

"He's a smart dude, Jake."

"Nobody's *that* smart, or lucky, Harv. No, We're the problem."

"How so?"

"Look, we've figured out where he would go, what, four times now, and we haven't stopped him yet. We're not doing enough."

"I don't follow."

"Look, we've figured out where he was going, and rushed there, and started searching for him. If we took it to the next level, we had the clues to stop him."

"Jake, I don't have a clue what you're talking about."

"Don't you see, when we followed him to Ocean City, the first time, we stopped thinking, and started searching. We *had* the information that he was a pilot. This guy has his exit planned, when he starts his plan. Even if we didn't know about him being a pilot, we should've thought that there isn't a more deserted place than that airport. If we had locked it down from the start, the three people he killed there might still be alive. And then, I said that he would most likely land that plane in a field, or road, somewhere he knew. My God! In his back yard. He practically told us! There's only four people living on that road. He knew before he went to that airport that he was flying out of there, and he was going to land on Farmers Landing Road, where he could steal a car relatively easy. Instead of driving up that way, we should have known he'd go there, and have the PA State Police sitting there waiting for him. So, then, we figure out he's coming down to Villas. We even figure out that he most likely rented a place down there."

"Well, we were right."

"Except that we already know his MO is teenage high school girls. We should have been watching that school. There's a good chance we could have prevented Elana Montez from being taken and gotten Reeves. And, again, he had a plan to get away, before he even got to Texas Ave. So, we think he took Kari up to Ocean City."

"And he did!"

"Yes, but in our haste, we screwed up. Harvey, we never should've gone into that house, once we saw there was no vehicle present. We should've put eyes on it, until the Tactical team showed up, or dodge Ram showed up. If we had waited fifteen minutes, Reeves would've been back in the house, when we breached."

"Okay, Jake, you're right. We screwed up all the way around. How does that help us now?"

"This guy isn't as smart as he thinks he is. This time, this morning, we caught him off guard. Oh, yeah, he had a plan to get away, but he never expected us to figure out where he was so soon."

"Does that help you figure out where he's going?"

"Yes, he's going back to Pennsylvania."

"We already figured that."

"Right, and then we stopped thinking."

"Huh?"

"Harvey, I think I know where Reeves is."

"You do?"

"I do. Hear me out. He had an escape plan for this house today, but I can't believe he'd thought out where he'd hole up next, when he took off this morning. We can't just think where he'd go. We have to think what he'd go there for. Right now, I think he's going somewhere to lay low, until he can make new plans."

"That makes sense. Keep talking."

"Okay, he knows we'll check surveillance on every bridge and ferry. And we might even post police at all of the free bridges. So, if I'm Harry Reeves, I want to get across the Delaware river without being seen, and then hide somewhere, until I make my next couple of moves."

"So, what does he do, Jake?"

"He drives up to Lindenwold, NJ, and takes the PATCO Speedline, over the Ben Franklin Bridge, into Center City Philadelphia."

"Okay, but then he's in Philadelphia, with no ride. It's not so easy to steal a car in Center City Philadelphia, on a Sunday, no less, as it is in one of the residential areas."

"Exactly right, Harvey."

"Doesn't that shoot your theory down?"

"Not exactly. We know he goes places he's been before, that make him comfortable. What if he's going somewhere he doesn't need a car to get to?"

"Jake, what the hell are you talking about?"

"Charlotte Foster. Reeves has been to her house. It's a place that's comfortable to him. And he can walk from the PATCO station to the Frankford El, take that to Allegheny Ave, and then a five-minute ride on the route 60 bus, and walk a half block south on Salmon St. He could stay there a few days, until he's ready to move on. Getting a car, in that neighborhood, should be no problem."

"That sounds good to me. Let's call Brandon."

"Yeah. About that. No."

"What?"

"Look, Harvey, if I'm right, he's been up there for at least a couple of hours. By now, Charlotte Foster is dead already. If I'm wrong, we'll have sent everybody on a wild goose chase. Brandon hired me and told me to do my own thing. That's what I plan to do. As for you…"

"No way I'm not going with you, Jake. When do we leave?"

"Right after we go check out of our motel."

"Let's do it."

They were on the Atlantic City Expressway towards Philly, by 3:30 pm. "Harvey, how are you going to handle Brandon?"

"I was just about to do that now." He dialed a number. "Brandon. Hi. Just checking in to give you a sit rep. Jake and I are headed up to Philadelphia. He called some guy he knows up there, who might be able to give us a line on Reeves. We should be there in less than an hour. I'll call you back when I know more." And he hung up.

"You hung up on him?"

"Hey, if you're right, it won't matter that we came up here. If you're wrong, well no harm, no foul, really. And it's easier to ask for forgiveness, than permission."

"Well, all right then."

By 4:45 pm, they were getting off I-95, at Allegheny Ave. Jake parked on Edgemont St., just around the corner from Charlotte Foster's porch front row home, on Salmon St. "Okay, what now?"

"Now, we have to get into her neighbor's house, without him seeing us. Follow me." Jake made his way past the Foster home, then crossed over to her side of the street. He knocked on the door a few houses down from Charlotte Foster's house. He showed the elderly man who answered, his badge, and asked if he could come in.

Once inside, Jake asked the old gent if he knew Charlotte Foster. When he said he did, Jake explained that she might be in danger, and they would like to get into Charlotte's neighbor's house to try and help her. Did he know Charlotte's neighbor? "Sure, The Westons. Tom and me belong to the Polish American Club."

"Do you have their phone number?"

"Sure."

"Can you call them for us, and have them talk to us?"

"Consider it done."

"Tom, you old bastard. It's George. Don't give me 'George who?', I'm the only George you know. Listen, Tom, I got two FBI guys here, in my house. What? No, I didn't do anything wrong. They actually want to talk to you. No, I'm not kidding. I'll give him the phone."

Jake took the receiver. "Mr. Weston. No, sir, you are not in any trouble at all. It's your neighbor, Ms. Foster. We're worried she might have an intruder. What I wanted to ask you, sir, is if you could unlock your front door, so my partner and I could hop over the porches, to your house, and come in, you know, undetected. Then we have listening devices we can use to hear if Ms. Foster is okay. Would that be all right? Okay, Mr. Weston, could you go, and unlock your front doors. No, don't open them. Right. And come back when they're unlocked. They are? Great. My partner and I will be there in thirty seconds. Thank you." He gave the phone back to George. "Thank you, George."

Harvey and Jake went over the twenty-inch dividers between each porch and slipped into Tom Weston's house. "Mr. Weston. Jake Miller, and my partner Harvey Caldwell. "

"Nice to meet you. Can I help?"

"Yes, you can, Tom. Could you get me a tall glass?"

"Sure. Iced Tea?"

"No sir. Empty will be fine."

When Tom Weston left the room, Harvey asked "What kind of listening devices do we have?"

"We don't. Tom Weston does." With that, Tom handed Jake an eight-ounce drinking glass. "Perfect. He turned the empty glass over and put the open end against the wall, and the other end to his ear.

"What the hell are you doing?"

"Look, Harv. I grew up in a Port Richmond row house. You can hear what your neighbors are doing all the time. You put a glass against the wall, it's like you're sitting in their lap. You listen."

Harvey did as he was told. After a few seconds, he pulled away from the wall.

"Well?"

"There's definitely a male voice in there."

"Sound like a TV show?"

"No. It was like he was talking to himself."

"We're going to assume it's Reeves. I'm going out the back, and you go over the porch. Crawl under the bay window and wait until you hear me go in the back. When you hear that, you go in the front. And Harvey, whatever else happens, Reeves doesn't walk out of there."

"Roger that."

As Tom Weston opened the back door for Jake, Harvey went out the front, and over the divide. He crawled on his belly under the window, and eased up against the wall, with his hand on the front door.

At the same time, Jake hopped over the three-foot-high fence between the yards and made his way to the back door. This presented a problem that Jake hadn't anticipated. The back storm door was full glass, and the inside door was open. With a railing on either side of the tree steps leading up to the door, Jake would have to expose himself getting to the door itself. If the door was locked, he'd have to pick the lock, and if Reeves was anywhere near the kitchen, he'd have at least ten to fifteen seconds notice to arm himself. This was an unacceptable option. He decided to go with option #2, which was to fire through the glass door, up high, and follow the bullet into the house.

Harvey heard the shot, and the glass breaking and burst through the front door. "FBI! Freeze!" The living room was empty. "Jake?"

As he emerged from the basement, Jake answered "Clear."

"How do you want to take the stairs to the 2nd floor?"

"Hold up a minute, Harvey. Look." On the kitchen counter, Harvey saw an old-fashioned reel to reel tape recorder, with a tape playing 'on a loop'.

"What the hell?"

"He recorded a bunch of crap, and put it on a loop, figuring if we came here, we'd hear it, and think he was here, and wait for an Entry Team, or at least work up a plan, before we came in."

"You mean he's gone?"

"Most likely. Let's search the rest of the house." They went upstairs and cleared the back and middle bedrooms. When they entered the front bedroom, they found Charlotte Foster, lying on the bed, next to Robbie, her Chihuahua. It might have been a Kodak moment, except that their heads were almost completely severed.

"Jesus, Jake. What a mess! Look! He left the straight razor on the nightstand."

As the two men turned to glance at the nightstand, a drop of blood fell from the razor, and ran down the side of the table. Jake sprang into action. "Harvey, this way!", as he tore down the stairs, and out the front door.

"Jake! Stop! What are we doing?"

"Don't you get it Harvey? This happened within the last couple of minutes! The blood was still dripping off the razor!"

"And?"

"And he just left. He must've seen us come around the corner. That means he took off in the last five minutes. Listen, you take this side of the street, I'll take the other. Knock on every door. Find out if they own a car and is it here."

Jake ran across the street and up the porch steps of the corner house. "Jake! Stop!"

"Why?"

"Look, you said the reason we haven't caught him yet is that we stop thinking. Well, assuming he already had an exit strategy planned, and his seeing us caused him to run, would he run out the front door, where he might run straight into us?"

"Shit! You're right Harvey! That's why the inside back door was open. He left it open when he ran out the back! We gotta go check for a stolen car on Emery St."

"Hold on, Jake. Take a beat here. If we figure out where he's going, we can beat him there. Now, you've been pretty much right on the money, figuring out Reeves' next move. What does your gut tell you?"

"Okay. Let's see. We know that he always has his next move planned, and he's going somewhere that he's familiar with. Knowing that he probably can't go into Buck's County, and that the I-95 South entrance is a block and a half away from here, that's most likely where he headed."

"All right, so he's on 95 South. Where's he headed?"

"From what we know about him, the only place he's familiar with south of here, is Baltimore. He's headed for Baltimore, Harvey."

"Right. And if he gets to Baltimore, the only place we know he's familiar with is the U of Maryland campus. He could be familiar with a dozen places in the surrounding area. It seems logical that if we don't get him before he gets there, there's a good chance, he'll go off the grid, and we'll lose him."

"Well, you're on a roll here, Harvey. How would you proceed?"

"Logically, if we spooked him, he just boosted a car, and took off. He wouldn't take the time to swap plates out. We go knock on doors, like you said, on that street behind these houses, and see if we can discover what he's driving. I'll call our Philly office and have our helicopter on stand-by."

"FBI has a helicopter?"

"Yeah. Down on Penn's Landing Heliport. It can have us at the Delaware/Maryland border, in less than fifteen minutes. I'll have a car there waiting for us, we'll be there before Reeves, and we'll know what he's driving."

"Brilliant. I see why Brandon keeps you around."

As they made their way around the corner, Harvey called Brandon Wright with an update. Brandon made all the arrangements that Harvey told Jake about, as well as having Maryland State Troopers sitting at each of the four Baltimore exits, along I-95.

The third door Jake knocked on was answered by Gordon Wallace. Jake could hear young children laughing in the background, and also detected an older, female voice. "Good afternoon, sir. My name is Jake Miller. I'm working with the FBI. May I ask if you own a car, sir?"

"Why do you want to know?"

"Well, Mr...?"

"Wallace. Gordon Wallace."

"Mr. Wallace. There have been a rash of stolen cars in the area, and..."

"Okay. You're interrupting my dinner. Yes, I own a car."

"Do you have possession of your car, sir?"

"Possession?"

"Yes sir. Is the car here?"

"Oh. Yeah. Right over…", his voice trailed off, as he pointed to the empty parking space across the street from his house. "Son of a bitch! Marge, somebody stole our car!"

"What!?"

"Mr. Wallace. May I come in? This is literally a matter of life and death."

"Yeah, sure." Jake motioned for Harvey to join him. Marge Wallace joined them in the parlor and offered them seats.

"Mr. Wallace, what kind of car do you have?"

It was Marge who answered. "A 2018 Hyundai Elantra."

"Color?"

"Tan."

Marge corrected him "Desert Sand."

"Marge, it's tan. They can call it whatever they want. These guys don't care about Desert Sand. It's a tan car."

"Do you know the license plate number?"

"Sure. FSH-IN."

"FSH-IN?"

"Yeah. I bought the car a month ago, with my retirement severance. I got one of them personalized plates. I plan to be down the shore, fishin'. Paid $60 extra for that plate. Now some bastard stole it."

"Yes sir. When was the last time you saw the car?"

"About a half hour ago, when I parked it. We got the grandkids this weekend, and we were at our place down the shore. We just got back up here, and I dropped everybody here, and went to McDonalds, to feed the kids. They don't eat anything else. My wife Marge gets worried about feeding them good food, and I tell her that we're not the food police. Let their mom and dad worry about them eating the right foods. I just want them to eat when they're here. Period. Am I right?"

"Yes sir. And you're sure you saw it a half hour ago?"

Gordon looked at his watch. "Not even a half hour. It's 7:05 pm now. I remember Marge told me my son would be here to pick the kids up at quarter after seven, so I had to hurry to get them something to eat, since we didn't get home until 6:25 pm. I remember after I parked the car, I looked at my watch, and it was 6:46 pm, so, that was, what, twenty-four minutes ago."

"Thank you, sir. The Philly police will be here to fill out a stolen car report. You've been very helpful. Thank you. Oh, one more thing, sir. You just drove up from the shore. How much gas was in the tank?"

"Under a quarter tank. I was gonna gas up, but Marge told me to hurry with the food. I figured on doing it in the morning. Guess I saved $25, huh?"

Jake and Harvey sprinted the block and a half to where Jake's car was parked. Jake pulled into the Sonoco station, on the corner of Richmond and Allegheny, a half block from the I-95 entrance ramp. "What are you doing, Jake?"

"Reeves would've looked at the gas gauge, and wouldn't chance a 75-mile trip, on two gallons of gas." He ran into the mini-mart and showed the girl at the cash register Harry Reeves picture. "Did this guy buy gas in the last half hour?"

"I only had two customers since I came on. Yeah. $10 cash. Creepy looking guy. In a huge hurry."

"Okay. What time did he get his gas?"

"Started pumping at 6:51:36 and stopped pumping 6:52:18."

Jake jumped back in the car, and raced to I-95, exited at the Columbus Blvd. exit, and screeched into the Penn's Landing Heliport parking lot in less than ten minutes. The men raced to the waiting helicopter and were quickly on their way to the Maryland/Delaware State line. Harvey had called all the information on the stolen car, and Maryland State Police were set up at the exits. They also had a car where Jake and Harvey would be dropped off. Since there was a toll at the Delaware/Maryland border, there happened to be a State Police Barracks there.

Jake and Harvey settled in behind the wheel of the unmarked car waiting for Reeves at the toll booth plaza, at 7:35 pm. With them were two Maryland State Troopers. Harvey had been on the phone with Brandon Wright the whole helicopter ride, and only now made sure he and Jake were on the same page. "We're about forty miles from where Reeves got on the highway, so about a forty-five-minute drive. He should be no more than five minutes, or so, away from our spot."

The Troopers, who had been in place for the last twenty minutes, had assured both men that a tan Elantra, with a personalize PA plate of FSH-IN, had not passed the toll booth. "Yeah. Extremely well-lit area. We should spot him easily. Good thinking, Harvey. If you hadn't spoken up, we'd still be knocking on doors on Salmon St."

"I just took what you said earlier and ran with it."

Traffic was fairly light, for a Sunday night, in early April. Harry Reeves was one mile away from the Delaware/Maryland border toll booth. He had a bad feeling in the pit of his stomach. He was nervous. He had narrowly escaped early this morning, down in Ocean City, and again, only an hour ago, at that slut Charlotte's house. Miller! He was smart. How did he find me so quickly in that old biddy's place? No matter. Miller might be smart, but he isn't smart enough to outsmart me. A slight smile crossed Harry's face. He was quite pleased with himself, at besting Jake Miller once again. This last time was close. Too close. He had just finished up with Charlotte, and that barking rat of hers, when he glanced out the upstairs window, and noticed two men making their way around the corner. They seemed out of place here. Like they're looking for something. Might that something be me? Harry's rules kicked in. Rule number 1: Plan your work and work your plan. It's 'spur of the moment' decisions that get most people caught. Rule #2: Always have an exit strategy in place, before you do anything else. Rule #3: Always assume the worst. This was the most important rule and had served him well over these last nine years. This was the rule that kicked in, when he saw those men. Get. Out. Now. Harry knew that if they were policemen, he might only have a few minutes to escape. He had to leave his favorite straight razor on the nightstand, because he didn't have time to clean it. Well, better to leave it, than to have it, with Charlotte's blood on it, found in his possession. Not to worry. There were no prints. He always wore gloves…Rule #1. He had grabbed his backpack, and sprinted out the back door, and was only halfway down the block, when he heard the gunshot. They *were* cops. Luckily, he spotted a car that suited his needs. No time to switch plates. Just get it and go. He breathed a sigh of relief as he merged onto I-95 South. He remembered thinking 'No speeding. Don't want to get pulled over for speeding.' Always obey the traffic rules. Maybe that should be a new rule? He allowed himself a smile over that. He was still smiling, when he paid the young toll taker. "Thank you."

"Have a nice night." A polite young man. Harry was relaxing now. Another ten minutes, and he'd come to the exit he was looking for. Ten minutes after that, he'd be in Elkton, MD, and he'd be free. No one knew about that place. Another smile.

Suddenly the night was filled with flashing lights, and sirens. Two MD State Troopers, and an unmarked police vehicle pulled out of the plaza in front of him, causing him to pull over on the shoulder of the road. He watched, eyes bulging out, as they surrounded the car, guns drawn.

How did they know, he thought? Then out loud, "Miller really is a smart one. I'll bet a tough guy, as well. I'd hate to be the guy driving *THAT* car", as he pulled out and passed the scene. Then he allowed himself a short chuckle. "Aren't you glad you're not in that car, Mary?" All Mary could do was cry. "Now, now, dear. They're not going to hurt your husband, as long as he does what they say. I think maybe they pulled him over for having a license plate that says FSH-IN." This thought caused him to laugh out loud.

Harry now thought about how much smarter than these cops he was. It was rule #3 that saved him. As he rode down I-95, he thought. "What if they find out what car I took? They could set up roadblocks." Harry was too smart to allow that to happen. First, he needed to find the right car. Maryland plates were preferable. It took him halfway through Delaware until he passed Mary and Tim, on their way back home, to Baltimore. It was perfect. The road was empty, except for Harry, and Tim and Mary Short. Harry pulled about a half-mile ahead of them, and when he rounded a curve, pulled over, put his flashers on, and got out, and flagged them down. Tim pulled over, right behind him. "Thanks for stopping. I don't have my phone. I broke down."

"Want me to take a look at it? I'm a mechanic."

"Would you? This must be my lucky day." Tim was halfway to Harry's car when he felt the knife in his side. "Okay, Chief. Here's what's gonna happen. You get in my car, and you drive into Maryland. You get off at exit #100. If there are no problems, I'll get off behind you, give you your car, and wife back, and you can get on with your lives. If you try anything, I'll butcher your dear wife. Understand?"

"Y-y-y-yes."

"Good. Ten minutes, and it'll be like this never happened." With that, he opened the door for Tim, closed it after him, and jogged back, and slid behind the wheel, beside Mary.

"Where's Tim?"

"Oh, he noticed that it's running rough. He wanted to drive it for a while. When we get to exit #100, we'll switch back."

A little over two minutes later, Harry put his right turn signal on (obey all the traffic laws). "Wait! This is Exit #109. You said exit #100!"

"I did? My bad. I meant #109."

"But Tim…Tim is going to Exit #100."

"Honey, Tim isn't going anywhere near exit #100, unless that's the exit for the Maryland prison." With that, Harry deftly removed the needle from his backpack, flipped the plastic sheath from the steel, and shot Mary Short with enough anesthesia to put her to sleep for several hours. He then congratulated himself on his accomplishment. "Oh Harry, you're a genius! Those cops thought they had you! I give them credit, they figured out you'd be heading South, but when will they get the message that they're no match for you? Not only did you anticipate their plan, and thwart it, but you picked up the lovely Mary Short along the way. Now, when you get to the farm, in ten short minutes, (pun intended), you'll show up bearing gifts. Pure genius!"

CHAPTER 21

Brandon Wright approached Jake and Harvey. "Harvey! What the hell happened?"

The Maryland State trooper barracks was pure bedlam. Reports were being repeated, the State Trooper Brass was screaming at everybody in a brown uniform. This caused so much confusion that it was rumored that the Governor had called. Jake grabbed Brandon by the arm and led he and Harvey into the barracks shower area, which was relatively quiet. "Listen, Brandon. Reeves outsmarted us…again. This isn't on Harvey."

"Oh, it's not? Well, my bad then. I'll repeat: What the hell happened?"

After Jake relayed Tim Short's encounter with Reeves, Brandon remarked, "It's like this bastard reads our minds. So, where do we stand right now?"

Jake nodded to Harvey Caldwell. "Jake and I have been trying to figure his next move. Reeves told Mr. Short to drive to Exit #100, where he'd give him his wife and car back. We both think he never planned to do that. We believe he stumbled upon this couple and saw an opportunity to get a 'clean' car, and his next victim. Now, if Short pulled over at Exit #100, and Reeves went past him, he could easily follow him. No, Reeves most likely planned to leave the highway before he got to Exit #100. The only exit between the toll here, and exit 100, is exit 109. We figure that's where he got off."

"Okay, what's there?"

"Really, nothing. Elkton is about 10-15 miles away. Lots of farming communities."

"So, you're saying he's in the wind, with a hostage."

"Basically, yeah."

"So, we're screwed."

"Not completely."

"How so, Jake?"

"This guy is on another level. We not only have to figure his next move, but the four after that. All we know is that he is consistent. He has to know that we know what he's driving, and where he got off the highway. We know from his past, that he's not going more than 10-20 minutes. Our search area should be a twenty-mile circle, with Exit #109 being the center point."

"Jake, you're talking about a ton of square miles!"

"I didn't say it was a very good option, but it's all we have. How many people can we put on the street?"

"I'm sure the Maryland State Troopers will want to help. They got as much egg on their faces as we did. Between them, the agents we have available to us, and the local Law Enforcement, maybe fifty? What do you think Harvey? Harvey?"

"Huh? Oh, yeah, I guess."

"What's going on, Harvey?"

"Just thinking. Listen, Brandon, I'm gonna head into the Baltimore office. I might have a way to narrow the search."

"Well, are you gonna tell us, or make us guess?"

"No, it's a long shot. I don't want to take any resources away from your search. I'll only be gone eight hours or so. I'll let you know what I find out." And with that, Harvey Caldwell headed out the door.

~~~

Brandon Wright quieted the room down. Between FBI, Delaware, Maryland State Troopers, and local police departments, there were sixty-five officers assembled. The Commander of the Maryland State Police had just introduced Brandon and given him the floor. "Listen up everyone. In a minute, Sergeant Ross is going to call your name out, and direct you to one of the duty stations. We've divided our search area up into four quadrants. We're looking at five, three-man teams for each quadrant. Each team will have a specific area to search, each day. You've all been provided with pictures of the suspect, Harry Reeves, and his captive, Mary Short. Leave no stone unturned. Time is of the essence. Stay alert. Reeves is to be considered armed, and extremely dangerous. He already has a list of ten deaths in the last two weeks alone, one of them being his own mother. So, be careful, and good hunting. Sgt. Ross..."

As the Sgt. started calling out names, Brandon made his way over to Jake. "It's 7:10 am. Harvey left around midnight. Have you heard from him, Brandon?"

"Only to tell me he got to our Baltimore field office. That was around two o'clock this morning. Any idea what he could be up to, Jake?"

"No, but I gotta tell you Brandon, he's really sharp. He nailed Reeve's plan for coming down here. If I didn't listen to him last night, we wouldn't be anywhere right now. Hey, where do you want me?"

"You're with me, Jake. By the way, I talked to Tom Hansen on my way here last night. He's at the hospital, with Detective Weaver. She's doing better. Doctor said she might be there 3-5 days. She should be fine."

"Physically, yeah, B. But you didn't see what those bastards did to her. I don't know how long it'll take her to get her head right."

Jake and Brandon drove down to Elkton Md. and joined in the search down there. It was the most populated search area, and two extra bodies would be best used there.

The group stopped for a quick lunch, in a diner, in the center of Elkton. While they were waiting for their food, Jake suggested that Brandon give Harvey a call. "No use, Jake. I've known Harvey for just about eight years now. The minute he finds something, we'll know. Before that, we'd just be interrupting him, and holding him up. Don't worry, he'll call." Twenty minutes later they were back at it. Knocking on doors, checking out garages. Showing pictures and asking questions. The plan was that the search teams worked until 5:00 pm, when the sun started to go down. They'd head back to the Trooper barracks, and mark off the areas they had cleared.

Jake and Brandon made their way back to the motel they were staying at. Both were tired and drifted off to sleep fairly early. Their sleep was interrupted by agent Wright's cell phone ringing. "Hello? Harvey? Yeah, I can hear you. Hold on a minute. Harvey, it's 11:30 pm. What's up? You're what? We're at the Motel 6, right as you get off Exit #109 of I-95. Room #210. An hour? We'll leave a light on."

"What's up?"

"Harvey's on his way here. He might have something. Looks like it's gonna be a long night, Jake."

"Well, then, I better go over to the Dunkin' Donuts, and get coffee, and some donuts. Want anything special?"

"No. make sure they give you plenty of sugar. Harvey uses a ton of sugar."

"Roger that."

Harvey Caldwell showed up just before 1:00 am. He got a coffee and opened the box of donuts. "A dozen old fashioned Dunkin' donuts?"

"Ask Jake."

"Jake?"

"Old habit. What do you have for us, Harvey?"

"Okay. We know that if Reeves is in this area, it's because he's familiar with it. So, it must be a place he's been to enough, to feel comfortable. He found those places in West Virginia, and Tennessee through the Computer Science Geeks, the group he started in U. of Maryland. I went back and started checking all the members of that group, to see if any of them were from this area."

"And?"

"And there were three Maryland residents in the club. Two from Baltimore proper, and one from Chevy Chase."

"So, no luck."

"No luck, at first. I looked into all three backgrounds. We may have gotten lucky with one. Joseph Carlyle. Grew up in Baltimore. Father works for the Dept. of Agriculture. Born in Akron, Ohio. No family in the area. His mother is Amy Reed-Carlyle. Grew up on a farm two miles outside of Elkton. Her sister, Barbara Reed, lives there. Joe Carlyle mentioned in his Bio, for the Computer Science Geeks, that he spent summers, growing up, working the farm, with aunt B."

"Bio?"

"Yeah. The Computer Science Geeks put out a yearbook, and it had a thumbnail, if you will, of its members."

"And you think Reeves is there?"

"Well, I *know* Carlyle is there. I went to his parent's house, looking for him, and they said he's lived there since he was a Senior in College, three years ago."

"Good work Harvey. What do you think, Jake? First light, the three of us pay Mr. Carlyle a visit?"

"No, Brandon. If Reeves is there, I don't want him slipping away. I think at first light, we surround the place and *then* we pay Mr. Carlyle

225

a visit. We have a force of, what, sixty? We take the dozen or so FBI guys you have here, and grab a dozen Maryland Troopers, and we block off every road in the area. Hell, we'll put guys in the corn fields, if we have to. Reeves has had an escape plan at every turn, so far. We have to assume he'll have one for this place."

"I'll make the calls. Show me on the map where this place is, Harv. Okay, about two minutes North of Elkton. There's a state park on the edge of the town, with an information center. I'll have everybody assemble there, at 0600. We can deploy our roadblocks North of the farm, via this dirt road, so they won't be seen while they're setting up. Am I missing anything?"

"No, but why don't the three of us head out there now. It's 0330. We won't get there until 0400. We can do a little reconnaissance. I brought my night vision equipment with me."

"Good idea Jake. If nothing else, we can sketch out the number of, and location of, any buildings on the property."

Harvey's intel showed the farm next door, was an eighth of a mile away from the Reed place. They pulled over there, and Brandon and Jake made the last part of the trip, on foot. It was an overcast night, so there was no moon. It was so dark, in fact, that Harvey Caldwell lost sight of the two men, before they had gone fifty feet. The plan was for Jake to call out buildings, and distances, and Brandon would sketch everything out.

It was 0515, when they got back to the car. Harvey doubled back and went down the dirt road that was just West of Route 279, where the farm was located. When they got to the Elkton State Park information center, they were the last ones there. A detailed topographical map of the area had been laid out on the four tables that had been pushed together to accommodate it. Jake was impressed with how well the FBI worked. Brandon had simply told one of his Agents how many resources they would have, and what he wanted, and Agent Morris took care of everything. Everyone knew where they would be deployed, and what their job was, by the time Brandon got there. All that was left was for Brandon to look over the plan and give it his blessing. When the perimeter people were gone, Brandon studied around the 8 ½ x 11-inch sketch he had made, based on Jake's estimates. There would be four vehicles, with four FBI agents in each. Three of the vehicles would form what amounted to a triangle around the place. One vehicle would come South on Route 279 and set up on the North corner of the property. A second vehicle would come North on 279 and set up on the South corner. The third vehicle would enter the property on the access road, and set up on the back, or East side of the property. The last vehicle, containing Jake, Brandon, Harvey, and Bob Morris, would follow in the same access road, but would stop at the front of the farmhouse. On a predetermined signal two agents would go in the back of the house, from their positions on the East side of the house, and Brandon, and his team would breech through the front. With any luck, they'd catch them off guard.

As with any forced entry, speed is of the utmost importance. The idea is to throw a flash-bang grenade in as you enter, causing momentary blindness, and hopefully catch your suspects with their pants down, so to speak, and take them down with as little risk to your team as possible. Everyone knew that the minute the two SUV's hit the dirt driveway, time was of the essence. When the two teams were in place, on either side of the house, on route 279, Brandon gave the green light. The lead SUV, driven by agent Morris, and containing agents Wright, Caldwell, and Jake, raced up the driveway, cut across the grass, and skidded to a halt just off the steps leading to the front porch. All four agents hit the ground running. At the same time, the second SUV followed the driveway along the side of the house, past an old, broken-down wagon, that was once the family's mode of transportation, a hundred years ago, and stopped at the back corner of the property. Four agents exited. Two took up defensive positions, behind their vehicle, and the other two sprinted towards the back door. The entry plan was relatively simple. Agents Morris and Caldwell would throw flash bang grenades through the front window, on either side of the door, and all four would crash the door. When the agents in back heard the entry, they'd flash-bang their way through the back door.

So far, so good. On Brandon's signal the two agents hurled their grenades through the windows. Three seconds later came the concussion of the explosion. Brandon hit he door with the battering ram, and they were inside, without incident. Jake heard the window break, as the rear entry team came in. He saw movement in the dining room, and the house was filling up with smoke, very quickly. Jake wondered if they were burning the place down. In his earpiece, he heard a strange report from the teams set up on the road. "Lost visual of house, and surrounding buildings! Smoke pouring everywhere! Report, team leader!"

"Hold your positions!" was Brandon's answer.

Ten minutes later, the smoke had cleared, and the officers cleared the farmhouse. It was empty. Walking back outside, Jake and Brandon made eye contact. "Son of a bitch!"

"What is it, Jake?"

"Look!" Jake pointed to a wire they had tripped, when they came in the front door. "We did it." Now that it was completely light outside, and the smoke was 90% gone, Jake could clearly see what had happened. "His own version of a security system. There's got to be a dozen smoke machines throughout this place. Probably twenty more outside, and around the other buildings. We set them off, when we came in. This guy is unbelievable! We couldn't see six inches in front of us. Reeves could have walked right past us, and out the front door."

"Why smoke? Why not just trigger an explosion?"

"Because then he couldn't get away. The smoke gave him cover. When we came in, as the smoke started, I saw movement, in the dining room, moving towards the window. Let's check it out."

They walked around the side of the house and saw that the old wagon was positioned directly under the window. "Damn! He thought of everything. The whole area fills with smoke, and he goes through the window, and lands in this wagon."

"Yeah. Look. Blood. He must've cut himself going out the window. Looks pretty bad, too." Brandon motioned for agents Morris and Caldwell. Our suspect is bleeding. He finally made a mistake. His trail leads across the driveway, and into that field. Go get him!"

Five minutes later, the walkie-talkie crackled. "Team Leader. Come in."

"This is Team leader."

"Brandon, it's Harvey. We found him. About two hundred yards into the field. He's dead. Bled out. Call the M.E."

"Roger that Harvey. Agent Morris, you will stay with the body until the Medical Examiner arrives, which should be shortly. Harvey, come on back."

They were making their way to check out the barn, when Harvey came out of the field. "Brandon! I didn't want to say over the air, in case he's listening, it wasn't Reeves. Pretty sure it was Carlyle. It was a set up!"

"How so?"

"He only had a couple little scrapes from jumping through the window. But there was a deep puncture wound, which must have severed the Femoral Artery. Reeves wanted us to follow the blood trail. He lived long enough to get us to follow him."

"So, where is Reeves? Was he even here?"

"Okay, Brandon. Let's look at this logically. If somebody stabbed Carlyle, it had to be Reeves. So, he was here. We can't find him. If he is out of the house, he is on foot, somewhere in that field, behind us."

"Why that field?"

"He wouldn't go the same direction as Carlyle. If he went West, he'd have to cross the road. The agents out front would have seen something. No, he went East. We have the surrounding roads manned. We need to search from the edges of this field in towards the center." As Agent Wright picked up his walkie-talkie, to give those orders, Harvey Caldwell stopped him.

"Jake, wait. Remember how you told me we would figure out his location, and then stop thinking, and start searching, and how that was why we hadn't caught him yet? Isn't that what we're doing now?"

"What are you thinking, Harvey?"

"I know if I was Reeves, and I set up this elaborate security system, I'd have a better plan than to run into the field. He'd have to assume we would expect that."

"I don't understand."

"No, Harvey's right, Brandon. He produced all that smoke. We couldn't see six inches in front of our faces. Of course, he went into the field. That's why he didn't!"

"He didn't go into the field? Well, where the hell did he go?"

Jake looked at Harvey, who nodded in agreement. "He didn't go anywhere. He's still here. In the house. In one of the buildings. He's got some kind of hidden room, or something. Someplace he'll hide out in, until we've moved away."

"So, what do we do?"

Before Jake could answer, one of the other FBI Agents, came out of one of the other three buildings on the property. "Agent Wright! Over here!"

Brandon muttered "Now what?", as he, Jake, and Harvey made their way over to what appeared to be a twenty-foot square building, a tool shed, maybe. "What is it, Agent Green?"

"In there, sir. I-I-I think it's a woman."

Inside, the tool shed had three walls covered with what appeared to be over a hundred different kinds of tools. The floor was bare, except for the torture station, in the center of the room. Attached to that station, was what was left of Mary Short. Her arms, still hanging from the ceiling, had been ripped from her body. Her left ear was lying on the floor, next to the pruning shears, that Jake assumed were used to remove it. A dozen teeth were strewn about. Most of her skin had been peeled from her body. The look of sheer terror on her twisted face made Jake turn away. Brandon spoke. "This is bad. The high school girls were all, basically, sexually abused, and eventually smothered, which is bad enough. He's morphed into dismemberment, and torture, more and more. We need to catch him now!"

"You're right, Brandon. Jake, what do you think?"

"I'd probably rip that house apart. Take down every wall and try to find his hiding place. Same goes for these other buildings."

"I agree. Your call, Brandon."

Agent Wright slowly turned towards the farmhouse. "Right idea, but wrong way to go about it. I'll be right back." He walked towards the mobile command post that had been driven in, as Jake looked at Harvey Caldwell, and shrugged his shoulders.

CHAPTER 22

By 2:00 pm that afternoon, all of Mary Short's body parts had been accounted for and collected, and the Medical Examiner had released hers, and Joe Carlyle's bodies. They were now gone, and the forensic team was going through the tool shed, collecting evidence. Brandon Wright was overseeing the job. "Okay, you have one more hour. Let's wrap this up."

Outside, Jake and Harvey were scratching their heads. When Brandon came outside, they approached him. "What are we waiting for, B?"

Brandon held a finger up, as he answered his cell. "They are? Fine. Send them right through." After he disconnected the call, he spoke to the two men. "Harvey, we're not waiting for anything. I just don't want to send anybody in there, poking around. Who knows if he has any booby traps set?"

"Then what?"

"Then, this…"

The three officers turned to watch a crane lumber up the driveway, followed by a half dozen oversize dump trucks. It took several minutes for the crane operator to maneuver the large machine into position. The operator then got out and walked over to Brandon Wright. "You in charge here?"

"Yes sir. What can I do for you?"

"Can you get one of them SUVs over there, to push that wagon out of my way?"

"Where do you want it?"

"Just out of my way. Have them push it into that field back there. If not, it'll just be in my way again, when I start knocking down all the other buildings."

Brandon instructed Agent Morris to move the wagon, so the crane could get closer to the house. Thirty seconds later, the way was clear, with the wagon now forty feet into the back field, and the crane was in position. "Uh, Brandon? Do you mind telling us what you're doing?"

"I'm checking the house, Harvey, for hiding spots." Brandon took hold of the bullhorn, and shouted, "Harry Reeves, this is FBI! We have heavy equipment here, to clear this entire lot. If you are in one of these buildings, you have one minute to surrender. If you do not surrender in the next minute, we will commence razing all buildings on this property."

After what seemed like only a minute, Brandon signaled to the crane operator to begin. Jake and Harvey walked to the street, and leaned on the car, and watched the crane rip the house apart, and load it into the waiting dump trucks.

~~~

"What's up, Jake? You been quiet all afternoon."

"Nothing really, Harvey. Just thinking."

"About what?"

"About Reeves. I know we were all jazzed when we came up with this idea of him still being in the house, but think about it. He'd know that we would search that field. And it's not *that* big. I mean, they're searching anyway, just not as many men, and they're almost done, right? A little over four hours."

"Yeah?"

"Okay, you're Reeves. You have to come up with a plan to escape. That's your M.O. Now, you create a diversion; to make everybody think you ran into that field, but you're hiding in the house somewhere. Now, you're a real smart guy. You must know it's only gonna take a few hours to comb through that field, and we're obviously not going to find you. You can't come out of your hiding spot until you're sure we are all gone, right?"

"Right. What are you getting at, Jake?"

"When you're thinking this through, what do you think is going to happen, after we all come up empty out there in the field?"

"I, uh…"

"Ideally, we go away, and after dark, you can sneak out. Maybe go to the neighbor's house and steal their car."

"Makes sense."

"Except that it's not going to be dark for another 2-3 hours. He *has* to think that we're going to think that if he didn't go through that field, he didn't go anywhere, and we'd check the house, and he'd be trapped."

"So, you don't think he's in the house?"

"Right! It doesn't make sense. He's too smart to be trapped like that, not leaving himself a way out."

"Okay, Jake. Let's assume for a minute that you're right. What happened to him? Where did he go? Did he just disappear?"

"That's the part I haven't figured out yet."

It took two dump truck loads to clear the rubble that used to be Barbara Reed's home. While a bulldozer finished clearing the lot, the crane moved over to the tool shed. In twenty minutes, it was splinters. By 4:00 pm, every building on the property was gone. A tired Brandon Wright approached Jake and Harvey. "No luck. He must've split before we got here. Somehow, he knew."

"No, he didn't leave before we got here. The M.E. said Carlyle bled out in less than five minutes. He didn't stab himself like that. No, that bastard was here. We just didn't see him."

"Couldn't be, Jake. Everything that was here, is gone now. Look out there! Everything is gone!"

Suddenly, Jake pushed away from the car, and sprinted into the yard. "Not everything."

Jake was now tearing through the yard, dodging the heavy equipment, that was now done its job. He flew into the field behind the property, with agents Wright, Caldwell, and Morris behind him.

~~~

Harry Reeves could not contain himself, as he crossed the Delaware Memorial Bridge, into South Jersey. "Brilliant, Harry! Simply brilliant! That poor excuse for law enforcement is no match for someone as smart as you, Harry! You made them do exactly what you wanted them to do. In fact, they even helped you, by pushing the wagon you were hiding in, into the field. That way, you didn't even have to wait for it to get dark, before you made your escape. Imagine, in broad daylight, you open the false bottom in the wagon, and drop down into the field, not thirty yards away from two dozen FBI agents. Since they had already searched the field, it became a simple matter of crawling on your belly five hundred feet, or so, until you had put the neighbor's house between them and you. And on top of that, as boys will, the morons stationed in front of the house, were so engrossed in watching the crane tear down the house (another distraction you didn't expect), that you could've paraded across the road behind a brass band, to the spot in the field where you had dear Mary Short's car waiting, and they probably wouldn't have noticed. Okay now, that's enough gloating, Harry. If you get caught up in reveling in your victory, you'll be off your game, and get caught. All right, now, what are they going to do next? Hmm, that Miller is smart. He'll find the wagon, and he'll realize I duped him again, and since none of the neighbors' cars are missing, he'll assume I'm still driving Mary Short's car. But I doubt they'll realize that I switched license plates, with the neighbor's tan Accent. Perfect for the brown Elantra I'm driving. They'll assume I'm headed into Baltimore. Sure, I wouldn't *dare* go back to Jersey, or Philly. No, they'll concentrate their search efforts in the Baltimore/Washington area. It'll be at least 3-4 days before one of the 'smart' cops suggests that I might have gone back to Jersey, and they widen their search. It'll take a couple of days for them to get organized, and that gives me just about a week of 'free time', before I have to get out of Dodge. That's way more time than I need to find what, and who, I need to find, before I leave."

Turns out Harry Reeves was dead on about Jake finding the wagon. As Jake, Brandon, Harvey, and Agent Morris stood looking at the old wooden wagon, whose undercarriage was now hanging open, revealing the 12" x 6' space that Harry Reeves climbed out of, sometime in the last 4 hours. Agent Morris was beside himself. "Damn it! I pushed the son of a bitch out here, and now, we have no idea where he's at."

"That's not completely true, Morris."

"What do you mean, Jake?"

"Look, Harvey. See where the flowers and weeds are all bent and broken? He crawled on his belly. That way...", pointing to the neighbor's house. The four men quickly followed the path to where it exited the field. "Look. There. Next to the house. Footprints in the soft dirt, and mulch, by the wall. When they got to the front of the property, it was easy to see the opening Reeves left, when he crossed the road, and ran into the field on the opposite side. Jake led them, single file, through the path Reeves made, until they came to the opening, about fifty feet from the road. "This is why we didn't find the Short's car on the property.

Look out there. Reeves drove the car in here, turned it around, and left it, for his escape."

"But how did he know we'd push that wagon into the field?"

"Don't think he did know. He couldn't possibly know that Brandon would call in the heavy equipment. No, I think he was prepared to stay in there, until nightfall. I think he was planning his escape after it got dark. All we did was allow him to execute his plan sooner."

"Okay, Morris. Head back to the mobile unit and get an APB out on the car. Harvey, you coordinate with our Baltimore Office. I want a hard target search; at every location we know he's familiar with."

"Roger that."

When everyone was back at the road, Brandon Wright turned to Jake. "What do you think, Jake?"

"I don't know, B. I think the way this guy plans is that when he leaves a place, he tries to anticipate what we are going to do, then he makes his plan accordingly. I gotta tell you, he's been right on the money every time, so far."

"So, what's his next move?"

"He'll expect us to find the wagon and follow his trail. He made no attempt to cover his movements. We'll assume he's still driving Short's car, and that he'll head into Baltimore. That will be where we focus our search for him."

"So, if he didn't head into Baltimore, where did he go?"

"That's the million-dollar question. From what we know about him, it will either be somewhere down the shore, or where he grew up. While it's true the place he knows best is his mother's house, he's holed up there at least twice, so I'd say he's at the Jersey shore, where towns are carbon copies of each other. He knows Ocean City, and Villas, but he could be in *any* town down there, from Wildwood, up to Long Beach Island. So, if you put a gun to my head, I think he's down the shore, somewhere, and I think he figures he's safe for a few days. That means he'll spend that time making his next plans."

"Okay. Good enough for me. I'll pull everybody out of Baltimore and pour bodies into some of the shore towns."

"No, don't do that. There's no guarantee I'm right. Besides, he's sure to spot a large presence of cops, and FBI guys. No, this is a job for a small group. You stay at Baltimore, in case I'm wrong. I'll get help from Tom Hansen, or Wilt, or somebody, down there."

"Well, take Harvey with you. He's a good man, and it'll give him a chance to visit that lady detective he's smitten with."

"Roger that. I'll stay in touch."

After catching up with Harvey Caldwell, they decided to stay overnight at their motel, and head back to Jersey in the morning. By the time they had said goodbye to Brandon, and the other agents, who were packing up, and heading into Baltimore, it was after 8:00 pm. When they got to Motel 6, Jake called Tom Hansen, to fill him in on what was happening, and to ask for his help looking for Harry Reeves. He asked how Kari Weaver was. Tom said he had been up to Ocean City to see her earlier in the day, and she was much better, physically. Most of the swelling had gone down. Most of the bandages she was covered in, on Sunday, were gone. Her state of mind, that was a different story. Next, Jake asked Tom about his sister, and niece. "I'm at your place right now, with them. Ask them yourself."

"Jimmy! Are you okay?"

"I'm fine, sis. How are you, and Kathleen doing?"

"We're good. I'm staying here with her. It's like a vacation."

"That's good, sis. Tell Kathleen I love her."

"I will Jimmy. What about Tom?"

"What about Tom? No, you don't have to tell him I love him."

"No, you knucklehead. Do you want to get back on the phone with him?"

"No, just tell him I'll see him at work tomorrow. Good night, sis."

"Good night, Jimmy. Drive carefully."

"Is Hansen going to help?"

"Yeah, Harvey. In fact, when we get down there in the morning, we're going to his office, to plan a strategy."

"That's good. How is your family?"

Jake laughed. "My family is fine, Harv. Why don't you ask me what you really want to know?"

"How is Regina?"

"There you go. That wasn't so hard, was it? Tom went up to see her this afternoon. Physically, she's doing wonderful. She will probably be released Thursday, or Friday. He said she's still really messed up, as far as her state of mind."

"Well, that's to be expected, right?"

"Absolutely. She went through one hell of an ordeal. Who knows how long it will take her to recover, emotionally. She will most likely need to talk to a shrink."

"Whatever it takes."

"Amen to that. Good night, Harvey."

"Night Jake."

~~~

While Jake and Harvey were calling it a day, Harvey Reeves was just getting started. He had just settled into his room at the Lollipop Motel, at 23rd and Atlantic Ave, in North Wildwood. He fired up his laptop. He smiled as he said to himself "Time to make the donuts." What a wonderful thing the Internet was! You could find out anything, about anybody... and most of the time, you could do it for free! Harry felt power when he was surfing the web. Nobody could bully him on the internet. No woman could say no to him. This was his place. He was the bully on the web. Tonight, though, was not for fun. Tonight was business. He brought up the search engine, and typed the name in. There were probably twenty-five hits. Most of them newspaper stories. Good. They always had lots of pictures. He anxiously opened the first one and started reading about the newest police officer on the Cape May Courthouse Police force. The year was 2002. A nice bio. Hmm, ex-Navy SEAL. Harvey jotted this down on his legal pad. A scant three hours later, and Reeves had read everything on the net there was to read about his subject. This would be easy. He was single. His wife was killed in an explosion. The only other family he had was a divorced sister, and her daughter. Next was to run a search on them. Harry Reeves turned the page and wrote the name Margaret Miller across the top of the page.

It was just after 3:30 am in the morning, when Harry Reeves shut down his computer. He was very pleased with himself. "I know everything there is to know about James Miller. But more importantly, I know everything there is to know about his lovely sister, and beautiful niece. I'll be paying them a visit, soon."

Harry decided to get some sleep and start planning his little party that he was throwing for the Miller girls.

CHAPTER 23

As Harry Reeves was drifting off to sleep, Jake was waking up. He tried to not make any noise, so as to allow Harvey Caldwell to sleep a little longer, but it was to no avail. "Jake? What time is it?"

"A little after 5:00 am, Harv. Go back to sleep for an hour. I didn't mean to wake you up."

"No, that's fine. I like to travel as soon as the sun comes up. I'll be ready in twenty minutes."

At 5:50, Jake checked out of the Motel 6, and the two-vehicle caravan started the journey to Cape May County.

About two hours later, they pulled into the parking lot, at the CMCPD. Jake noted that Tom Hansen's car was already there. The pair made their way to Hansen's first floor office. After getting coffee, and taking a seat around Hansen's small conference table, Jake began the strategy session. "Tom, this Reeves is diabolical. He's figuring out what *we* are going to do and planning accordingly. And he's been right every single time."

"Slow down there, pard. So, what does Mr. Reeves think we are going to do now?"

"As I told agent Wright, he made no effort to cover his trail. He wanted us to figure out that he drove away from the place near Elkton. He knew we'd expect him to go into Baltimore and focus our search there."

"And so, instead of going to Baltimore, he came here?"

"Well, not so much here, but to the shore. It's still relatively quiet here, being early April, and he likes to be alone."

"And, so, of all the shore towns in Jersey, how do we know where to start?"

"We don't know where, for certain, but it makes sense that since he likes Ocean City, and he likes the Delaware Bay area, that he would go to a town in between those points. And since he was closer to here, than he was to Ocean City, it's logical that he went somewhere down here. Now, the way I figured, he thinks that he has 4-5 days, before somebody decides to start looking down here for him, so this is not his end game. He's going to use this time to plan his next move, or moves. With that being said, it doesn't make sense for him to rent something long term or take a chance of getting caught because the homeowner, whose house he broke into, came down to open the place up. So, I believe he'll…"

"Stay at a motel for a few days. Only problem is, where at?"

"I've been thinking about that too, Tom. Reeves will assume that when we start looking for him down here, that we'll believe he's in a motel, so he'll want to be in a town that has the most motels, making the haystack a little bigger."

"Well, pard, Cape May, all the way up to Margate, all have plenty of motels."

"Right, but only one place has the benefit of having triple the number of motels, than any other place. The Wildwoods."

"Good thinking, pard. Between the Crest, N. Wildwood, and Wildwood proper, there's way more motels than in any other single shore town. But where do we start?"

"Been thinking about that, as well. Figured we check the Crest, then North Wildwood, and Wildwood last."

"Let's have at it, then."

Armed with the latest picture of Harry Reeves, they started out towards Wildwood Crest.

Jake started out in Diamond Beach. He knew it was a long shot that Reeves would be there, but he didn't want to leave any stone unturned. He walked into the rental office at SeaPointe Village, and was greeted with a warm smile, and a friendly good morning, by the receptionist, who's nametag identified her as Sally. "Good morning, Sally. I'm working with the FBI. I was wondering if you could help me?"

"Sure. What is it you need?"

"Well, I'm looking for this man." He gave her Reeves' picture. "Have you seen him in the last day, or so?"

"No, he hasn't come in here."

"Well, he would've been trying to rent a place, for a week, or so."

"No. I'm certain this man was never here. Can I keep the picture, and if he comes in, I'll call you?"

"That would be great. Thank you very much."

It was like that all day. By 3:00 pm, they had completed checking all the motels in the Crest. They still had a few hours of daylight, so they decided to head up into North Wildwood. They drove up to Anglesea and started making their way South. They had just finished up the Sahara just off of Ocean Ave, a little after 6:00 pm. All three were tired, so they decided to start fresh in the morning.

Since Tom's wife Maggie was already at Jake's, and Harvey was staying with Jake, they stopped at the butcher, and Jake fired up the grill. It was still a little too chilly to eat outside, but that didn't stop anyone from having a good dinner. Tom and Maggie went home about 8:30 pm, and Jake and Harvey turned in a little after nine o'clock.

~~~

Jake and Harvey were ready to go, the next morning, when Tom brought Maggie over to Jake's house. Art Kaufman had gotten there early. Jake had arranged for Art to guard the women. He also had arranged for Phil to take Assault and Battery for the day.

The Florantine motel was the first stop of the day, with no luck. It was just after 11:00 am, when Jake walked into the Lollipop Motel. "Would you like a room?"

"No, just some information." Jake flashed his badge (fake though it was).

"How can I help?"

"Have you seen this man? He would've checked in, maybe Wednesday?"

"Oh, yes sir. He's staying with us until Sunday. Mr. Lyons. Andrew Lyons. Room 204. Go outside, up the stairs, fourth door."

"Thank you. Do you know if he is there now? "

"Well, he signed in his car as a brown Hyundai Elantra, with Maryland plates. I believe that's his car down on the end."

"Thanks. I'll need a pass key."

As Jake left the office, he waved for Tom and Harvey to join him. "Room 204. Clerk thinks he might be in there. That's his car down the end of the lot."

"Okay, pard. How do you want to do this?"

"We're taking no chances. Harvey, you go around back, in case he has an escape plan out the back window. Tom, you and I go up, you stay outside, in case he's got a way into the room on either side. I'll go in, okay?"

"You got it Jake. Give me thirty seconds to get around back."

"Let's have at him, pard."

A minute later, everyone was in place. Tom motioned to Jake to check the door for trip wires. Jake gave him a thumbs up, turned the key, and cracked the door, enough to check if it was booby-trapped. It wasn't. He entered the room low and fast. Empty. Next stop, the bathroom. Also empty. Jake motioned to Harvey Caldwell, through the bathroom window, to join him and Tom Hansen, and gave Hansen an 'all clear.'

Harvey entered the motel room as Tom Hansen said "He's gone, Jake. Nothing here."

"Almost right, Tom." Jake had opened the drawer on the nightstand to find a cell phone.

"Don't think that's a coincidence, pard. He left that for a reason. Check the last number called."

Jake did just that. "Only one number called on this phone. Five times, all within a couple minutes."

"Call the number, Jake."

Harvey Reeves was driving the silver Explorer he stole from the Lollipop parking lot, after he switched plates with a Chevy Bronco, of course. He had spent most of Thursday planning his next move, and by supper time, he was ready to go. Pack everything up, and into bed by 8:00 pm, then out the door just after sunup. What was that saying? Early to bed. Early to rise. Makes a man... something. Harry was in too good a mood to worry about remembering nursey rhymes. He was very pleased with himself. He had done it again. He was jolted from his daydream by his cell phone ringing. He looked at the incoming number. 'Well, I really didn't expect them to find my room this quickly.' "Hello. Is this the famous Jake Miller?"

"Is this you, Reeves?"

"Come on now Jake, don't be so formal. Are you angry because I've bested you so many times?"

"Why did you leave this phone here?"

"I wanted to talk to you, of course. I have to say, I want to thank you. You're very good. You've forced me to step up my game."

"Is that all you wanted, was to tell me how fantastic you are?"

"Certainly not. I wanted to tell you how my day has been. I checked out of my motel, but I guess you already know that. I put the key in the drop box when I left. I guess they haven't looked in there yet. Tell me, how did it feel, to think you had me trapped, only to find out I was gone?"

"Kind of the way you're gonna feel, when I *do* catch you."

"It's good you can stay so positive, with as many times as you've failed. But that's not why I wanted to talk to you. I wanted to tell you that I am a man of my word, and that everything that's happened today is because of you. I told you to leave me alone, but you wouldn't. And so, you had to pay." Jake silently mouthed Tom Hansen to call his wife.

"What are you talking about Reeves?" Tom Hansen opened his contact list on his phone, and hit the button marked 'Wifey-Poo'.

"Just what I said Jake. You have to... wait, I have a call coming in on my other phone. Margaret Hansen's phone. Margaret can't come to the phone right now; can I take a message?" Jake grabbed the motel notepad, and scribbled a phone number on it, wrote the phrase *'ping it'* under the number, and shoved it in Harvey Caldwell's chest. He ran out of the room, as he took out his phone.

"Reeves! What are you doing with my wife's phone?"

"Her phone? Mr. Hansen, I think her phone is the last thing you should be worrying about right now. But I'm being rude. I'll have to let you go Mr. Hansen; I have your brother-in-law on my other line." Harry disconnected the call to Tom Hansen, and when he rejoined Jake, he had a completely different demeanor. "Here it is, Miller. I was at your house this morning. Parked half a block away, waiting for you three stooges to leave. Then I marched right up to the front door and knocked. Your charming niece answered, and when I told her I was broke down, and my cell died, and could I call AAA from your house, she let me in. Who was the old man? I think I killed him. Sorry, if he was a friend. Sadly, you sent your dogs away for the day. I was almost looking forward to dealing with them. It's been a long time since I dealt with an animal. Anyway, your sister, she's a tough son of a gun. Well, she was tough, right up until I grabbed her daughter from behind, and pushed the point of my knife about an eighth of an inch into her right side. Then, well old Maggie did whatever I told her to. They're both here with me. I'd let you talk to them, but I gave them both a pretty strong sedative, and they're both out like a light. Well, so far, today has been fun, but the real fun will start in a couple of hours, when we get set up, at my next destination." Before Jake could say a word, the call was gone.

Jake and Tom stared at each other, in complete silence, until Harvey Caldwell re-entered the room. "Guys! Snap out of it! I pinged the phone. It went to voicemail, but that doesn't matter. When the voicemail answered the phone, we got a lock on it. Maggie's phone is about forty-five miles away. It's stationary. Let's go. I also sent EMT's to your house, Jake. Come on! Lets' go find that phone!"

"Hold it, Harvey! Before we go running off after him, we need to find out what he's driving. He left his car here, so he most likely stole one from this lot." They ran down to the lobby. Jake grabbed the guy behind the check-in counter. "How many guests did you have here overnight?"

"What?"

"I'm going to say this one more time, I don't have time for any bullshit. How many guests did you have overnight?"

"Hold on a second. Seven. No, eight. There were eight guests here overnight."

"Did any of them check out today?"

"Two."

"The six that are still here, did they all have cars?"

"Yes sir."

"I need to know what kind of car each registered." While the clerk was getting that information, Jake scanned the parking lot. There were only four cars parked out there. One was Reeves'. "Come on! First person. What kind of car?"

"Uh, red Toyota."

"It's out there. Next."

"Silver Pontiac LeMans."

"Here."

"Green Ford pickup."

"Here. Next"

"Silver Ford Explorer."

"Not here! Room number!"

"212."

Jake nodded, and Tom Hansen took off for room 212. "Next."

"Brown Hyun…"

"Here. Next!"

"White Chevy Bronco."

"Room number."

"103." Jake and Harvey ran out and knocked on room 103. No answer. As the went back to the lobby, they met Tom Hansen coming down the stairs.

"Got it Pard. Silver Ford Explorer. NJ plates. BMJ-25R."

"Let's get it out on the air."

"Hold on, Harvey." Jake went back into the lobby. Guest in room 103. White Bronco. Did they leave a license number?"

"Sure. 38R-TM5."

"Ok, Harv. Put it out there, with both plate numbers. Now, let's go find that phone."

Jake took off, with Tom next to him, in front, and Harvey in the back seat. He flew West, out of Wildwood, on Rio Grande Ave. He ran the light at Route 9, and Route 47, and narrowly avoided getting smashed by a sixteen-wheeler. "Which way Harvey?"

"Keep going the way you're going. I'll let you know when you should change direction."

Jake made the twenty-one-mile trip to where Rte. 47 turns into Rte. 347, in fifteen minutes flat. "Jake, we're too far south. You need to head in a northerly direction."

"We will be, in a few minutes Harvey. Pretty sure he went North on Rte. 55. Ten minutes later, Jake was driving north on route 55. "Okay, Jake, straight ahead, about 8.5 miles." Right after they passed Exit #27, Harvey told Jake to slow down, that they were within five hundred feet of the phone.

"How close can that thing get us?"

"Within ten feet. Stop! Right here!" Jake pulled to the shoulder and stopped. Harvey got out, walked to the guardrail, and stepped over it. Less than a minute later, he was back over the rail, with the phone in his possession.

Back in the car, Jake turned so he could face both men. "When Reeves said he'd be at his next destination in two hours, I looked at my watch. It was 11:45 am. Harvey, you pinged the phone two minutes before he said that, and it's been in that spot since then?"

"Yeah."

"All right, then. He's not going to Baltimore. There's a massive manhunt for him there. He's just about an hour from the Walt Whitman Bridge. Considering traffic, in another forty-five minutes, or so, he would be in the vicinity of Farmer's Landing Road."

"His mom's house?"

"Why not? It's perfect. He killed three of the four people that lived on that road, and the fourth is still in the hospital, so that whole road is deserted. That's where he's headed."

Tom Hansen spoke for the first time since he got off the phone with Reeves. "Jake! If you're wrong about this, and we don't find them, you know what will happen."

Jake flashed on the memory of the carnage inside the toolshed, where Mary Short was butchered. He felt a chill, and more than a little doubt. "Tom, I..."

"Hold it. Tom, I've been with Jake most of this case. He's been right every single time, on figuring Reeves' moves. Back at the motel, you and I were ready to hit the road. Jake was the one who thought clearly enough to go find out what kind of vehicle we were chasing, and the possibility he switched plates, and what that plate number would be. No, I say he's right. If he says he's at his mom's house, that's our best chance of getting him."

Jake swung back around and hit the gas. "Harvey, get hold of Brandon. Have him check the toll cameras at the Walt Whitman, Ben Franklin, and Betsy Ross bridges, from 12:15, this afternoon, until they see the silver Explorer."

"Already done, Jake. He'll call as soon as he sees something."

No one spoke for the next 40 minutes. Jake crossed the bridge into South Philly a little after 1:00 pm. He made the turn onto the I-95 north entrance ramp and sped towards Bucks County. As they passed under the Ben Franklin Bridge, Harvey Caldwell got a call from Brandon Wright. "Yeah, B. Twenty minutes ago? Betsy Ross Bridge. Route 413, five minutes ago. Thanks, B. No, Jake is afraid Reeves would spot a trap. Just have them stand by. Roger that."

"Well?"

"Reeves crossed the Betsy Ross, and went North on 95, twenty minutes ago. He exited at Route 413, five minutes ago."

"Way to go, pard."

"Yeah, now all we have to do is get there, and kill the prick."

"Well, pard, you take care of the first part, and I for sure will take care of the second part."

Jake was doing 85 mph when he got to the 413 exit, eighteen minutes later. "How far is it from here to his mom's house?"

"Less than ten minutes."

"That means he'll have been there for twenty minutes, when we arrive."

"Think positive Tom. Nothing can happen to them right away."

When they breached Harriet Abrams home, Jake found it just the way he remembered it, neat as a pin, only with a month's worth of dust. What he didn't find was her son, Harry Reeves. "He's not here, Jake!"

"I can see that, Tom. Maybe one of the other places on the road. Let's go!"

As they started out, Harvey Caldwell kicked something that clanged against the metal kitchen chair leg. "What was that?" Jake picked up a set of keys.

"How did these get on the floor? They go up here, with the other set. Wait! There's a set of keys missing. Harriet had two sets of keys hanging here. Now there's one. And it was on the floor. That means somebody took one set of keys and knocked this set on the floor doing it. Keys open things. He's in one of the outside buildings! The barn. Hurry!"

Jake and Tom headed to the barn, while Harvey went to the garage. Nothing. "This place is empty. He must've driven to one of the other places." He started towards the car.

"Hold on there, Pard."

~~~

Harry Reeves finished tying Maggie Hansen to the bed. "Finally! All that's left to do now, is wake you two up, and we can start having

251

some fun." Maggie, and her daughter Kathleen, were each tied to a single bed, positioned so that they could see each other. They were gagged, and still dressed. That would soon change.

Reeves started with Maggie. He slapped her into consciousness. "Good morning, Mrs. Hansen. Glad to see you're awake. Excuse me for a minute. I want to go wake up your lovely daughter. I wouldn't want her to miss anything." He walked over, and woke Kathleen, the same way he woke her mother. "Wakey-wakey Katie. Time to wake up." Kathleen came to and struggled against the ropes holding her to the bed frame. "Calm down dear. You're just going to hurt yourself, and that's my job." A cruel smile came over his face. "Don't worry. Your mom is right over there. I'm going to go play with her for a while. I woke you up so you could watch. Don't worry, I'll be back shortly, and we can play."

Reeves hovered over Maggie Hansen, waving his straight razor, like it was a baton, and he was an orchestra conductor. "First we need to get rid of these clothes." He quickly sliced through her pants, on the top of each leg, from hip to ankle, also cutting into her flesh about a quarter of an inch. He deftly pulled the slacks out from under her, much in the same way someone would pull the tablecloth from under the plates, in a parlor trick. Both Maggie's legs were now bleeding, from hip to ankle, and she was uttering a muffled scream. Kathleen was crying. "Don't worry Maggie. Those cuts aren't too bad. Besides, in about an hour, you'll be thinking that the pain you're feeling now, isn't so bad, compared to what comes next. Now, let's get that blouse off, shall we?" He went about removing it, the same way he removed her slacks; slicing down each arm, and then cutting her chest, until he could peel everything back, and pull it from under her. "There. That's better! Let's see what we're going to play with first. He picked up the bone saw. "This? No, that's for later. Near the finish. We have to start small. Can't have you dying too quickly. Ah! I know." He picked up the long handled pruning shears, that someone would use to cut small branches from bushes and hedges. "Yes. Now, what first? A toe? Maybe a finger? How 'bout an ear? Decisions, decisions, decisions. Don't worry though. I'll get to all of those, eventually."

The crashing of the front door startled him. He turned to run out the back door, only to come face to face with Tom Hansen, who grabbed Harry around the throat. Reeves instinctively thrust the pruning shears forward, into Hansen's stomach. Tom released his grip, and fell to the floor, as Jake, who came through the back door behind Tom, fired a shot into Reeve's midsection. Harry Reeves recoiled, clutching his stomach. He had a bewildered look on his face. He stared at the barrel of Jake's Glock. "No! It can't be! How?!"

"You're just not as smart as you think you are, asshole." Jake shot him in the face, and Harry Reeves was dead before he hit the floor.

Harvey Caldwell rounded the corner from the living room, saw Reeves dead, and went to Tom Hansen, who was on the floor, covered in blood. "Tom, lay still. Paramedics are on the way!"

"I-I think I'll be alright, Harvey. It only went in about an inch. Don't think it hit anything. Just hurts like a mother."

Meanwhile, Jake had untied his sister, and covered her with a sheet. She threw her arms around him and cried into his shoulder. "Oh, Jimmy! It was horrible. I knew you'd find us, though. Thank you!"

"Thank your husband, sis. We were at Reeves' mother's house, about five miles from here. We knew a set of keys were missing from the house. All of the seven properties on that road are empty, so Harvey and I wanted to search each one. Tom stopped us. He figured that since the set of keys still there were for the doors, and such, in her house, and none of her other buildings, like her barn, and garage, had locks on them, that the set of keys missing had to be somebody's house keys. Tom suggested they were more likely keys to a relative's house, and did

Harriet Abrams have any relatives nearby? I remembered her nephew, Eddie Abrams. This is his house. This is where this whole thing started. Jamal King and I rescued two high school girls in this same room, a couple of weeks ago. We killed Reeves two partners, but he got away. Never expected him to come back here. Guess that's why he did."

"Tom! You're hurt!"

"I'm all right, Mags. Bastard jabbed me in the stomach with those pruning shears. Didn't go in far enough to do any real damage."

"Looks like that spare tire you've been sporting may have saved your life, Tom."

"Very funny, Jake. Hey, wait! I thought you said this Eddie guy lived here with his family."

Harvey finished untying Kathleen, who now threw herself on her mother, crying tears of joy now. He spoke up. "Yeah, about the family. It's a mess in the living room. Two bodies. Adult. Male and female. Make them to be Eddie Abrams, and his wife. Throats cut. Neat and quick."

"Makes sense. They were family. That's why he killed them quick. Kids probably are not home from school yet. It's 2:30 pm."

By 3:00 pm the property on Pine Road was a flurry of police activity, again. EMTs tended to Maggie and Tom's injuries and checked out Kathleen. After each was deemed to be stable, they were ambulanced away, though Jake had to threaten his niece, in order to get her to agree to go to the hospital. FBI Agent Brandon Wright showed up fifteen minutes after the first wave of law enforcement did. "Give me a sit-rep, Harvey."

"Not much to tell, Brandon. Jake got us in the right church, and Tom Hansen got us in the right pew, so to speak. I entered the property via the front door and discovered two dead adults. Turned out to be the owner of the home, Edward Abrams, and his wife Mary. They have two children who were at school all day. The children are with child services. Mrs. Abrams has family in the area. Child services is trying to reach out to them. While I entered the front, private Investigator Miller, and Police Captain Hansen entered the rear door. They encountered the suspect, Harold Reeves, in the act of torturing two victims. Kathleen Miller, and Margaret Miller. Captain Hansen received a stab wound in a physical confrontation with the suspect. Mr. Miller entered the scene and shot the suspect dead."

"Excellent. Good work, Harvey. Jake? You okay?"

"Yeah, Brandon, I am. Just thinking what almost happened here. If Tom hadn't triggered the thought of Eddie Abrams, we would still, right now, be searching houses on Farmer's Landing Road, and my family..."

"But he did, Jake. And you got here in time. And that sick son of a bitch can't ever hurt anybody else."

CHAPTER 24

Jake invited Brandon and Harvey to stay at his place a few days, which they agreed to. They arrived at Alexander Ave just after 7 pm. Jake had called Phil, and asked him to bring his dogs home, and Phil was sitting on the porch, when Jake and the FBI guys showed up. He had also called the hospital to check on Art Kaufman, who Reeves had failed to kill. Art was listed as being in stable condition. After calming down the dogs, and getting Harvey and Brandon acclimated, Jake took off to see his former boss, in the hospital. He found Art sitting up and chatting quietly with his wife, Irene. "Well, this is a sight for sore eyes. I was worried about you, Lou."

"He caught me off guard, Jake. Slashed my throat with his razor. I was able to get my hand up, and deflect enough of the blow, so that he missed the artery in my throat. Your sister was like a wild animal, and I think that caused him to not get as deep as he would have liked. I got lucky, Jake."

Jake resisted the urge to tell him 'No such thing as luck', a phrase that Jake had heard Lt. Art Kaufman use dozens of times. He instead turned to Irene. "How is he really, Irene?"

"He's fine Jake. They're sending him home tomorrow!"

"That's great! Call me, and I'll come pick him up."

"Not necessary, Jake. Our son Dave is here with me. He just went to get something to eat. He'll bring his father home."

"Good. anything I can do for you, Lou?"

"Just tell me you got him, Jake."

"Not for nothing, boss, but I wouldn't be here yet, if he was still out there. Harry Reeves is dead. My sister and niece are fine. Maggie got sliced a little, from his straight razor, but it wasn't deep enough to warrant stitches. Her husband is bringing her and my niece home, probably as we speak."

"Well, that's cause to celebrate."

"You're right, Lou, it *is* a reason to celebrate. Sunday, at my house. Big party. I hope you'll feel up to coming for a while. Tom Hansen will be there. I'll invite Wilt, Denise, and the girls. Regina is home. I'm sure she'll come, if she's able. Chuck and his family. I'll even go get Becky Lachowicz. What do you say?"

"That's up to the boss here, Jake."

"Irene?"

"We'll see, Jake. If Artie is up to it, we'll gladly come."

"Well, I better get going. I got a party to plan, and only one day to do it. I really hope to see you two this Sunday."

Jake spent the next hour making calls and inviting people. Wilt King said sure. Jake could hear his daughters, Angela, and Patty, squealing with delight in the background. Wilt even offered to pick up Irene Lachowicz on the way. "I haven't called her yet, Wilt."

"Don't worry, Jake. I got this. Even if she says no, I'm strong enough now, thanks to her, to pick her bony ass up, and carry her to your place."

"Great! Hey, how does it feel being back on the job?"

"Fine. We'll talk on Sunday."

"Good night, Wilt."

"Night, Jake."

The next call was to his ex-SEAL buddy, Tommy Williams, who happily accepted. He was glad Jake had called because he had what he called, *huge* news, to share. After Tommy, Jake called Kari Weaver. "Hey baby girl. How you feeling, K?"

"Better, Jake. I'm in my own house, so that helps. All the swelling is gone. My mom has been here with me, and Harvey is here now. Oh, Jake, Harvey said to tell you not to wait up for him tonight. He's staying here, on my sofa."

"Okay, Kari. I'm gonna stop over tomorrow to see you, if that's all right. Anything you want me to bring?"

"No, Jake. It'll be good just to see you."

"All right K. And you know, the invitation for Sunday includes your mom, too."

"Thanks Jake. I'm gonna try my hardest to be there. Night, Jake."

"Good night, Kari. Rest easy."

When he got off the phone, he joined Brandon Wright, Tom Hansen, his sister, and niece, on the deck. It was an unusually warm night, considering it was April 12th. "So, Uncle Jay. Dr. Randy is coming down Sunday. Is it okay if he brings Tiffany and Harley with him?"

"Only if Harley eats before she comes down. Otherwise, I might run out of food."

Saturday went by in a flash, but with Kathleen and Brandon's help, everything was ready for Sunday.

The weather gods were kind on Sunday. It was sunny, and the temperature reached 69 degrees, a full 10 degrees warmer than average. Tommy and Carmen Williams were there, sans children. His big news was that he was going to be a millionaire. He had partnered with two other entrepreneurs, and the two mile stretch of road that was known as Farmer's Landing Road, was, in two short years, going to be home to forty single townhomes, to be known as Farmers Landing Estates. Realizing that all but three of the properties were in the hands of the bank, Tommy and his partners bought everything, and very cheaply.

If only twenty of the expected to be priced around $300K homes sold, Tommy's end would be $2,000,000. "Good for you, Tommy. Maybe I'll look into moving up there."

"Not for nothing, Jake, but we really don't want your kind in our Estates."

Hector 'Chuck' Alvarez, and his now wife Anna, announced that the pair were starting their own marketing group. Anna would get a chance to put her Marketing Degree to use, and Hector would run the office. True to his word, Wilt showed up, with his brood, and Irene Lachowicz, the widow of his old partner, Simon, who was affectionately known as 'Fatso'. Art Kaufman showed for a short while, as did Kari Weaver. Max and Billy, Jake's across the street neighbors were there. Dr. Randy, Tiffany, and Harley were the last to arrive, at noon.

~~~

About 5 pm, as people were milling around, getting ready to leave, Kathleen's friend Harley said, "Hey, Mr. M! No dessert?"

"My goodness! I forgot. Everybody wait here a minute!" Jake ran into the house, and a few minutes later reappeared with a sheet cake, that contained the words 'Happy Birthday', and the number '27' in red icing, and one large candle. "Thanks for the reminder, Harley. For that, you get to blow the candle out."

After Harley blew out the candle, she asked "Whose birthday is it?"

"Ahhh. It's actually a belated birthday. The birthday we're celebrating was the first."

"April first? Is this some kind of April Fool's Day prank?"

"No, it's not, Harley."

"Well, shouldn't we know whose birthday day it is?"

"Yes, you should."

"Well, is it anybody here?"

259

"I don't think so."

"Well, aren't you going to tell us?"

"No, Harley, I'm not."

Jake's sister laughed, and said "Jimmy, you are an ass."

"Not one more word, Mags."

"Mom? You know, don't you? Tell us who."

"No, Kathleen, your uncle would kill me if I did. Give them a hint, Jimmy."

"Okay, April first, is the birthday of the greatest player ever to play for the Philadelphia Phillies."

"Jimmy! That's pretty vague. Be more specific."

"Okay, but last clue. This gentleman holds the Phillies' team record for homeruns in a season, by a rookie. Now everyone grab a piece of cake. Take some home if you want."

"Come on, Uncle Jay. Tell us who it is."

"No Kathleen, if I tell you, you'll forget. If you work to find it, you'll remember it. Right, Tom? Look it up!"

As Jake went in to get a beer, he couldn't help but smile at the sound of his sister laughing.

Printed in the United States
by Baker & Taylor Publisher Services